when grandma smokes a pipe

a totally weird comedy

FSC
www.fsc.org
MIX
Papier aus ver-
antwortungsvollen
Quellen
Paper from
responsible sources
FSC® C105338

Wallenda

when grandma smokes a pipe

a totally weird comedy

Impressung / Imprint:

©2025 – W. T. Wallenda
M. J. Wallenda

Titelbild und Rückseite / Cover and back cover:

Fotos/Bilder – Photos/Pictures:

grandma smokes

©by Sophia Wallenda

Weitere Mitwirkende / other contributors:

Umschlaggestaltung und Verlag / cover design
and publishing:

BoD · Books on Demand GmbH,
In de Tarpen 42,
22848 Norderstedt, bod@bod.de

Druck/print:

Libri Plureos GmbH,
Friedensallee 273,
22763 Hamburg

ISBN: 978-3-7693-7619-7

Chapter 1
How it all began

More had gone wrong in her life than is normally possible. This sentence would have said everything that had happened so far. Nothing else had happened until that day. Her life was comparable to zero, nothing, nichts, niente, nada.

Like every day, the earth rotated both on its own axis and around the sun. Like every day for millions of years, the sun rose in the east in the morning, displaced the night and the moon and set in the west in the evening to make room for the night and the moon in its wake. This was and is the same procedure all over the world and is therefore no different in Bavaria.

Good old Germany. Somewhere near Munich and yet away from civilization, there was a small village where there wasn't really much apart from a church, a bakery, a few standard houses and several farms. It smelled permanently of manure and, at regular intervals, of slurry or *odel*, as they say here in Bavaria. Although the term *smell* was very flattering. *Stinking to high heaven* would be a more appropriate term.

Every day, the farmers milked their cows and then drove them out to pasture. Nothing ever seemed to change in the village. Everything stayed the same and always would. It was probably better that way. Because any change, no matter how small, could only harm the village, where twenty percent of the villagers were human, fifty percent cows, ten percent chickens, five percent cats and the remaining percentage was made up of horses, donkeys and other types of animals.

It is unnecessary to mention the name of the village, as you neither know it nor can you find it quickly on a map. Even *Google Maps* struggles forever to find it in its mountains of data, only to place a dot somewhere in the vast Bavarian pampas.

The main road led into the village and out again on the other side. Those who crossed the village hardly noticed it. Except, of course, for the smell. It lingered inside the car for a while.

Recently, the villagers also included the three biggest chaotic people in the world. To call them chaotic was extremely polite. They were the type of people who, although not stupid in terms of IQ, were still pretty simple-minded.

If they were left to their own devices, they would probably barely survive for more than a week in any big city. If you were mean, you could say they are fools, idiots or dolts, but that wouldn't be fair. It would be more accurate to describe them as simple minds. Friendly, kind-hearted and likeable. That probably sums it up best.

No, a big city would be their downfall. Here in this village, however, they were somebody. Here they almost felt like little heroes. Here they lived very close to the ass end of the world, but undisturbed by all evil in their quirky shared flat. A shared flat the likes of which the world had never seen before. Strangely enough, it worked. Each of the three friends had a skill that complemented those of the others. This allowed them to live together smoothly. Or should we call it *survival?*

It wasn't always like this for the three men. They grew up apart from each other. But as life would have it, all three of them found themselves in the same town one day and went to the same bar. And as luck would have it, all three were sitting next to each other on their stools at the counter of this bar, mulling over their problems. Each for themselves. At least at first. That was the birth of what is probably Bavaria's most curious flat-sharing community.

Their names were Willy, Ernest and Tommy. Objectively speaking, the three of them didn't fit together at all. They had different lives, different interests and, above all, different characteristics. Nevertheless, fate had brought them together because all three had one thing in common. They were born *losers* who had managed to end up right here in this bar because of bad decisions. But on this day, the lives of the *three zeros* were to change completely.

Willy was a trained car mechanic and knew more about engines than about women, finances and the daily demands of life in a civilized world, such as cooking, ironing and washing. His life plan had always been to meet a wealthy woman so that he could squander the fortune she brought into the marriage with her. Part one had worked. At least in part. He had met and married Sylvia, who was not very pretty, but all the wealthier for it. Willy had quit his job at *Izmir's car service* and lived his dream from then on. He went on vacation three times a year, bought old American cars, repaired them in his own small garage workshop, sold them on at a loss and financed his *lifestyle* with Sylvia's money.

However, she had other plans than Willy. While his wife wanted him to take more care of her, Willy preferred to work on cars. So it was not surprising that Sylvia considered the marriage a failure after just two years. Thanks to a prenuptial agreement, Willy was left penniless after the divorce.

With his assets of 53.85 euros, he hadn't gotten very far. The job at *Izmir* had of course long since been filled and there was nothing new to be found. Willy had kept his head above water with odd jobs. The beer that had been on the bar in front of him had also been the barman's reward for repairing his car. A casual acquaintance of Willy's.

Ernest had the appearance, or rather the figure, of a Japanese sumo wrestler. His excess weight was also the reason why it never really worked out with women. He didn't get the girls he wanted and he didn't like the ones who wanted him. Ernest was therefore born to be single.

He quickly had to give up his dream job as *a police officer* because he didn't even make it as far as the sports test. His personal hurdle had already been set at an unrealistically high level during the medical examination.

"Lose 70 kilos and you'll be back," the police doctor told him at the time.

"No problem, I know a diet from *Woman's Health*. I'll stick to it and I'll see you again in a few weeks, Doc," replied the overweight police fan full of self-confidence.

That was three years ago. Ernest was still working on the task of reducing his weight enormously. He had lost two kilos since that examination. At least temporarily. However, he had never given up hope of reaching his dream weight.

Ernest made a living from what his uncle from Canada sent him each month. Uncle Eddie was rich. Filthy rich, in fact. He owned two hotels and a supermarket chain. Ernest was Eddie's godchild and his rich uncle sent him an even thousand every month. Too much to die for, too little to live on.

Ernest used to sit in this bar because you always got a free bowl of peanuts with a drink. The heavyweight laughed a lot, was a pleasant fellow and was very tidy. Secretly, Ernest felt like an *undercover cop* and sometimes he told that to the women he was chatting up. None of them had believed him yet, but he was still working on this tactic.

The third guy was called Tommy. There wasn't much to say about him. Tommy was the youngest in the flat share and the unluckiest guy known to mankind. Whenever there was a blunder around, he would take a running start and shout: "Ass bomb, get out of the way!" and *then he* was in. Tommy had messed up everything in his life that could be messed up. He had neither a school-leaving certificate nor any training, and he had also messed up his temporary job as a paperboy because he had *smashed* at least two letterboxes on every delivery round.

For this reason, he had never managed to stand on his own two feet. The only thing Tommy was good at was talking to his houseplants. They understood him and he nurtured and cared for them.

His father had been putting pressure on him for some time. "The boy has to get out of the apartment. Once he has his own place, he'll learn how to earn money. Namely through hard work!"

His mother, on the other hand, had always believed that her son's breakthrough would come. "Once he meets the right woman, things will go uphill for him."

And so his parents had argued about him every morning, every lunchtime and every evening. He had ended up in this bar to get drunk with his 20 euros pocket money or to meet a woman or both. Of course, neither had worked out. Instead, he had met Willy and Ernest.

The catastrophe took its course. Fate sat invisibly in the far corner, rubbing his hands together, laughing and thinking: "This is going to be great fun!"

All three men, for whom nothing had ever gone really well in their lives, met in this bar. You can either like it or dislike it. But one thing is certain. If they hadn't happened to be in the same place at the same time that evening, they would probably never have met. Then they would each have gone their own miserable way to end up in front of their own personal mountain of problems at the height of *Mount Everest*.

Tommy would have gone *over* Mount Everest, Ernest *around* Mount Everest and Willy *through the middle*. As a team of three, they were now free to choose which route they would take.

It had been Ernest who had been sitting in the middle of the three guests, nibbling on peanuts, looking through the daily newspaper for apartment offers. He had found one advertisement so interesting that he read it out loud. "Looking for a new tenant, small house in the village, shared flat possible, cheap." He paused for a moment and muttered: "Shit! Now I need two more flatmates, then that would be something for me."

Tommy's ears perked up and he looked at the fat newspaper reader. He seemed likeable. The bowl of peanuts in front of him was empty. Tommy pushed his bowl over and asked: "You're looking for an apartment? What a coincidence. Me too. I can't afford one on my own, but a shared flat would be feasible," he said, hoping that his father would pay the rent. At least for a while. As the price for moving out, so to speak.

"Shared flat for three?" came from the other side immediately afterwards. "I'm newly divorced and looking for a cheap room. Guys, if you want, I'll be the third in the group."

It was a done deal and Ernest had bought all the drinks that night. After that, a third of his monthly allowance from Uncle Eddie was gone, he and his new friends were drunk and life was full of stars and hope.

Willy had spent the night in his old BMW and picked up his two new buddies the next morning. Ernest had paid for the necessary tank of gas and Tommy had brought sandwiches that his mom had bought.

When they had passed through the village for the third time without finding their destination, it was Ernest who said: "Guys, we have to keep going. I have a good feeling. I like it here."

"Really?" exclaimed Tommy and Willy simply said: "Pretty much in the middle of nowhere, but idyllic."

After another half hour of searching around, they finally found the address and marveled wide-eyed at the little house and garden.

"Ring the bell," Tommy asked Ernest.

He scratched the back of his head. "You ring the bell, I'm too excited," he passed the task on to Willy, who would prefer Tommy to ring the bell. "You look really nice. If she sees you first, we'll get the tenancy agreement."

They agreed to play puzzles. While they were still playing Schnick, Schnack, Schnuck, and Tommy had already lost the first round, the front door was literally ripped open. A woman stood in the doorway. Mid-sixties, peasant clothes, gray hair, headscarf and a piercing gaze. She eyed the three prospective tenants suspiciously. "You three model boys want to rent my house?" she said in a military tone reminiscent of a *drill sergeant* from Hollywood's US Army films.

The woman's appearance had been enough to put the three zeros in a kind of *figure-of-eight position*. Their eyes lingered on Willy, the oldest of the three friends.

"Uh, yeah," he huffed. "We ... well, that's Ernest and Tommy and me." Willy immediately realized that his halting flow of speech was making anything but a good impression. *Shit, messed up*, he thought.

"He means that his name is Willy," Tommy added, trying to smile as politely as possible. "He's great at fixing cars."

The landlady's eyes pierced the three friends again. However, her expression relaxed a little. "Well, well," she said deliberately, "come in then, but clean your shoes. I don't want to have to wipe them again. And don't touch that plant back there. It's a leftover from the previous tenants. It's hemp or stuff like that. I found it in the barn."

"Hemp? You have a marijuana plant in the barn?" Tommy had asked incredulously, staring at the elderly lady.

"Friend, if you think you can pluck something to make yourself a bag, you're wrong. The police were there last month. They arrested the previous tenants. They weren't just selling marijuana, they were probably selling other things as well. While they were still in the patrol car, I of course gave them immediate notice to quit. That's why I'm renting again. The policemen overlooked the one plant. I'll throw it on the neighbor's dung heap later," she pointed to the other side of the street with her right hand, then said: "So, one more time for everyone! Any of you who think you can happily smoke a few bags of weed can leave your bags packed and turn yourselves in immediately."

Tommy immediately waved his hands away. "I don't smoke."

"Me neither," Willy added immediately.

"Not me anyway. I'm already half policeman anyway. I just need to lose a few kilos," panted Ernest. He was a little out of breath as he had covered the few meters from the garden door to the front door faster than usual. Small beads of sweat were forming on his forehead and dark patches were spreading under his armpits.

The landlady stopped at the end of the corridor, turned around, put her hands on her hips and asked: "Which one of you three boys is responsible for the rent?"

"Him," Willy replied, pointing at Ernest.

"Him," Tommy immediately imitated him.

"Uh... I," Ernest stuttered, thinking at the same time about sending his Uncle Eddie another postcard.

"No women, no drugs, no loud parties and I want my rent on time."

"Perfect," Ernest beamed, "that's exactly my thing. I hate parties," and held out his fat hand to her with a broad grin.

The landlady looked at the mountain of meat, turned away and walked on. "All right, the pug will take care of everything. Come along then. I'll show you the house." She stopped, turned back to the men and asked another question: "Or do you like men and think you can throw pink parties here? Or do you belong to some cult and attract crazy freaks?"

"No," Ernest abruptly waved him off.

"Neither!" Tommy confirmed.

"We are just normal men who are setting up a quiet and orderly shared flat. We want to work and live together peacefully with everyone in a village community," Willy reassured us.

That was convincing enough. You received the rental contract.

The house was small, but very cozy. Sometimes you don't need a lot of space to feel comfortable, you just need the right flair. This house had flair. And lots of it.

For the first time in a long time, all three chaotic people finally had the feeling that they had achieved something. They had done it together and won the bid for a house to rent. They had each played their part. It was clear to them that they were an unbeatable team. The future could come. They were ready. The rental contract was signed and all was right with the world.

Ernest took over the rent and paid the deposit. As Ernest and Tommy didn't have a driver's license, Willy borrowed a Delivery van, picked up all his friends' belongings and drove them here. Tommy diligently helped with loading and unloading. This meant that after a box of glasses had slipped out of his hands on the top floor, tumbled down the stairs and the broken glass was scattered everywhere, he *helped* by holding the doors open so that his friends could carry the rest of the boxes without barriers.

Willy had recognized Tommy's *talent* and knew from that day on that his buddy helped best when he sat there quietly and did nothing.

At the end of the evening, Tommy stood in front of his flatmates with the aforementioned marijuana plant under his arm and said: "Our landlady forgot this."

Willy first eyed Tommy, then the plant. "She wanted to throw it on the neighbor's dung heap. Why don't you do that and it'll be gone."

Tommy was uncomfortable. "We haven't even introduced ourselves yet. I can't just go over there and throw something away."

That sounded logical. You should already know someone if you dispose of your organic waste there. "That's right again. Then bang it on our compost heap."

"Okay," Tommy nodded and went outside the door. As he stood in front of the compost heap, he looked at the little plant. "I'm sorry, but you're not allowed here. I have to dispose of you." He stared at the delicate greenery. He felt as if the baby plant was talking to him. *Have mercy. I'm still so small and innocent. What can happen if you plant me in the garden? Besides, I have healing powers.*

Tommy reached out and picked up the plant, but didn't have the heart to throw it away. "All right, but you'll behave yourself," he whispered, looked for a suitable spot and planted the hemp. "You'll be comfortable here and no one will see you," he said. "Elephant grass is growing in front of you and sunflowers are already sprouting up next to you. You'll have nice neighbors."

Satisfied with this solution, the plant lover went back into the house.

All three chaotic people were happy. For once, life had been kind to them. They had a cozy house with a beautiful garden, a garage and a barn. The latter was more like a large shed, but the term barn sounded much better. There were two apple trees, two cherry trees and two plum trees in the garden. The vegetable garden was divided into a flower bed, a vegetable bed and a herb bed. Elephant grass grew next to it, framed by sunflowers and the newly planted hemp.

A hunter's fence had been erected around the property, with a holey thuja hedge planted behind it. Everything looked quite tidy. Except for the lawn. It grew and grew and grew.

The landlady had noticed this during her regular inspections, but had always left without comment. When she once saw Tommy working in the garden, she mentioned it, but when the amateur gardener explained to her that the lawn had not been mowed in order to provide food for the bees and that all kinds of useful insects felt at home there, she was satisfied, especially as the subject of *bee mortality was repeatedly in the press.*

However, the lawn wasn't actually mowed because the three men didn't own a lawnmower. After this conversation, Ernest and Willy knew that Tommy had made a very positive contribution to the shared flat. It was important to have a gardener in the house when you live in the country.

Just two weeks later, the landlady had brought them cake for the first time. She had stopped at the garden door in amazement and had noticed with approval that Willy was in the process of painting the old shutters. She looked around and noticed that everything else had also been spruced up.

When their old Mercedes once again failed to start as they were saying goodbye, Willy played his joker. He stepped in front of the car. "Open the hood."

A few minutes later, the engine was humming. "I need to fix a few more little things on the engine, then it'll be like new again. But for now, you can drive," he concluded. "That doesn't cost anything either. I'm happy to do it. However, I do need a few small spare parts."

The landlady's handbag then opened. Willy waved a hundred towards her. "For the materials."

"That's easily enough. There must be 20 euros left over."

She looked at the house, pulled another hundred out of her wallet and said, "Nice color. Maybe you need some more. If it's not enough, just give me a call. And if there's anything left over," she winked, "you can keep it." As she drove away, she hummed a song, grinning and in a good mood.

"There's nothing like a good relationship between tenant and landlord," Willy had told his buddies when he showed them the two banknotes. "For the paint."

Willy's old BMW was parked in the garage. Apart from his high-quality tools, it was his only possession worth mentioning. The garage was Willy's kingdom, so to speak. He could spend hours there tinkering with his car. Of course, he would like to have a larger garage, perhaps with two or three more cars to repair and sell later.

He also dreamed of a lifting platform, even more tools and perhaps even his own small workshop, where he would also repair customers' cars.

"One day I'll open *Willys Autoservice* here," he had once said, setting himself a new goal with this dream. A much better one than catching a rich woman and squandering her fortune.

But for the time being, he was content to keep his old BMW running or look after the landlady's Mercedes. And Willy did that perfectly.

"We should divide up the work in the house so that everyone has roughly the same amount to do," was the initial suggestion.

The plan was good, but the implementation failed miserably. Even the shopping had become a challenge. All three of them had to go. Willy, because he was the only one with a driver's license. Ernest, because he paid with his credit card and Tommy, because he couldn't be left alone in the house. Unless he was in the garden. That's where he did the least nonsense.

The situation was similar with washing, cooking, cleaning and chopping wood. The latter was needed for the small stove in the living room. No matter what work had to be done, they did it together. And as none of the three slobs had a job, it wasn't a problem. It was also extremely effective. Everyone did their part. Willy was the brains of the flat share, Ernest was the only one who really knew his way around the housework and Tommy, because he simply belonged and was easier to look after when he was with them. In short, they had grown into a perfect team of three.

The relationship with the landlady, who had the stupid double name Müller-Meier, was fantastic. She was almost affectionately called *Mrs. M.* and brought cake round almost every Sunday.

The neighbor to the right of the chaotic shared flat was called Alfons. He was around 60 years old, a board member of the small animal breeding association and a hobby chicken breeder. Alfons was politeness personified and unfortunately also extremely talkative. He kept bringing the three friends eggs of different sizes and colors.

"Great, you don't have to paint any more for Easter," Tommy had said and placed them on the living room table as a decoration the first time. That went well until they rotted and started to stink terribly. Since then, the eggs from Alfon's chickens have either gone straight into the pan or into the fridge.

There was no neighbor to the left of them. There was one of farmer Huber's cow pastures. His farm was diagonally opposite. When the wind was unfavorable, the smell of dung heaps spread like wildfire. We always had to *close the windows.* Apart from this typical country smell, which city dwellers had to get used to, the three friends felt at home in the village.

The garden beds also proved to be useful. While Willy repaired everything and Ernest kept the house tidy, Tommy lovingly looked after the garden and the plants. That was his world. He made himself useful here and you could even let him handle gardening tools on his own without causing a disaster.

Summer flowers, lavender, rosemary, tomatoes and zucchinis flourished. But the hemp plant had also shot up.

The hemp plant was a gross understatement. A small field of hemp plants had formed around it in the meantime. The previous tenants must have scattered a number of seeds in the soil, which gradually sprouted and grew into magnificent perennials within a very short time. The small hemp field could not be seen from the road. Surrounded by elephant grass, bamboo and sunflowers, the forbidden *grass grew* in secret. The telltale, typical smell of marijuana that the plant exuded was permanently masked by the almost permanent scent of odel and, of course, dung heaps in the air.

Tommy had never felt so much fun and joy in his life. He looked after his garden, smiled in a friendly manner, greeted everyone and everything and was simply happy.

At first, the villagers who strolled curiously along the garden fence gave him funny looks. He was an outwardly withdrawn member of the human species and quite the opposite of the polite Tommy. When he greeted the walkers with: "Hello, good morning" or: "Have a great evening. Just take a look at the enchanting sunset", they were flabbergasted. You would have thought they thought Tommy was an alien who spoke their language.

Over time, the strangeness subsided and one or two walkers smiled when Tommy came out of the house and greeted his plants by cheerfully shouting "Good morning, garden" or "Hello, my plants, did you sleep well". If he then greeted the walkers, they even dared to greet him back. Tommy liked this and it made him feel more and more at ease.

Of course, the avowed hobby gardener had also informed himself extensively about his new, exotic favorite plants with the peculiar smell and convinced his two living buddies of the positive use of this plant.

"The botanical name of this medicinal plant is *Cannabis sativa*. It originates from India and was used medicinally in China over 4000 years ago, for example as a remedy for rheumatism."

"I'm bored of your herb stuff," Willy had responded, looking in the newspaper ads for a used lawnmower. "Maybe I can find one to repair."

"Tell me, isn't your hemp *weed?* The stuff that people in the drug scene buy, make a bag of and snort?" asked Ernest, who sensed a criminal case and already had the headline in mind. *Trainee policeman finds the drug bunker of an imprisoned gang!*

Tommy raised his hands vehemently and shook his head in denial. "I'm only looking at the whole thing medically. I'm not a drug dealer."

That made sense to Ernest, and his criminal case deflated like a soap bubble. Especially when Tommy read out from one of his books that marijuana could also be used in cookies and cakes.

"You can really eat this stuff?"

"Sure, but only if you're ill. Otherwise it's useless."

After this explanation, all three men were of the opinion that it couldn't be harmful if Tommy continued to tend the plants horticulturally. At least for the time being!

As far as the use of marijuana was concerned, chance had led the way. On a warm summer's day, the grandmother from the Huber farm opposite had stopped in front of the Chaoten's house during one of her walks, leaned her walking stick against the garden fence and watched Tommy plucking herbs for a while.

"Young man," she had said to him. "You have lots of herbs in your garden. We used to have a herb garden when I was your age. My grandmother had a suitable herb for every illness. Unfortunately, I never acquired this knowledge myself."

Tommy raised his head, grinned and replied. "I know quite a bit about that. I've even read a book by *Hildegard von Bingen*. It took me a while because," he hesitated, "well, because I'm not very good at reading. But never mind. Anyway, she was the number one herbalist in the Middle Ages. She had it down to a tee. She was all the rage back then."

Grandma Huber smiled. "Yes, that's what my grandmother used to say. Only she used different words." She exhaled audibly and groaned a little. "Oh, you know, I have such terrible rheumatism and nothing from this pharmacy really helps me. The quack doctor has no idea either. Do you happen to know if any of your herbs would be good for me? I'll pay for it too."

Tommy felt sorry for the old woman. He spontaneously decided to help her. "I already have an idea. My medicinal herbs could actually bring you some relief."

Grandma Huber's sad face brightened. She had long toyed with the idea of turning her back on the doctor and his pills in order to see a naturopath, an alternative practitioner or a Chinese healer. So why shouldn't she give this young man and his herbs a tiny chance? Her already good mood lifted once again. "What's your name, young man?"

Tommy stood up and walked to the garden fence. To clean his hands, he rubbed his palms against the legs of his jeans. He then held out his right hand. "Hi, I'm Tommy and *you* can leave out the *you*. I've always been on first name terms with everyone."

"Elisabeth Huber," said the old woman, shaking his hand and adding: "You can call me Grandma Huber. That's what everyone here in the village says."

"Grandma Huber, I can give you ..."

"You! We'll leave out the *'you'* for me too and be on first-name terms," she interrupted him. "What applies to you also applies to me."

The old lady's smile was extremely pleasant. Tommy liked this woman straight away. "Gladly," he replied. "I already have an idea of how I can possibly help you. I'm putting together a special herbal mixture. With a bit of luck, it will work against the rheumatism."

"As tea?" she asked.

"You can make a tea out of it, bake it in cakes and cookies," he thought for a moment and then said, "but it will probably be most effective if you smoke it."

"As a cigarette? Boy, I smoked a cigarette once when I was 16. I felt sick for three days. In contrast, I took a puff of my dad's pipe every now and then. Tobacco with a hint of vanilla. I liked the taste. But I was only allowed to do that when he had a pint of beer and was in a good mood," she laughed.

"A pipe is a good idea. I'll get straight to work and put together a mixture for you. You just have to get yourself a pipe."

"I've kept my dad's old pipe. But tell me, how much does it cost?"

Tommy thought about it for a moment, shrugged his shoulders and said: "Nothing!"

"Only death is free and even that costs life. I'll try your herbal mixture and if it helps me, I'll pay you one euro per pipe filling."

Tommy's face brightened. "Agreed! But I can't manage the vanilla flavoring."

Grandma Huber winked at Tommy. "That's medicine, too. It doesn't have to smell or taste like vanilla," she laughed and waved goodbye.

Tommy looked after the old woman. His thoughts turned to his plants. He sensed that this was the start of something really big. And with one euro per pipe portion, he would also be able to contribute something to the household budget.

"My friends, we're a team! From now on, I'll earn some extra money," he said aloud to himself and immediately set to work.

Just one week later, five euros and five pipe bowl fillings changed hands. Another week later, Grandma Huber visited him again, smoking a pipe and in a great mood. Tommy had just watered the tomatoes and put the watering can to one side. As she walked through the garden door, he called out to her in amazement: "Grandma Huber, where's your walking stick?"

The pensioner raised her whistle demonstratively. She walked normally, didn't limp, didn't drag her leg and, if Tommy wasn't mistaken, she even walked at a relatively athletic pace.

"I no longer need the walking stick. Your medicine works wonders. I'm already thinking about who I should dance with at the Sportsmen's Ball."

Tommy clapped his hands. "That's wonderful."

Grandma Huber strutted straight through the garden. She stopped at the columbines, admired their colors, glanced at the bamboo and the elephant grass sprouting behind it and bent down to pick up a small stone. She threw it to the side into the gravel bed that bordered the house. She even gamely took the small step that led to the raised tomato bushes. When she reached Tommy's house, she explained the reason for her visit in no uncertain terms. "Your medicine is extremely good for me, and that's why I'm here. My dear, good, very best new friend, I need another supply. Do you have any more of the herbs?"

The young hobby gardener's joy was clear to see. At last there was someone who appreciated his gardening skills and made him feel really important for the first time in his life. "No problem," Tommy replied. "I've already prepared a few pipe fillings."

Grandma Huber was beaming with happiness. "Great," she rubbed her hands together. "And since I'm here. My friend, Mrs. Korner, also has an ailment. She would also like to try your herbal mixture. And old Anna Schwinghofer, the fruit farmer's wife who lives at the other end of the village, needs it too. You know, she often has a bad back. All that bending over and then carrying the heavy fruit baskets."

Tommy wasn't exactly a brainiac, but he knew that growing his medicinal plants, i.e. the marijuana plants, and selling his so-called herbal mixture made from them wasn't exactly legal. Nevertheless, he didn't have a guilty conscience. After all, he was doing something good by passing on his harvest. To make it clear to the old lady that what they were doing was illegal in and of itself, he asked carefully: "Grandma Huber, do you know that we have to keep this a secret? I mean absolutely secret."

She winked at him. "Don't worry, Tommy. We girls from the pensioners' coffee party are as secretive as the graves our heirs have already chosen for us."

Suspicious glances rested on Grandma Huber, who corrected her statement slightly. "Better said, we're secretive when we know we have to be. Otherwise, of course, we gossip behind closed doors about this and that, about whoever it is."

Tommy fumbled around a little. He decided to be clearer once again. Although they were both alone in the garden, he whispered: "I think that a not insignificant part of my medicinal herb ..." He couldn't think of the right word. "So ... it could be that the police ... I mean to say that ... so if someone ..."

Grandma Huber clamped her pipe between her teeth and demonstratively put her hands on her hips. "How do you like it!"

"What did you say?"

She took the pipe out of her mouth. "We are secretive! That's it!"

The amateur gardener nodded. This statement was clear and his fears were thus dispelled. The young man's facial features relaxed. "All right, if I can help, I'm happy to help."

Just three days later, Grandma Huber was back and reported that Tommy's medicine had also had a positive effect on Mrs. Korner and Anna Schwinghofer. "The stuff just works!"

Tommy was very proud. "That makes me happy."

"And because your medicine seems to help against all aches and pains at our age, I thought I'd take some for everyone in my senior ladies' group for next Thursday. You know, Tommy, since I've been taking your medicine regularly, or should I say *smoking it*, I've been feeling great. I can't keep that from my other girlfriends. Otherwise they'll start whispering about me."

Tommy, who would have preferred to keep the dispensing of his herbal medicine a little smaller and therefore more discreet, conceded defeat without objection. "And all your friends smoke pipes?"

The pensioner shook her head in the negative. "No, of course not, but they're herbs, so I can use them in the kitchen. I bake cakes or a few cookies for our non-smokers," she said confidently.

"Wait here." Tommy disappeared and returned a few minutes later. Grandma Huber bagged up a few pipe fillings, three portions for rolling cigarettes and four bags of herbs as ingredients for baking mixes. Tommy was given a Zwanni and they both felt great.

Thanks to Grandma Huber, Tommy's special herbal medicine gradually reached her entire group of senior citizens. The miracle cure was first presented to their two closest friends and when they were unconditionally convinced of its effectiveness, they decided to present it to the rest of the group over coffee. In the Village-mug-Inn, the only inn within a ten-kilometer radius, the senior citizens met every Thursday afternoon to chat, gossip and complain about each other.

From the time Grandma Huber supplied the ladies with Tommy's special medicine, the meetings were brought forward by half an hour. However, the unusual clique did not meet directly at the inn, but behind the bus shelter at the bus stop.

It was a great place to enjoy a communal pipe or two, a home-made bag or a few cookies with special ingredients from Tommy's herb garden. Afterwards, the group returned to the *Village-mug-Inn in* high spirits and laughing.

From then on, they no longer talked about aches and pains, doctors and boring raffles, but instead chatted about vacations, the Caribbean and the handsome men who are supposed to be there and who should be eaten.

"This is Thailand for women," said Grandma Huber with a mischievous look. "I can check how much a trip like that costs. It's always better than those coffee trips to South Tyrol," she suggested, earning roaring applause.

Tommy had given the pensioners something very special. Joie de vivre!

He had become their beloved *herb boy*, who, from the old ladies' point of view, had brought some zest into the formerly monotonous village life. Tommy had sweetened their boring lives in a pleasant way. Or should we say *greened it?*

A pipe filling cost Tommy just one euro. Just like the bag for smoking or the baking ingredient. And you could afford such a portion of happiness for a mere euro, even on a meagre pension.

When the senior citizens invited Tommy to the village pub from time to time, he naturally brought the goods for free for the *warm-up round* behind the bus shelter.

Tommy loved his garden, and the ladies loved the grass that grew so wonderfully in Tommy's garden. Tommy's herbal cures were the new highlight in their lives.

From then on, the ladies had a motto for their weekly get-together: *La vita é bella - life is beautiful.*

The constant good mood of the grandmothers in the village also ensured a generally better harmony among the inhabitants. Farmer Huber received freshly baked cakes three times a week, without Tommy's herbs, of course. Grandma Korner raised the wages for her temporary workers in high spirits. Anna Schwinghofer reduced the price of the cider she sold to the other villagers. The queues at the doctor's in the neighboring village became shorter, so he came home in time for lunch.

When you add it all up, Tommy's herbal mixtures brought harmony to village life as a whole. Everyone was happier than before and no one was at a disadvantage.

Chapter 2
A completely normal day

The day was perfect. It was neither too hot nor too cold. A few white clouds drifted across the blue sky, and they were so elegant to look at that you would have thought you were staring at a painting by *Monet* or *van Gogh*. They floated above the village like giant cotton balls. The pleasantly mild wind seemed to lift the sun upwards so that it could spread its rays over the Bavarian village. In two words: Bavarian village idyll.

Like every morning, the three friends were woken up by the loud *cock-a-doodle-doo* of Charles, the name of neighbor Alfons' rooster. Charles belonged to the *Friesian chicken* breed and was therefore always greeted by Tommy with: "Morning!".

At seven o'clock on the dot, Charles crowed like crazy. Apparently he was having a duel with farmer Huber's rooster, who was strutting around on the dung heap there and also crowing like crazy. However, his crowing was not nearly as disturbing as that of the Frisian cockerel living next door.

"Morning, Charles," Tommy called out of the window, waking Alfons, who had become accustomed to the cock-a-doodle-doo but not to his new neighbor's response. Shortly after Tommy had shouted out his *Morning*, the echo followed.

"Good morning, Tommy!" replied Alfons, sticking his head out of the window, taking a deep breath and exclaiming: "A beautiful blue sky. Do you know why the sky is blue?"

Tommy looked up. "Eh," he pondered, "maybe because it's not raining?" He was also a little proud of the good answer. Unfortunately, it was wrong. Alfons solved his riddle without waiting for another answer and replied: "No, of course not. It's so blue because it's mainly blue light that is scattered in all directions by the smallest air particles. And that's why the cloudless sky appears so blue to us."

Tommy frowned. That was too much information for this time of day. At the same time, he heard the voices of his buddies: "Shut up Tommy!"

"Tommy, shut up, otherwise Alfons will come over again."

Tommy followed the instruction, waved to Alfons with a grin and said: "Great, I'll remember that," and closed the window.

As in *"Groundhog Day"*, this procedure took place every day. As mentioned at the beginning, Alfons bred chickens. In addition to the *Friesians*, he also kept the *Onagadori* and the *Dutch Owlbeard*.

Alfons was friendly and meant well, but he was friendly in a particularly intrusive way. It was exactly this kind of politeness that was completely annoying in less than 60 seconds. He was the kind of person you should never look directly at. Once you had made eye contact, it acted like a magnet. Not just any magnet, but the notorious *douche magnet*. True to the motto: "Don't look at a douchebag, otherwise he'll come here!"

You could set the clock by it. Willy and Ernest had already done this a few times and kept count.

"Three, two, one ..."

And then there was a knock at the door.

Tock tock tock

"It's me, Alfons. I've brought you fresh eggs. This time it's three green ones and a blue one."

Alfons lived alone, which didn't surprise Ernest, Willy and Tommy, because no woman could stand his constant chatter for more than a few hours. He talked and talked and talked.

He even included boring topics such as past election results, the weather in northern Canada or synchronized diving at the Olympics in his speeches. He jumped from one topic to the next and never found an end. The *end* had to be forced, otherwise your neighbor would never stop.

The fact was, the three slobs thought Alfons was nice, but avoided any unnecessary contact. When they saw that he was in the garden, they quickly scurried back into the house or didn't go outside at all.

"Alfons talks more in three minutes than I do in an hour," Willy once said.

Tock tock tock

"You sleepyheads, how much longer will it take you to get to the door?" shouted Alfons.

"I'm in the loo," Willy replied.

"Me too," came from Ernest, whereupon Willy said, "We have two toilets," to immediately rule out any misunderstandings.

"And I'm taking a shower," Tommy cheated.

"But not while I'm in the loo," added Ernest.

"This is taking too long, I still have coffee on the table. I want to enjoy it warm. I'll put the eggs outside the door. We can have a chat another time."

Breathe a sigh of relief.

Later, it smelled of fresh coffee and fried eggs. As he did almost every morning, Ernest browsed through the newspaper for accidents, bank robberies and other violent crimes that he hoped to solve before *his colleagues* did.

It was always fascinating for him to see what was happening in the world. Every time he imagined himself as a policeman being called to a serious accident or a burglary. In his mind, he was a superhero. He rescued seriously injured people, successfully hunted down gangsters, investigated murderers and caught them before they could carry out their escape plans.

Willy almost felt as if he was assimilating with the villagers and becoming just like them within a short space of time. For four weeks, the same scenes had been played out every day in the same rhythm.

"At some point, you won't be able to tell us apart from the people who live here," he said, reaching for a piece of toast.

"Yes, yes, not much happened yesterday," muttered Ernest, reaching for his coffee cup and taking a loud sip. It rattled as he put the cup back on the saucer.

Willy looked at the laid table. In addition to the fried eggs, he saw sausage and cheese, butter, jam, honey, toast and, of course, coffee. "Tommy, hurry up. The coffee's getting cold!"

A muffled voice could be heard from the bathroom: "I'm coming!"

Almost a little disappointed, Ernest leafed through the newspaper and finally looked for the crossword puzzle. "Nothing happens here, not even an accident," he complained. "Not even a little shoplifting or anything like that," he added.

"Be happy," said Willy.

"Nothing happens here! The same routine every day. The most exciting event since we've lived here was when Farmer Huber's piebald cow escaped and was almost hit by a car."

"It's nice. Everything is peaceful and everyone is happy."

"If you say so," Ernest replied and picked up the pen he had already put away. It was crossword time. He had opened the guessing page and placed the paper on the table next to his plate. "Personally, I find it boring as hell. A little more action would do us all good. You know, I'm more of an action guy. A little power under my butt and off we go!"

Willy found that hard to imagine. If there were two things that didn't go together, it was *action* and *Ernest*. "Just wait until you're my age, there's nothing better than a wonderful, quiet and undisturbed morning where you can enjoy your coffee," said Willy.

Ernest looked at him askance. "You're just three years older than me."

"And you can tell," Willy said smugly and leaned back. "After all, that's three times 365 days. So," he started to do the math, but quickly gave up and replied: "That's a lot of days!"

Tommy came out of the bathroom and sat down at the table. Ernest poured the coffee. Tommy took the cup and sipped cautiously.

"Don't be so careful. It's already cold anyway," Ernest replied. "You really are always the last one to turn up in the morning."

"If you always occupy the loo for so long in the morning," Tommy countered.

"Then you'll just have to get up earlier," Ernest grinned.

Tommy reached for a sugar cube. He put the sugar cube in his coffee, stirred, sipped again and picked up two more lumps of sugar. He dropped them into the cup and stirred again. Two more sugar cubes followed, then Tommy was satisfied and took a slice of toast.

"Five sugar cubes?" Willy wondered.

"I don't know, I don't have a calculator to hand."

"How can you only put five sugar cubes in your coffee?" asked Ernest.

"How can you eat sausage at the crack of dawn?" Tommy grumbled at him, pointing to Ernest's thickly topped bread. He demonstratively took another sip of coffee before putting his cup back down. "Mmm, delicious!"

"There's nothing better than a well-filled sausage sandwich," Ernest countered. "It contains all the vitamins and proteins that a healthy body needs to wake up."

"What a load of garbage. You must have read that in the newspaper on April 1st."

Ernest tapped the newspaper with his index finger. "Yes, that may be true, but what's in the paper is true!"

"They've taken the piss out of you. They write nonsense on April 1st. And apart from that," Tommy explained, taking a short pause to deliberately send the second half-sentence in such a way that it was perceived correctly by the recipient, "*you* should watch your diet. Otherwise your police figure will never work out!"

"At least I don't have a brain made of tar."

"Why tar?" Willy wondered. "Is there something wrong with Tommy's brain?"

Ernest was perplexed. "I don't know!"

"Then why did you say it?" Willy shook his head.

Tommy didn't find it funny at all, but kept quiet.

Ernest concentrated on the puzzle again. "I think it sounds great! I could also have said that there are more brains in every one of Alfon's chicken eggs than in Tommy's head," he grumbled and took a provocative bite of his sausage sandwich.

"Are there really brains in the eggs?" asked Tommy. "I thought there was white and yellow stuff in there. That's not what brains look like."

"Forget it Tommy, that was a joke," Willy explained.

Tommy laughed. "Ha, ha, I see."

Ernest was engrossed in the crossword puzzle again and asked the group: "Capital of Italy with three letters. I've never been to Italy, have any of you ever been there?"

"No, but I've had Italian food before," grinned Tommy. "At *Bella Roma*."

"What kind of aroma?" asked Ernest.

"That's right, Rome! Rome is the capital of Italy," Willy answered the question.

After breakfast, they cleared the table. As they didn't have a dishwasher, they had to wash up by hand. Tommy was just a spectator, as this was the least he could do wrong.

"I have to go out again today. I need two-stroke mixture for Bauer Huber's old Zündapp. I've actually got the bike running again," said Willy.

"We'll come with you. The fridge is almost empty," said Ernest.

"Almost empty?" asked Tommy, puzzled. "We only went shopping on Saturday.

Ernest shrugged his shoulders. "So what? There was Sunday in between. Have you forgotten? Today is Monday. No wonder it's empty again. And besides, I have to go to the bank and then to the post office at the EDEKA store."

Willy put the dried cutlery away. "What do you want at the post office?"

Ernest pulled the plug. The washing-up water ran out. "Finally send Uncle Eddie the postcard with the new address."

"If you're going to the bank, can you withdraw an extra fifty? I have to fill up. You'll get it back as soon as I bring the Zündapp to Farmer Huber. He promised me a hundred."

Nodding in agreement. The heavyweight's cheeks flushed. "No problem."

"Great. When are we leaving?"

All three looked at the large wall clock, which adorned the otherwise bare wall in station style with Roman numerals.

"Now!" Ernest decided and rubbed his voluminous belly.

When the three mates went shopping, they drove to the village five kilometers away, which supplied all the other villages around it with everything they needed to live.

There was a bank and a *corner store*, which also had a small post office. The store was run by Grandma Korner from the senior citizens' group. Despite her 72 years, she still worked hard and did as much as possible herself. Only when she had doctor's appointments or went to the regulars' table did she leave the business to her helpers.

Next to the EDEKA-Food-Store was the *Korner bakery* and diagonally opposite, behind the pretty village fountain, was the *Korner butcher's shop*.

The Korners were probably the only long-established family in the village who did not own a farm, but had nevertheless established themselves as an indispensable part of the village with their business. Only the petrol station did not belong to the Korners, it was run by old Brennauer, whose wife was also one of Grandma Huber's friends.

Then, of course, there was the obligatory Italian restaurant, which also delivered pizzas. And just over a year ago, a Turkish family settled here and, after some initial difficulties, ran a kebab stand quite successfully. Both families have now been fully integrated into rural life, are very popular and have become indispensable here.

The elderly general practitioner and an even older dentist took care of our health. Both, how could it be otherwise, brothers of course.

A construction company, a carpenter, an old print shop and a disused quarry are also worth mentioning. That was it. Apart from that, it was a *dead zone* here. Except, of course, for the fire department festival, the shooting festival and the footballers' ball. The whole village celebrated at these mega-events.

Another major event was carnival. Every year on Shrove Monday, the Village-mug-Inn hosts a fun, so-called "*cap evening*". The guests put funny caps on their heads, feel dressed up and dance to the sound of a cheap Hammond organ and everyone roaring along: "... on the North Sea coast ..." or "... here the holes are about to fly out of the cheese ...", a polonaise through the restaurant.

Willy had removed the front passenger seat from his BMW weeks ago so that Ernest could sit more comfortably. What's more, without this seat, the heavyweight was able to get in through the passenger side and roll himself onto the back seat like a crawler. He had already practiced this so much that he was able to get in and out of the car perfectly.

Willy drove off. Although he and Tommy were sitting behind each other, the BMW was leaning slightly to the right. Ernest was firmly convinced that Willy had the tools and first-aid kit in the trunk on the right-hand side and that this must be the reason for the uneven weight distribution. Willy was therefore responsible for the BMW's lean.

"Are we having a snack there?" Ernest wanted to know.

Tommy thought he had heard wrong. "We've just had breakfast," he countered immediately.

That wasn't an argument for Ernest. "But a trip like that makes you hungry."

Willy was more on Tommy's side, took a deep breath, turned onto the main road and accelerated. "We've been on the road for less than five minutes and you two are already talking about food again. Is that necessary?"

Annoyed, he switched on the radio.

Beautiful maiden, do you have time for me today? Ho-ja-ho-ja-hooo, blared *Tony Marshall's* voice from the speakers.

Willy was shocked. He frantically tried to tune in another station. "Who was playing the radio and saved this grandma station? If I listen to it any longer, I'll have to pull over and throw up."

Tommy grinned. "Stay cool, Willy. I sat here with Grandma Huber and listened to music while I gave her some medicine packets."

"You're selling drugs in my car?"

"What nonsense. This is medicine. Herbs from my herb garden. And if it helps Grandma Huber and her friends, then I'm doing something good with it."

"The old women smoke weed because there's nothing else to make life better here in the country, except maybe boozing. That's the truth."

"Don't be so mean, Willy. The stuff helps them and nobody else gets it either. Besides, I'm not really dealing because I only take one euro for a pipe filling. You really can't call that a profit. I'm no *Walter White* from *Breaking Bad.*"

Ernest spoke up. "I'm the policeman among us and of course I've checked the whole thing from a forensic point of view. I declare it to be medical *hemp* and I'm of the opinion that Tommy isn't doing anything illegal," he said rather confidently, then thought about it for a moment.

"Except that he might not have a license to grow the stuff, but that's ridiculous compared to the Colombians or other cartels in the real narcotics scene. Besides, the proceeds are just enough for us to be able to order food from an Italian restaurant or buy a kebab once a week. So we leave the money in the community. From that point of view, it's nothing more than a barter deal," he explained, taking Tommy's side. Then he skillfully returned to the initial topic. "Speaking of food, have we decided where we're going yet?"

Willy gave up. Jimi Hendrix's guitar riffs thundered out of the radio and that improved his mood considerably. "Okay, we'll go shopping now, then we'll get something to eat, but Italian is out of the question. We're short of cash. However, a tasty kebab would be no problem for anyone."

"It's not even twelve yet," Tommy wondered. "I thought you didn't want to buy a kebab before lunch. Last time, all the vegetable soup tasted of garlic because you had to eat a kebab beforehand."

"So what? When I'm hungry, I'm hungry. And then I don't care whether it's seven in the morning, twelve at noon or one in the morning. And I think that a kebab is a first-class starter and goes perfectly with vegetable soup," countered Ernest, who was afraid that his buddies might decide against the kebab stand.

"Guys, but let's go shopping at EDEKA first, shall we?" Willy interjected.

Silence.

"What's going on?" Willy asked and shifted down a gear. A tractor with a slurry tanker attached was chugging along in front of them.

"I'm already hungry," Ernest sulked. "If we go shopping first, the kebab won't be enough, so we'd better go to the Italian restaurant." He rubbed his stomach and squeezed out a long, drawn-out "Mmmmh".

"We've already had pizza twice this week," Tommy complained. "We'll do as we agreed and eat kebabs!"

"Today is Monday!" Ernest interjected. "And since it's the first day of the week, it's clear that we haven't even gone out to eat this week. And we could eat kebabs on kebab day."

"Kebab day?" Tommy repeated thoughtfully.

"Thursday is kebab day from now on," explained Ernest, proud of his skillful play on words.

Tommy felt defeated and a little offended. "Then we just had pizza last week. I don't really care. Anyway, we're having pizza far too often these days."

"It's delicious, too."

Tommy became grumpy. "That may be. But not if you eat them every day," he hissed angrily.

"We're not," grinned Ernest.

"But almost every day!" Willy remarked, shifted down a gear again, put the blinker on and pressed the gas pedal. He swerved and overtook the tractor. A faint smell of liquid manure permeated the BMW's ventilation system. Willy rolled down the side window a little, which let in even more stench. Sighing, he closed the window again.

"So what? It's damn tasty too!" Ernest repeated.

"That may be. But not if you eat them every day," Tommy insisted.

"That's what you just said," came from Willy, who had reached his recommended speed of 80 km/h again. The old car didn't have much more to offer when Ernest was driving along.

"So what! But he also said earlier that it's delicious."

"So what?" interjected Ernest, who thought he was in the right and wanted to annoy Tommy.

Tommy sulked. "Oh, why don't you leave me alone?"

"Italian?" Ernest suggested again, but this time with a nice, conciliatory tone of voice. He grimaced and rubbed his hands over his voluminous belly again. He looked at Tommy questioningly.

He turned away demonstratively and looked out of the window, still offended.

Ernest began to sing. "O sole mio .... O my pizza ... how I love you ... O ..."

Tommy, who had to stifle his laughter, turned to Ernest. "Stop singing, it's all right. I agree, but next time I'll decide what we eat all by myself."

"Agreed," came from Willy.

"All right, and I suggest we go back into town on kebab day, then you can decide that we get a kebab."

Tommy thought about it for a moment. "Okay, it's a deal! That's fair!"

Willy parked in front of the village store. *EDEKA-Korner* is written on a sign. Blue lettering, yellow background, illuminated at night. Seen from a distance, it gave the impression of a large supermarket. In reality, however, the store was only about a quarter of the size of a conventional supermarket.

They got out and picked up a shopping cart. Then the three friends entered the village store.

"Good morning," greeted Ernest.

Mrs. Korner, who was also responsible for the post office counter and the cash register, looked at her watch with a wry expression. In her opinion, it was far too late for a *good morning greeting*. In keeping with Bavarian custom, she grumbled: "Grüß Gott!" before lowering her eyes again and sorting a few sheets of stamps.

The small store had just three aisles, in which the shelves were filled with drugstore items, food and other stuff. Everything was neatly lined up and restocked, as if someone went through after every purchase and straightened the goods with a ruler.

The shopping list was quickly completed and the friends stood in the small queue at the checkout that had formed in the meantime. The word *queue* is a relative term. It consisted of two people, but they needed about as much time as a twenty-meter-long queue in a large discount store. This was because Ms. Korner had conversations with all the customers, which were longer or shorter depending on how well known they were.

The unlikely friends waited patiently until it was finally their turn. In the meantime, three rather gloomy-looking guys who were probably passing through had queued up behind them. Neither Mrs. Korner nor the other two customers greeted them, but simply looked at them suspiciously. That was the clear sign to the villagers that they were strangers.

To be on the safe side, strangers were not approached at first. It was comparable to a western in which a rider came into town and was made fun of by the sheriff. The rider was allowed to buy himself a whiskey because he had a dry throat, had to hand in his weapons beforehand

and was told to leave town as quickly as possible after the drink. When he rode away, a tangle of bushes blew through the street, the bad guy met up with his gang, turned back and there was a fierce shootout, with the good guy winning.

Here and now, of course, Mrs. Korner embodied the good guys and the strangers at the back of the queue were the bad guys. At least that was the impression they got from the looks they were given at regular intervals.

After what felt like a quarter of an hour, it was finally the friends' turn. The goods were placed on the mini treadmill, typed in and ended up back in the shopping cart. After the last item had passed through the checkout, the store manager said: "53.80!" and, without looking at the bill held out to her by Ernest, squinted at the three people passing through.

Ernest cleared his throat. Mrs. Korner showed no reaction. The situation was frozen. Frozen in shock. The good girl aimed at the three bad guys. The Winchester lying imaginary under the counter was loaded, her hand on the stock of the gun. The air was as tense as in a western.

"Hello Mrs. Korner," Tommy tried his luck.

The store owner's frowning face brightened when she heard his voice. She immediately paid attention to him. "Hello Tommy, how are you? Would you like a doughnut? They're from yesterday, but they're still delicious. I'll give you one."

"Gladly!"

Mrs. Korner reached behind her and handed Tommy the pastry.

"Thank you very much."

"Tell me, I'm meeting Grandma Huber again soon. Have you given her the medicine for me yet?"

"Sure! She picked up the herbal mixture on Saturday."

The older lady rubbed her hands together. "Very nice." Then she changed her expression again, looked at Ernest, repeated: "53.80!" and reached for the banknote that was still in her customer's hand. At the same time, she continued to stare at the three strangers.

Ernest opened the change compartment of his wallet. He shook his head in the negative. Although the movement was only slight, his cheeks wobbled for a moment, reminiscent of a St. Bernard dog wiping the water from its fur after a downpour. "I'm afraid I'm not 3.80."

"I can give out."

Ernest squinted behind Mrs. Korner. "Are there any doughnuts left from yesterday? I could eat one too," he grinned.

"No, but my brother over at the bakery probably still has some. There are so many, they even have to sell them," Mrs. Korner joked and was the only one to laugh at her joke. Then she put the change on the counter.

Ernest was disappointed. A doughnut like this would have been just the thing for in between. "I need another postcard. You know, I have this rich uncle in Canada. Uncle Eddie, the one with the supermarket chain and the hotels. I need to send him my regards again and finally tell him where I live now. He sends me money every month."

"Nobody cares, Ernest," came from Willy.

Ms. Korner reached under the counter and placed two postcards with motifs of the market town on the counter. "Two euros with a stamp!"

Ernest looked at the postcards. "Hm, which one should I take?"

Tommy compared the motifs. One card showed the EDEKA supermarket, the other the village fountain. "Take the fountain," he suggested, but Ernest had already decided on the EDEKA card.

"It's great. I'll text him that I'm in this store right now."

Willy was bored. "We'll go to the car and put the stuff away," he said and pushed the shopping cart towards the exit.

"I have to go over to the bank right now. That was the last of our cash," Ernest called to him.

"Sure, then you just follow me. We'll go to the Italian restaurant."

The bank and the pub were opposite each other on the other side of the street. So from Ernest's point of view, the distance he had to walk was no problem. In addition, he counted every movement as exercise, which brought him a little closer to his goal of training every day for the next police recruitment test. "Okay, I'll have a family pizza with everything."

Willy turned around. "This is a family pizza," he said in a stern tone, discreetly pointing out to his buddy that this huge slice would usually feed a family of four.

Ernest nodded. "That's exactly right. *Family pizza* is a stupid name, isn't it, but it simply tastes the best," enthused Ernest, feeling his mouth watering.

"You can also have a ..."

Ernest raised his hand in objection. "I'll have a family pizza with everything and extra cheese," he grinned, ignoring his roommate's objection.

Willy gave up. "Okay! Before you start bitching at home again," he made a disparaging hand gesture and pushed the shopping cart out of the village store. "A family pizza then," he grumbled quietly.

"With everything and extra cheese!" Ernest called after him admonishingly, paid for the postcard, moved aside to make room for the three guys and filled out the postcard with a customer pen lying around, which was secured against theft with a thin parcel string.

The three guys who had been queuing behind the flatmates at the checkout had also left the village store after shopping and were in the parking lot. They had their heads together and were whispering. In general, they didn't seem very likeable. It was exactly the kind of group of people you would usually cross the road to avoid trouble.

To all appearances, it was a family. A father with his two sons, because all three had the same elongated, horse-like face. One of them even had a revolver in his pocket. As he bent down to pick up something shiny, the pommel of the gun poked out from under his jacket for a moment.

"Look, a lump of gold," the guy said happily.

The old man poked him briefly in the side and said grimly: "Hide the gun, you fool! The handle's sticking out. Besides, that's not gold, it's the wrapper of a chocolate."

"What a shame!" the finder exclaimed, took a closer look at the find and threw it away again. "You're right Dad, it's garbage."

The old man pointed covertly towards the store. "I looked in the till, there are only a few paltry bills in there. Not even 200 euros."

"But that's not enough. Shouldn't we rob the bank instead?" suggested his other son, who seemed a little more intelligent.

"So they can film us again and we can see our faces in the papers and on TV? Forget it. The last two years in prison were enough for me. Besides, we said that the next robbery would bring us the big money," the father objected and repeated: "Not 200 euros! That's not enough loot!"

"And what now, Daddy?"

The old man grinned mischievously. "I already have an idea of how we're going to get a lot of money."

The sons clapped their hands. "How then, Pop?"

"You've seen the fatso, haven't you?"

"Yes," they both nodded.

"We kidnap the guy and demand a ransom."

Two heads flew around and stared in the direction of the supermarket. They were looking for the victim. "Is he rich? Do you know him?"

"Don't look, you fools!" the old man scolded.

Her eyes were immediately drawn back to her father's, who continued: "It's not him, it's his uncle who's rich. Don't you listen when people talk?"

Shaking his head in amazement. The somewhat more intelligent son asked: "That's a great idea. How much money will we get?"

"Certainly a grand each," said the man with the gun happily.

The father slapped his forehead lightly with the flat of his hand. "Oh man! I don't know what I've done wrong with you. But you don't know anything about business. We're asking for 100,000 euros! And with that, we'll retire in the south."

Both sons stutter. "One-hundred-hundred-hundred thousand?"

"Right!" The old man breathed in proudly and puffed himself up like a peacock that had just flapped its feathers.

"And how do we do that?" the one with the gun wanted to know, scratching the back of his head.

"It's quite simple. We watch the guy. When the fat bastard comes out of the store, we grab him, put him in the trunk and get out. We send the blackmail letter to his two buddies. They seem to live together. Tell them to contact his uncle and he'll send the money."

Pause. Thinking. "But we don't even know where they live."

"Idiot! Of course the fat guy tells us that!"

Broad grins on everyone's faces. "What a great plan! Mom will be delighted when she's released from prison in a few days."

"The plan is mine too," the father boasted.

"And where are we going with our hostage?" pondered the cleverer of the two sons.

"Exactly where we've been hiding all this time. In the quarry."

Ernest squeezed his text onto the postcard and slid it across the sales counter. "I'll leave it here."

Mrs. Korner nodded wordlessly.

The heavyweight squinted at the two doughnuts again, but again refrained from asking for them and left the store. The corpulent police fan was in high spirits. He had written a postcard to Uncle Eddie, was exercising by walking to the bank and the Italian restaurant, and was looking forward to the reward. A family pizza.

He strolled leisurely across the parking lot. He warbled the tune of Maya the Bee and began to sing softly: "... and this bee I mean, her name is Maya ..."

Suddenly, tires squealed next to him. A small Fiat Panda stopped. Two men with balaclavas pulled over their heads jumped out of the small car. The driver remained seated. Ernest was shocked and stood still. The Maya the Bee song fell silent.

One of the guys pulled out a gun and pointed it at Ernest. He immediately raised his hands. "I ... I ... don't have any money. I'm on my way to the bank right now."

A rough voice, muffled by the balaclava, rang out to him. "Shut up, fat man! Get in the trunk with you!"

Ernest knew immediately that this was no game. While the first one was still threatening him with the revolver, the second perpetrator put a dark hood over his head. Ernest could no longer see anything. Everything was dark. Someone was scanning him. He had to laugh. "Hi, hi, hi, hi, hi. Stop it!" he giggled, wiggling his upper body impetuously. "I'm very ticklish."

"Shut up!" one of them shouted at him. "Stand still."

Ernest froze. His thoughts were racing. *What do these guys want from me? Hopefully nothing sexual!*

He felt his wallet being pulled out of his back pocket.

Phew, lucky me. They only want my money, not my body!

Anxious and unsettled, he said: "Look, there's no money in your wallet. You can keep everything that's still in it."

"Shut up, fat boy! Over to the trunk!"

Ernest had read a lot of books and watched a lot of movies. He knew what to do if you were the victim of a crime. At least in theory!

Stay calm, he told himself silently.

"Where am I?" he added, a little proud of his coolness.

"Stupid, still in the parking lot in the same town as before."

Ernest then heard a soft clap, followed by an "Ouch!" and a "Don't talk so much nonsense!"

The prisoner was maneuvered to the trunk of the car.

"Come on, get in there!"

Ernest felt the outline of the body and guessed that he was supposed to get into the trunk of the Fiat Panda. He turned around accordingly and sat down on the edge of the loading area. The small car was almost lifted up at the front due to its weight. The front tires just touched the ground. At the rear, on the other hand, the wheel arches sank down to the tires and came to rest on the ground. Ernest made an effort, but he had no chance of getting into the small trunk. "I can't do it," he said after a few attempts. He was starting to sweat under this stupid hood.

The kidnappers then tried to push him inside, but that was also doomed to failure.

"Shit, he's too fat!"

Ernest replied: "I'm not too fat. The trunk is too small!"

One of the kidnappers pulled the balaclava off his face and said: "The trunk's too small, Pa. We can't get him in there."

Gossip

"Ouch!"

"Don't call me Pa, you moron."

"Yes, Pa. You got it."

Gossip

"Ouch!"

"Come on, let's try it by lifting our legs up. Then it's bound to work!"

This attempt did not bring the desired success either.

"Too heavy," gasped the one with the raspy voice. It was the father of the three figures.

You just couldn't fit an XXXL parcel into an XS trunk or push a parcel through a letterbox slot.

They gave up. Their plan was impossible.

The old man thought for a moment, then ordered: "Go on, get him in the back. On the back seat."

Ernest stood up. The shock absorbers shot upwards, the front wheels touched the ground again completely. The hostage was taken to the rear side door. "Get in!"

The kidnap victim wanted to obey the order. He even put one leg into the vehicle to squeeze himself in completely, but his massive body got stuck at the entrance. "That's damn tight. What kind of mill are you driving?" grumbled Ernest.

"A Fiat Panda, you fat bastard!"

Gossip

"Ouch!"

"You don't say anything else now. Do you understand?"

"Yes, Pa!"

Gossip

"Ouch, why did I get that slap in the face again?"

"Because you said *Pa.*"

"Just because I say *Pa,* I get a slap in the face?"

Gossip

"Ouch!"

Both gangsters grabbed hold and tried to push Ernest into the vehicle. They pushed like crazy, but he definitely didn't fit in.

Attempt number three followed. "Come on, get in the passenger seat!"

They maneuvered Ernest slightly forward. He felt his way along the bodywork and the door. The command followed. "Get in!"

Ernest tried to get into the Fiat again. But no luck. "It's not possible. Your car is too small."

"You're too fat!"

Ernest got angry. He remembered that his family pizza was waiting for him. He was stressed. Stress made him hungry. And hunger made him grumpy. "No, the car is too small. You need a bigger car!" he groaned.

Silence. The gangsters seemed to be thinking. One of them became more and more nervous and panicked: "What do we do now? Hurry up, guys. If anyone sees us and calls the cops, we're fucked!"

The more intelligent son resigned himself. He had been watching from the driver's seat. "He really doesn't fit in, bloody hell. What do we do now?"

The father took the floor again. "Silence! Let me think!"

"Hurry up," urged the driver.

"I've got it," said the old man and turned to Ernest. "Watch out, fatso! We know where you live and we know that you're there with your gay buddies ..."

Ernest was really angry now. "We're not gay. We're a flat share and we're just mates!"

"Don't make a wave here!" one of the guys nudged him. It was probably the one with the gun, because Ernest felt something hard being pressed against his stomach. It could only be the revolver. "You don't need to justify yourself. We don't care if you're gay."

"But I do care. I want you to know that we're not gay! We're a decent flat share!"

The old man roared, completely exasperated. "Shut up!"

He took Ernest's ID card from his wallet and read his name and address out loud. Then he pocketed the ID card.

"I don't give a shit whether you're faggots or not! You'll get us exactly 100,000 euros by next Monday, otherwise we'll come by your place and put you down a meter. Understand? I have your ID. Your name is Ernest Kowalski and you have a rich uncle in Canada! So, Fetti, one more thing to remember! Get the money or we'll come and visit you and turn out the lights!"

"Pa, then we'll have to come at night. They don't have any lights on during the day."

Gossip

"Ouch!"

"Ernest, you're going to repeat what I told you!"

"My name is Ernest Kowalski and you don't care that we're not queers!"

Now the old man's collar burst. He ripped the hood off Ernest's head and shouted at him. "100,000 euros by next Monday or I'll kill you and your warm brothers!"

"They're not my brothers! And we're not gay, we're not warm and we're not faggots!"

The guy grabbed Ernest by the collar. "And no police, or I'll be standing by your bed one night! Do you understand me?"

That was clear. Ernest recognized in the old man's gaze that he was going to make good on his threats. He became afraid. Fear of death. His knees began to shake.

"We'll be in touch about the handover! One hundred thousand! Got it?"

Ernest's whole body was now trembling with fear. "Y-y-yes," he stuttered.

The younger of the two gangsters facing him reached into his trouser pocket and pulled out a cartridge. He held it between his thumb and forefinger and handed it to Ernest. "Here! I've got a whole load of these in my revolver. Each one has one of your names on it. I'll give you these so you don't forget to get the money on time. And no cops, otherwise ..." he indicated a cutting motion at the level of the genital area.

"No boo-boos!" confirmed Ernest, who felt hot and cold down his spine. He was fully aware that the gangsters were serious.

The men jumped into the Fiat Panda, the low-horsepower engine whined and they drove off. It took a good two or three minutes before Ernest was able to think reasonably clearly again. He was still shaking like a leaf.

I have to get to the boys and warn them, he thought, and started to run. That is, he took two or three quick steps, then fell back into his usual leisurely pace. However, he continued to breathe so excitedly that you would have thought Ernest had taken part in a marathon.

Dutiful as he was, he didn't forget to go to the bank first. After all, he needed cash to pay the pizza bill and Willy needed a penny for gas. Somewhat clumsily and with slightly shaky fingers, the voluminous man pulled his bank card out of his breast pocket. The moment he held it in his hands, he rejoiced inwardly. He had won a victory. Those bastards hadn't captured his bank card and therefore couldn't plunder his account.

Never keep everything together in one place. If something gets stolen, you still have reserves, he thought.

Ernest turned around several times. He wanted to make sure he wasn't being watched. Once he was sure he was alone, he inserted the card into the ATM, typed in the PIN and desired amount after a virtual prompt and grabbed the money from the dispenser.

And now for the Italian! Falling victim to a crime makes you hungry.

The Fiat Panda chugged along the country road.

"Pa, that was brilliant!" the driver praised the head of the gang.

"I know, kid. I'm the brains of our gangster family. Without me, you'd just be harmless muggers. But with me in charge, we're one of the big clans. We're the modern-day successors to Al Capone, Lucky Luciano, Jesse James and all the other gangster bosses."

"Bonnie and Clyde," the son, who was sitting in the back seat, pulverized to the front.

"They were lovers. They may have robbed a few banks and shot cops, but they weren't professionals," his father improved him.

"Yes, that's right. But then we're like our finance minister."

The driver rolled his eyes. "What's all this stupid talk? If you have no idea, then just shut up," he grumbled and pressed the gas pedal.

The speedometer needle wobbled its way up towards 90 km/h.

"We should use the money to buy a faster getaway car. If we make off with this car after a robbery, they'll catch us pretty quickly."

The old man turned around. "What do you mean, the finance minister?"

"Mom always said the finance minister was stealing all our money."

Silence.

"Pa?" asked the driver.

"What is it?"

"Where should I go?"

"Home to the suckers."

"And when they're at home?"

"Didn't you hear them eating pizza earlier? Man, if you didn't have me."

"What are we doing there?"

"Give me a pen and a piece of paper. I'll write them a little letter so that they actually know that we know where they live."

"Pa, you're simply the cleverest!"

The old man laughed maliciously. "They'll really wet their pants."

"What's more important is that they get the money."

"They will, boys, they will. And if they don't, we'll really light a fire under their asses," came the confident reply.

Willy and Tommy were sitting at their regular spot at *Da Antonio*. As always, Antonio served them personally. The landlord was a waiter and also stood behind the counter, while his wife worked in the kitchen and conjured up the finest Italian dishes. Her cooking skills were also reflected in her figure.

The restaurant was relatively small and if it wasn't located directly on the main street and therefore clearly visible to the few walk-in customers who occasionally strayed here, Antonio would probably have gone bankrupt in the first year.

Only gradually did the people here accept the *spaghetti*, as they first jokingly called Antonio when he opened his business and now with full respect. The villagers soon learned that there were other culinary delights besides schnitzel and roast pork.

By now, even people from the city were coming here to eat and you actually had to make a reservation at the weekends to get a seat.

An appetizing aroma wafted into the restaurant from the kitchen. It didn't take long for the two guests' mouths to water. Antonio came to the table. He twirled his voluminous moustache, which looked more Bavarian than Italian, and said: "*Buon giorno*, friends."

Tommy returned the greeting: "John Porno!" and was pleased with his almost perfect Italian.

Willy rolled his eyes in horror, Antonio ignored the slip of the tongue and asked about the third friend: "Without Ernest this time?"

"He's going to get some money, he'll be right there," Tommy replied.

"Do you already know what you want to drink?"

Willy waved him off. "Nothing today, Antonio. We've been shopping and the stuff will only break if it doesn't get into the fridge quickly. We'd like to order takeaway pizza."

The Italian placed two menus, which he had been holding in his left hand, on the table. "Here you are, Seniores, perhaps a small espresso on the house while you wait?"

Willy nodded, Tommy waved him off. "Ernest wants a family pizza with everything and extra cheese, but we both need to take a quick look at the menu."

"Don't be in a hurry. I'll make the espresso first."

The door literally banged open. Ernest came strutting in like a gunslinger in the Wild West. However, he didn't look so casual and cool, but was sweating like crazy. He seemed to be completely winded and was pale as a sheet. You would have thought a horde of wild rockers were chasing him to beat him up. Or worse. It was Sunday morning and the fridge was yawning empty. This was Ernest's worst nightmare. He quickly spotted his two buddies, headed for the table, sat down, turned to the landlord and said: "Antonio! Three grappas!"

Antonio beamed, Tommy and Willy immediately declined.

"Are you crazy? It's not even lunchtime yet and you're already ordering schnapps. I still have to drive!" grumbled Willy.

"They're not for you, they're for me!"

Tommy was confused. He had never seen Ernest this agitated before. Except perhaps the other day, when they were shopping in the big supermarket in the district town, when Ernest had had a look like this before.

"Ha, ha," Tommy chuckled as he remembered the scene and re-played it in his mind's eye.

Ernest strolled through the aisles with his shopping cart. He put pasta, tomato sauce and all sorts of stuff in the trolley. He had been looking forward to *Toast Hawaii* all day. Toast, slices of cheese, cooked ham and even a jar of cocktail cherries were already in the trolley. All that was missing were pineapple slices from the can.

Ernest spotted it and was startled to see from afar that there were only two cans of the beloved sliced fruit left on the shelf. His eyes immediately circled around like a radar device. Except that his radar wasn't detecting enemy planes, but potential rival customers who could still snatch the can away from him. And indeed. Ernest spotted an elderly lady who, like him, was staring at the cans and accelerating towards them with her shopping cart.

"The cans are mine!" he had shouted and suddenly stepped on the gas, which meant something to Ernest.

Well, as anyone who knows anything about physics knows, once a certain mass has started to move, it also requires a corresponding braking distance. For example, an aircraft carrier or a fully loaded container ship has a braking distance of approx. 15 ship lengths when immediately under full braking. If such a ship is 200 meters long, it therefore requires a braking distance of 3 kilometers. If you apply this to Ernest, he would have had to brake before entering the aisle in order to come to a halt at the level of the pineapple cans. The opposite was the case. When he entered the aisle, Ernest did not initiate the braking process, but sped off. An estimated 160 kilos of live weight plus the products in the shopping cart started moving at increasing speed. He hit full speed and didn't even come close to stopping at his destination. He also rammed the shopping cart of the elderly lady. Both trolleys toppled over. A mash of burst milk cartons and yoghurt pots poured over flour, toast and other things.

Ernest slid over this mass, lost his balance and slammed into the shelf of cans like a felled tree. He remained lying there, his belly fat wobbling violently for a long time.

His opponent was a little more skillful. When she saw the disaster racing towards her, she let go of her car, shouting: "Help! A madman!", and backed off. Unfortunately, there was a pile of eggs behind her. She bumped into it, lost her footing and ended up landing on the cartons of 6 and 10 fresh eggs, all of which came from free-range hens in the region.

While she was still brushing the yolk, egg white and splintered shells out of her hairdresser-styled hair, she set her sights on Ernest. Her gaze alone would have been enough to kill him. That's probably why he didn't look at her, but rolled around with a loud groan, grabbed the cans of pineapple and cheered loudly: "Toast Hawaii is safe, boys!"

Ernest had only noticed the misery at the time after he had held the cans up in a jubilant victory pose. His eyes froze when he noticed the utter misery around him. It almost took his breath away. He saw Personal run up, recognized the old lady's death stare, shook his head and had the presence of mind to shout, "Can't you watch where you're going? I could have hurt myself."

That was exactly the wrong thing to say, as the first eggs flew in his direction. Ernest tried to get out of the way and, believe it or not, his weight, thrown backwards with a bit of vigor, was enough to knock over another shelf. Ravioli, chilli con carne and various soups rolled through the supermarket.

Crack crash boom rumble

Dominoes of the unwanted kind. The shelf naturally crashed onto the next shelf, which in turn crashed onto the shelf next to it.

Shelf domination in the supermarket, you could read in the newspaper the next day. *Grandmother goes crazy*, was the second headline.

And thanks to the coincidence that the employees only arrived at the scene of the accident at the moment when the elderly lady was running after Ernest like a fury and repeatedly throwing objects at him, the newspaper report concluded: *Elderly woman admitted to mental hospital after rage attack!*

At that moment, Ernest also got the rushed look he had now and he was just as drenched in sweat then. However, he didn't need three grappas afterwards, but ate two more Hawaiian toasts than usual. "Because of the excess calories burned while running," he had explained. "It helps with sore muscles."

Since that day, they have only shopped at *EDEKA-Korner*, even though it was a little more expensive here than at the big discount store. Since then, they avoided the supermarket in the district town like the plague. Ernest had expressed concerns that the old lady might be lying in wait for them to take revenge.

Antonio put the three grappas on the table. Ernest still hadn't said anything. He had to calm down first. The dark sweat stains under his armpits had already taken on enormous proportions. Antonio handed Ernest a napkin so that he could dab the sweat from his forehead.

"Now tell me what's going on," urged Willy.

"First things first. First things first. Have you ordered my family pizza?"

"Yeah, sure."

"With extra cheese?"

"Of course! But now tell me what's going on!"

Ernest was relieved. The pizza would do him good later. "Well, boys, watch out. Our lives are in danger!"

Willy leaned back and Tommy leaned forward. "What?" they said at the same time.

Ernest took a grappa and downed it. He put the glass on the table and reached for the second. "You heard right. Our lives are in danger!"

"What makes you think that? Did you find out from a secret agent that a nuclear bomb will explode right here and World War III will begin?"

Tommy liked Willy's question and also thought of something clever to say: "Or did the dinosaurs from *Jurassic Park* make it this far?"

"They've all been taken care of," Ernest said casually.

"Exactly not. A few have survived!"

"Tommy, that was a movie," interjected Willy, who finally wanted to know what had happened to Ernest.

"The critters were real! Didn't you watch the movie in 3-D? I'm telling you, the dinosaurs are real!"

Ernest shook his head. As always, his chubby cheeks were flabby. "Those were tricks."

"What nonsense. I saw it myself at the movies!"

Willy appeased him. He really wanted to know what Ernest had to report. The subject seemed serious and explosive. Ernest very rarely drank schnapps, and when he did, it was definitely never before dinner. "Okay guys, I'd suggest we discuss this topic another day," he decided and addressed Ernest before Tommy added something else and the pointless discussion about dinosaurs continued. "Now tell me what's going on!"

Antonio came to the table. "The pizzas are almost ready. Shall I cut them into pieces?"

"Yes, please," Ernest replied.

Willy nodded in agreement. "As always."

"Si, as always, eight pieces and large family pizza in 16 pieces."

Tommy thought for a moment and raised his hand in objection. "Uh, please only cut mine into four pieces. I can't manage eight today. That would really be too much."

Silence. All eyes are on Tommy.

Antonio wondered whether he should laugh or answer. He decided not to do anything, waited briefly and spoke in Italian out of sheer confusion. "Quattro o otto pezzi, amico mio."

Tommy was now staring at Antonio. "Otto? No, the pizza is for me. I don't know any Otto."

Antonio gave up. "It's Italian and means four or eight pieces, my friend."

"Wow, guys, did you hear that? Antonio can speak Italian."

The innkeeper closed his eyes, took a deep breath and then said: "I think I need a grappa too."

Willy had to intervene. "You already know that it makes no difference whether you eat the pizza in eight or four pieces," he tried to explain to his buddy Tommy. "And by the way, Antonio *is* Italian." The emphasis was extremely strong.

Tommy shook his head vehemently and grinned in victory. "You're on the wrong track this time. Eight is more than four."

"But if you have them cut into four pieces, one piece is twice as big as if you have them cut into eight pieces."

It took Tommy a moment to come to his senses. "What are you talking about, old man? Eight is more than four," he repeated.

"But the two pizzas are always the same size. No matter how many pieces you divide them into."

"Huh? I don't check," Tommy shrugged his shoulders. "Why is the pizza the same size as the other one? You only have one. How big is the other one? And where did it suddenly come from?"

"It doesn't matter. Ultimately, this question doesn't arise, and if it does, then only as a rhetorical question," said Willy.

"A what?"

"A rhetorical question."

"What is a rhetorical question?"

Willy clapped his hand against his forehead.

Antonio rolled his eyes and Ernest intervened. "A question you don't expect an answer to," he explained.

Antonio was almost desperate. His head flew back and forth like in a tennis match. "Four or eight pieces? How am I supposed to cut now?"

"Four!" said Tommy.

"Eight," said Willy and added: "Then you can have a look at it at home."

Antonio left. "I think I'll have two grappas."

The pizzas were brought to the table, Ernest paid and they left the restaurant. He had a grappa flag and his stomach was growling. "I hope I make it home. That smells great again."

"You won't eat anything in my car."

"It's okay!"

"You also have to finally tell us what happened," Tommy urged.

They drove. Tommy had the pizzas on his lap to be on the safe side. This ensured that Ernest didn't start eating in the BMW.

"They just tried to kidnap me. But I didn't fit into the three gangsters' car."

Willy braked abruptly and pulled over immediately. Tommy had trouble holding on to the pizzas.

"You what?" Willy gushed.

Ernest told the whole story one after the other to get to the point at the end. "... and then they said that we had exactly one week to raise 100,000 euros!"

Chapter 3
100,000 euros is a piece of cake

The three buddies sat in front of their empty pizza boxes and pondered to themselves. They were deeply shocked when they found and read the letter at home. So the criminals knew where they lived.

Terrible! Devastating! Frightening!

Each of the three friends suddenly realized that the *worst case* had happened.

Ernest made a face as if the fridge was empty, Tommy looked as if his marijuana field in the garden had burned down and he could no longer sell his girlfriends medicine, and Willy stared as if someone had run over his BMW with a tractor.

Endless minutes of silence. It was Willy who finally broke the silence by lifting up the sheet of paper with the spidery handwriting and reading the blackmailers' lines out loud once more. "You have one week to get 100,000 euros or you will die one after the other. First the fat one, then the tall one and finally the slim one."

Ernest took an audible deep breath, looked around and asked: "Who do these assholes mean by *the fat one*? I'm the big one, there's no question about that." His gaze lingered on Willy. He scrutinized the car mechanic. "You haven't actually put on that much weight," he turned to the gardener. "Tommy's got a bit fuller. But to call him *fat* just because of that is really cheeky. Don't you agree?"

Willy screwed up his face, rolled his eyes and tried to say it as gently as possible. "Sorry Ernest, but they mean you. You're *the fat one* for them! First they want to kill you, then me and you die last," he said, looking at Tommy. Without waiting for a reaction, he lowered his eyes to the paper again and continued reading, visibly affected. "As soon as you have the money, send a text message to the cell phone number below. Then we'll arrange a handover date. The number is untraceable. Prepaid. We're not stupid! And no police! Remember, we know where you live and who you are. 100,000 euros! Payable in one week!"

Break.

Willy swallowed. His Adam's apple was clearly moving up and down. "And then they drew a hangman on it!" he squeezed out in a croaky voice.

Ernest grabbed his neck and rubbed it.

Tommy noticed this and wanted to comfort him. "Don't worry, Ernest. They won't hang you. The rope would break. Man, I'd love to be as fat as you."

Ernest glared at his buddy. "I'm not fat, I just have incredibly heavy bones. It runs in our family. But apart from that, they're serious, these gangsters can't take a joke. They showed me a cartridge in the parking lot and said that they had one for each of us and that it had everyone's name on it. My money's on the mafia. These guys are cold as ice!"

Willy hit the table so hard with his fist that the candle fell out of the candlestick. "Bloody hell! What are we doing? And where did these kidnappers get the idea of blackmailing us? We barely have enough money to get by ourselves."

"Maybe they think I'm part of some big drug cartel. Just because I sell my *health herbal mixture* to the ladies here in the village," Tommy interjected and tried to put the candle back in the candlestick. It took him a few attempts, but then he leaned back proudly. It had worked. The candle held.

"Nonsense! If this had anything to do with drugs, they would have shot us long ago," Ernest shook his head. He straightened the candle as it looked like the Leaning Tower of Pisa.

"Or blown up with a car bomb," Tommy confirmed. "Like in those movies you like to watch."

Ernest took a deep breath. "They want me to ask Uncle Eddie from Canada to give me the money."

Tommy laughed, slapped his thighs and stood up. "Great idea. Bingo, we've solved the problem. What's on TV? Would anyone like a Coke? I'm going to the fridge."

Willy looked at Ernest. He didn't look very relaxed. "Forget Uncle Eddie. He does pay me a thousand a month, but that's only because he signed a sort of contract when I was born. I think Mom got him to do that because she knows something about him that's better kept secret. You have to know that my uncle is stingier than *Scrooge McDuck*. He'd rather die than voluntarily pay a penny to blackmailers."

Willy couldn't believe it. "It's not about any business, it's about his nephew's life."

Ernest waved them off. "Do you know why Uncle Eddie lives a-lone?"

"Nah."

"No."

"Because his wife was kidnapped ten years ago. The perpetrators demanded a million dollars back then. Uncle Eddie just said that they should go to work for their money and that he wouldn't pay a cent. He wouldn't support something like that and couldn't be blackmailed."

"And how did that end?"

"His wife has since disappeared without a trace. He will not be blackmailed."

"You're taking the piss, aren't you? That must be a joke," gushed Willy.

Ernest wordlessly replied in the negative, swaying his head slightly back and forth. His cheeks wobbled as usual.

"What if he lends you the money?" suggested Tommy, who thought he'd had a stroke of genius.

"He doesn't. As far as that's concerned, he thinks that if you need to borrow money, you should go to the bank. If they don't lend you anything, he won't do it."

"Your Uncle Eddie is quite an ass," commented the amateur gardener.

"That pretty much sums it up!"

Tommy looked at Willy. "Your ex-wife? Do you think she could..." he didn't finish the sentence, because Willy's look was expressive enough. He said something like: *Shut up, never mention Sylvia again or I'll strangle you!*

Instead of saying another word about this option, let alone going into the idea in any detail, Willy got up and fetched a writing pad and a pen. He sat down again and began to make notes without saying a word.

Ernest squinted at the sheet of paper and read: *Uncle Eddie*. As soon as he had written it, Willy crossed out the words. Ernest became curious. "What are you doing?"

Willy was deadly serious. "We have to consider all the options that come into question. And so that we know we're not forgetting anything, I'll write it down. So, everyone thinks and we write everything down."

Ernest was thrilled. "That's called *brainstorming*! I wanted to suggest that too."

"Brain-what?" asked Tommy.

Willy grinned. "What other people have in their heads."

Ernest was nicer. "Just tell me your ideas on how we can get 100,000 euros," he said, but also refrained from giving an explanation.

Some time later, all the options that the three friends had come up with to solve the acute problem were written on the piece of paper.

Willy put the pen to one side and passed the solution sheet around. "Read it, then we'll discuss each individual point."

1. ~~uncle Eddie~~
2. inform the police
3. search for jobs
4. take out a loan
5. play the lottery
6. selling marijuana on a large scale
7. rob a bank
8. move away from here

"Do you really think we should call the police? The three gangsters are extremely dangerous and I don't want to take any risks," Ernest began.

"What Ernest says makes sense. What if the police only catch one or two of the guys? Then the third guy takes revenge and possibly burns down the house while we're asleep. Or builds a bomb in the BMW and we explode when we go shopping," Willy states soberly.

"And how do we do that with the jobs?" Tommy wanted to know.

Willy gave the answer. "I'll get us a daily newspaper. We'll read the job advertisement thoroughly and systematically. Maybe we'll find something."

"Good idea, please bring cake. I once read that you should eat lots of sweets when you're thinking. It stimulates the brain."

Tommy had a slice of apple pie, Willy a cherry turnover and Ernest an apple pie, a cherry turnover and a Black Forest gateau. "That's exactly the crucial link in my stomach between the apple pie and the cherry tart, you know, that's how I harmonize my inner values. It's called *feng shui* in the body," Ernest explained when he was accused of saving money in order to scrape together the 100,000 euros for the blackmailers.

The open daily newspaper lay on the table. Willy read it out. "They're looking for a nursery school teacher in the neighboring community."

"No!" came the chorus.

The finger wandered over three more job advertisements. "Bricklayer wanted. Do you think we could work in construction?"

Shake your head.

"Then there's a part-time janitor job at the town hall."

Ernest asked: "Is there nothing about a detective agency? I could use my police experience to get a temporary job there before I start my training."

Willy replied in the negative. "Unfortunately not."

Tommy wondered what police experience Ernest was talking about. After all, he had only been to the medical test. End of experience. But if Ernest could do detective work, he could also do gardening. "Or is someone looking for a gardener?" he asked.

"Not even that. No gardener, no detective, no car mechanic."

Ernest became nervous: "What are they looking for anyway?"

Willy turned the page and skimmed a headline. "They're looking for a sex offender who harasses women in the city park."

Tommy scratched the back of his head. "Do you think that would be a job for me? What do they pay?"

From the looks he received for this question, the hobby gardener quickly realized that this was not a job offer.

Willy put the newspaper aside. "There's no point. Nothing for us."

"And what about the janitor? What are they paying you?"

"450 euros a month."

Ernest thought about it for a moment. "If we take the job, pay off a loan of 100,000 euros at the bank and the interest rate is pretty low, we'd have to pay for around 300 months, then we'd be debt-free again. That's 25 years."

Tommy slapped his thighs. "Bingo! Let's do that. Problem solved!"

"No bank will lend us that much money. Forget it," came from Willy. At the same time, he lifted up a lottery ticket. "I played it with the last household money. If we hit the jackpot on Wednesday evening, we'll be out of trouble!"

Tommy slapped his thighs again. "Bingo! This time we've really solved the problem."

Tommy also understood Ernest's remark that you would have to fill in about 100 million lottery tickets with different number combinations to have a good chance of winning.

"And what do we do if we don't hit the jackpot?" he asked, his gaze falling on the next item. "Do you think I should go into the big marijuana business?"

All three got up and went to the window. They looked out at the hemp field, which was now growing lushly in the garden.

"Oh my God," Ernest, who had never noticed how many hemp plants were sprouting there, exclaimed. "You made all that from this one plant?"

Tommy was proud. "Not quite. A few seeds had already been sown by the previous tenants. But I took good care of the plants. That suits me."

Ernest began to do the math. "How many ... well ... joints ... do you get out of it?"

"If I take the herbal mixtures for my ladies as a guide, I guess ..."

"Stop!" raged Willy.

His two buddies looked at him in amazement.

"Do you remember what happened to our previous tenants?"

"Sure," replied Tommy. "They went to prison."

Willy raised a warning finger. "Exactly!"

"We're smarter than that," Ernest replied.

"It works here in the village. The group of ladies who consume Tommy's stuff keep their mouths shut, but if we grow and sell cannabis on a large scale, we'll soon not only have the drug squad on our backs, but also the drug cartels. Then we'll have the choice between prison and the cemetery. And in prison, sooner or later we'll meet the extortionists again."

Embarrassed silence. Nodding. Agreeing. "Willy's right. Besides, it would damage my police career," groaned Ernest.

Tommy's seconds-long dream of making it big in the marijuana business burst like a soap bubble. "Oh man! So what happens now?"

Willy lifted up the lottery ticket again. "We'll wait for Wednesday. If we hit the jackpot, we won't have any more problems."

"And if not, Willy?"

The car mechanic mumbled the next words somewhat reluctantly: "The next item on our list is: bank robbery!"

"Or move away from here," Tommy interjected.

"Is that what we want?" Ernest asked his friends.

All three agreed. No! They felt at home here in the village. They were recognized and had made friends with many people. So there were really only two things left to do to get money: rob a bank and run a marijuana business.

It was perfectly clear to Ernest and Willy that Tommy was better left out of the planning of a sure-fire bank robbery. With his talent for putting his foot in every little hole, he was far too big a risk. So they decided to work out a perfect plan for a bank robbery by Wednesday, while Tommy worked in his hemp field to make as many herbal mixtures for smoking and baking as possible.

Three friends, three options! They put the last options for getting money in a row.

Plan A - Lottery win
Plan B - Bank robbery
Plan C - Expand the marijuana business

Tommy worked like crazy in his herb garden. He watered here, plucked some weeds there. After tending to his herbs, he started harvesting. Hibiscus, peppermint, lemon balm, thyme and a few other herbs were neatly plucked or cut off. He put the harvest in a large basket and went to the barn. He spread everything out on a large table that was still here from the previous tenants. He looked at the ingredients for his medicinal herb mixture with satisfaction.

He wiped his hands on his dungarees, which reminded him of *Peter Lustig* and the construction trailer from *Dandelion*, grabbed the basket and went back outside. His destination was the marijuana field. The plants grew surprisingly quickly and bore impressive umbels. As he examined them and harvested them with a skillful eye, he was proud of himself.

"In life I'm a klutz and a loser, but here in the garden I'm the boss," he said. Gardening was in his blood and if it helped save his friend's life, he would work through the whole week without a break. He, Tommy the Full Chaot, knew how to do something that others could not. He had an indescribably good feeling for plants. He always used the right amount of fertilizer, which of course came from Farmer Huber's dung heap. The same dung heap that also masked the constant smell of marijuana in the air.

To everyone's amazement, Tommy was also able to handle gardening tools without any accidents. Perhaps this was because the young man didn't think when gardening, but acted purely on instinct.

He knew that he was often very clumsy and extremely untalented at ordinary tasks of all kinds. But he was also aware that he had probably discovered the perfect mixture of herbs, spices and marijuana to alleviate the everyday problems of the elderly ladies here in the village.

His medicine worked exceptionally well and the women had taken him to their hearts. A feeling that Tommy had never known before, apart from his family and of course his two best friends Ernest and Willy. They liked him here in the village and he was important to them all, and he also trusted Grandma Huber. She was old but sprightly. She knew almost everyone within a radius of 30 kilometers and had enormous influence. He knew that she could be secretive. And she was his great hope for saving his friends.

While Tommy had been cutting the herbs in the garden, this idea had matured in him. If the lottery jackpot plan failed, he would tell Grandma Huber about the blackmail. His idea was to make so many herbal mixtures that he could keep a whole army of pensioners fit.

In his mind, the amateur gardener saw himself dressed as a druid cutting mistletoe with a golden sickle. He was the modern-day *Miraculix* from the *Asterix and Obelix* comic. He was able to make a magic potion. Not as a potion, however, but for smoking and as a baking mixture. He would sell so many bags of his stuff that he could pay the blackmailers the 100,000 euros they demanded.

"If Grandma Huber knows 100 other grandmas, and they know as many other grandmas, and I have enough bags together, then I'll get," he used his fingers to do the math, looked at both hands, gave up and said quietly, "a hell of a lot of money!"

While Tommy was busy in the barn making his medicinal herb mixture on a grand scale, Ernest and Willy sat at the kitchen table and racked their brains as to how they could pull off a perfect bank robbery.

They agreed on one thing. Tommy stayed at home! He was the biggest risk, because the youngest of the three buddies was almost magically attracted to misfortune.

"One more time," Willy whispered, even though they were alone. "I'll park the BMW in the side street." His index finger was on the map of their neighboring market town. "You keep a lookout, I'll run to the bank, storm in, shout loudly: Robbery! Give me the money! Show my gun, have the money handed to me and get out! We then drive out of the town very slowly and go to EDEKA-Korner, buy something and get a pizza from Antonio. We drop Tommy off there before the robbery. He orders the pizzas and waits. He tells Antonio that we're still shopping. That's the perfect alibi!"

"That's right. The alibi is perfect," Ernest replied. "But you have a small flaw in your thinking."

Willy looked alternately at the city map, the edge of which was full of advertisements, and at Ernest. The latter leaned back and crossed his arms. The car mechanic waited for his overweight friend to continue talking, but Ernest remained silent. Annoyed, Willy asked: "What kind of mistake?"

"You wait in the car. You're the driver, I'm the one who storms into the bank and carries out the robbery!"

Now Willy leaned back. "I can't do that!"

"Oh yes I do!"

"Oh no!"

"Oh yes I do!"

"Oh no!"

"You bet I can!"

"That's just not possible!"

Ernest leaned forward again. "And why not?"

"Because ... because you ... well, I think I can ..." he thought about how best to express himself so as not to offend Ernest. "I think I can run faster than you. I got a winner's certificate at the sports festival at school and was the fastest in the 50-meter dash."

Ernest pondered. "That's a good point. I almost got a winner's certificate back then too, but I sprained my ankle in the long jump and therefore couldn't take part in the 50-meter run."

"How far did you jump?"

Ernest grimaced and stared at Willy, slightly angry. "That was a failed attempt, I tripped on the run-up and landed really badly on my jumping leg. The jump wasn't scored, so it wasn't measured! Is that enough of an answer?"

Willy raised his hands defensively. "That wasn't an accusation. It could have been that you only caught yourself on the third jump ..."

"No!" Ernest interjected. "At the first attempt, and now the subject is closed!"

Willy was silent. Ernest too. The car mechanic looked at his heavyweight friend, gave himself a jolt and asked again. "Okay, so ... what do you suggest?"

Ernest stopped sulking. "As you know, I'm the criminalist among us. Your mistake is that you're the *driver*, the man who waits in the car with the engine running and steps on the gas when I jump into the car after the robbery."

Willy gasped in and out at this thought. In his mind, he saw Ernest run quickly to the BMW, pull open the door and jump in. No! That could never work! "Well," he wanted to interject, but Ernest continued.

"Come to think of it, you and I should storm into the bank together."

"Why is that?"

"Back up! If a bank customer tries to play the hero, he could prevent me from escaping. Or worse still, one of the bank employees triggers the alarm because I can't keep an eye on everyone. If there are two bank robbers in the counter, one can get the money and the other can keep the customers and bank employees at bay."

Now Willy leaned forward too. A broad, confident grin flitted across his face. That sounded reasonable. He was convinced. "That's how we do it!"

Ernest was in his element. It was as if he was solving a criminal case, only backwards. He didn't solve the case, but devised a perfect plan that simply couldn't go wrong. "Now for the disguise! We have to cover our faces."

"Stocking masks?"

Ernest laughed. "Tell me, what century are you from? We're modern bank robbers. We wear costumes."

Willy was taking a sip of orange juice when Ernest said something about the costumes, he choked and coughed. "What, costumes? You're not seriously going to believe that we're going to storm into the bank as princesses or garden gnomes with pointed hats or, even worse, as unicorns. They'll all laugh themselves to death. I don't want to sit in prison and be greeted by every inmate with: *well, little princess.*" At the same time, he imagined Ernest in a princess costume with a little crown and began to laugh heartily.

"Why are you laughing so stupidly?" asked Ernest in amazement.

"I ... ha ha ha ... I ... ha ha ha," snorted Willy, "I imagine how you look in skin-tight white leggings and a tutu skirt and a crown on your head. And maybe you'll pull out a magic wand instead of a revolver and threaten to turn the bank employees into frogs ... ha ha ..."

"Idiot! They're fairies, not princesses. Oh man, I want to work with professionals for once in my life."

Ernest sulked again.

After Willy had made coffee and Tommy had served a packet of cookies, Ernest had calmed down.

The three of them sat at the table. Tommy wondered whether he should tell his buddies about the plan to take Grandma Huber on board. In the end, he decided to keep it to himself. That was his secret weapon. Instead, Ernest came up with the perfect plan to rob the bank. He had worked out the final details while Willy had put the coffee on.

"Listen up and shut up. I'll tell you beginners what we'll do if the lottery jackpot doesn't work out tonight!"

Tommy and Willy listened spellbound. Ernest put three cookies in his mouth at the same time and washed them down with coffee. Tommy poured tons of sugar into his cup and stirred for ages. Willy was curious to no end.

Ernest enjoyed the situation and delayed it again by reaching into the pastry bag once more. This time, however, he only took one piece in his fingers, put it in his mouth, chewed and swallowed it. Then he finally began to present his plan. "Here's what we're going to do: The three of us drive off. We'll drop Tommy off at Antonio's. He'll order pizza."

"What are you doing?" the gardener complained.

"That is important. Very important, in fact. You're our alibi. If you mess this up, we'll go to prison."

Tommy was silent at first, but then said in surprise: "Really? If I don't order a pizza, we have to go to jail? That's crazy." Thinking really wasn't his thing. He didn't understand, but didn't want to ask. He wanted the others to think he knew what it was all about. He was glad when Ernest gave him a short lecture about an airtight alibi and that he played an extremely important role in the bank robbery. Tommy felt like a hero.

"Go on," urged Willy.

"We both quickly buy something at EDEKA-Korner and then drive to the bank. We'll put on our camouflage there."

"What kind of cover?"

"We spoke the other day and talked about carnival."

"Carnival?" Tommy wanted to know.

"We call it carnival," Willy improved.

Ernest continued to speak. "Tommy was a cowboy."

"I was a gunslinger. Two guns in my belt," Tommy improved.

"Willy wasn't dressed up at all and I went as Batman."

"What's that got to do with the bank robbery?" asked Willy.

"We slip into these costumes, use Tommy's revolver and rob the bank. We cover each other. As soon as we have the money, we run to the car and drive to Antonio. We'll pick up Tommy and the pizzas there. Done!"

"Wait a minute!" Willy interjected. "You go as Batman, Tommy gives us the revolvers. And how do I dress up?"

Ernest nodded with a confident expression. "The Batman costume was a two-piece. Batman and Robin. I bought Batman in XXXL and Robin in XL because I wanted to wear it as soon as I lost some weight. You know, I'm in daily training for the police recruitment sports test."

"Batman and Robin," Tommy clapped his hands. "Nothing can go wrong. The two of them can do anything."

"At least they also have eye masks. Okay. I'll have a look at the costume. XL might fit," commented Willy.

"Then the BMW is the Batmobile," laughed Tommy, whose face suddenly stiffened. "Guys, my guns may look like the real thing, but they're not real Colts. You already know that, right?"

"Is that a problem?" Willy followed up and looked at Ernest questioningly.

He remained relaxed. "It's enough if they look like real revolvers! We only want to intimidate and not shoot anyone!"

Everyone agreed. The thing would work.

Wednesday evening. The lottery numbers were drawn live. Tommy held the ticket in his hand, Willy stared at the screen, Ernest wrote down the winning numbers on a piece of paper. Willy repeated the number drawn out loud.

"Score!" Tommy cheered at the first winning number.

"It's off to a promising start," grinned Willy.

The second number followed. Willy predicted it, Ernest wrote it down and Tommy compared it on the betting slip. "We did too!"

"Hey, great job Willy. Two right ones already," said Ernest happily.

When Tommy announced that the third number had also been marked, the joy almost spilled over. Willy was beaming all over his face. "Yay, we've already got three correct numbers and will get our stake back."

"Watch out, the fourth number is coming," said Ernest.

Willy read aloud. Ernest joined in and Tommy's eyes raced over the lottery ticket. "Right again!"

"Yay! Four right ones! Now it's getting exciting, guys!" shouted Willy excitedly.

Ernest broke out in a sweat with joy. His T-shirt turned dark under his armpits, small beads of sweat formed on his forehead and the hair on the back of his neck stuck to his skin.

Willy read out again and once more Tommy announced a hit. "Bingo!"

"A five of a kind! Friends under the sun, we've got five right! I can't believe it. Just one more number .... Attention ... watch out! Now it's being drawn!"

Ernest and Willy stared at the screen. Their pulses pounded, Ernest's beads of sweat rolled down his face. He reached into his trouser pocket. With a handkerchief, he quickly wiped his forehead and once around his head, then the handkerchief disappeared back into his pocket.

Willy said the last number in an almost shaky voice. Ernest wrote it down. Tommy's eyes sparkled.

"We've got them too, guys! All the numbers!"

Willy clapped his hands, jumped up, danced around the table and began to sing: "We are the Champions .... We are the Champions ..."

Ernest leaned back. He could hardly believe his luck. "Give me the lottery ticket. But be careful, it's the most valuable piece of paper you've ever held in your hands. I'm totally relieved."

Tommy stretched out his arm, Ernest took the lottery ticket and looked at it. Then he looked at his notepad, back at the lottery ticket and back at the notepad.

Willy danced into the kitchen. "Guys, do we have champagne in the house? I'd say we're celebrating!"

Tommy was now also dancing through the living room full of joy. "Juppi duppi dieh ... ha ha ha ... juppi duppi deih!" he sang, drowning out Willy, who didn't know any other lyrics by heart apart from the chorus of Queen's global hit.

Ernest turned white as a sheet. He took a deep breath, stood up and shouted as loud as he could: "Tooommmyyyy!"

Willy came back from the kitchen. Tommy was still dancing around, grinning at Ernest and singing in hip-hop style: "Ernest is standing there ... Tommy is dancing ... Willy is getting champagne ... the corks are popping! Yeah .... Antonio makes pizza .... We play the lottery ... he cuts them into Otto .... We get the millions ... yeah ..."

"Tooommyyyy!" Ernest repeated loudly.

Suddenly everyone fell silent and stared at the heavyweight.

"You're the biggest idiot I know. Have you ever played the lottery?"

Tommy was surprised. "No, why do you ask?"

"Because we have no profit. The numbers all have to be in the same box. We have all the numbers, but each one is in a different game. We haven't won anything, absolutely nothing!"

Willy's breath caught in his throat. "Like nothing?"

"Nothing," Ernest repeated.

Tommy scratched the back of his head. "I don't understand. We all have numbers. I'm not stupid!"

Willy went to Ernest and took the lottery ticket from his hands. He took a look at it, compared it with Ernest's notes and repeated: "Nothing!"

The good mood had vanished into thin air.

Tommy no longer understood the world. "You really mean ... nothing!"

"Nothing at all! Not even a threesome," came the depressed reply.

"Oh man, Tommy. I was so looking forward to it," Ernest cringed.

"I'm sorry about that, I really thought we'd won."

Ernest sat down. Willy too. Tommy's voice dropped. "I'm really sorry, guys," he repeated. "I really am a fool."

"I didn't mean it like that," Ernest rowed back his outburst of anger from a moment ago.

"And now what?" asked Willy, who had also regained his composure.

"Batman and Robin?" Tommy suggested.

"We have no other choice if we want to continue living."

Ernest clenched his right hand into a fist and slammed it into his left palm. "Batman and Robin! We'll pull off the robbery. We'll rob the bank tomorrow morning!"

Chapter 4
Batman and Robin in action

Tommy sat on the sofa and looked at his two revolvers. They were replicas of the legendary Colt *Peacemaker* from 1873 and were intended as decoration. "If they were real, we could wait for the gangsters and welcome them accordingly. Then we'd light a fire under their asses!"

"Oh yes," came the muffled sound from Ernest's room. "I could handle it without any problems. As a budding policeman, I'm a first-class marksman, of course, but I'd have my doubts about you."

"Where did you learn to shoot?"

Ernest's voice grew louder. "I'm a natural. I was born with it." He came into the living room. "And I started out as a marksman at the Munich Oktoberfest. The owners of the shooting galleries rolled their eyes out of respect when I arrived. Boy, those were the days."

Tommy had to look twice when Ernest stood in front of him in his Batman costume. He didn't know whether to laugh or cry. Ernest was wearing a pair of black leggings that were dyed blue from the knees down, imitating Batman's black boots. His upper body was also clad in a deep black, skin-tight long shirt. The Batman emblem on his chest looked extremely bulky, as it did not rest on Batman's six-pack but extended over Ernest's gigantic stomach.

The Batman mask with the strikingly upright bat ears was pulled over his head and covered his face. Only the mouth was exposed. A belt was fastened around his waist. The metal pin of the buckle was hooked into the very last hole. A cloak rounded off the costume.

"I ... I," Tommy huffed, "am impressed." He had to stifle his laughter. *Bat-Elephant-Man* was on the tip of his tongue, or *Bat-Hippo-Man* would have been even more accurate. But he remained silent. He knew how indignantly his buddy could react when he was asked about his figure, or rather his excess weight, so he stuck to his statement and reaffirmed it. "Yes, very impressive indeed."

Ernest was proud. He almost felt like the real Batman. It was as if the comic hero's superpowers had been transferred to him. The costume transformed him from Ernest, the budding super-policeman, into Ernest, the real Batman. Batman, the superhero who solved all problems.

"Ta ta ta ... taaaaa", it sounded and Willy hopped into the living room as Batman's sidekick Robin.

Tight lime green leggings, a tight-fitting long shirt with a red chest and back and lime green sleeves. An eye mask hid part of his face and a yellow cloak hung loosely down his back.

"Hello Robin!" Ernest greeted him, beaming with joy.

"Hello Batman!" hissed Willy in a firm voice.

"Hello Willy," replied Tommy.

"So, how do I look?" asked Willy.

"Perfect," came from Batman.

"You look like Willy in a Robin costume," Tommy said matter-of-factly.

Batman went to the table and took the Colts. He handed one to Robin. They both held up the revolvers, examined them and practiced aiming.

"Hands up! Give me the money! This is a robbery!" Ernest shouted.

"Up with the fins! Don't make a stupid move and get the dough out!" Robin imitated him.

"No counterfeit money in," Tommy whispered to them.

Ernest awkwardly slid the revolver into his belt. In other words, he tried to slide it in there, but failed because only the barrel fitted. The part with the cylinder was too wide or the belt too narrow. In other words: Batman was too fat. Depending on how you look at it. So Batman kept the deceptively real-looking Colt in his hand. "You don't get fake money at the bank, buddy."

Tommy insisted. "Yes, he did!"

"Watch out, Tommy. When I say you can't get counterfeit money at the bank, that's because you can."

"This time I'm right!"

Robin intervened. "What do you mean, *counterfeit money?*"

"Well, the money that becomes colorful after the robbery."

Ernest tapped his forehead. "Right, now I know what you mean. You mean the security packets they like to put in bundles of money. They explode and color the money and possibly the bank robber's hands. The banknotes are then unusable and the bank robber can't get the color off. That was a very good tip."

Tommy was delighted.

"Robin, we have to tell the bank employees not to slip us any *juice packs*, otherwise..." he raised the Colt and pulled the trigger. Of course, nothing happened because the decorative weapon had been rendered useless, but Willy, alias Robin, knew what was going on.

"That's right! Pack coal, but no security pack, otherwise ..." Robin repeated in a deep, frightening voice, also holding his Colt menacingly to the front.

"So, how were we?" Ernest wanted to know.

Tommy pulled a face. "Not so convincing. You need to practise that a bit more!"

"That's what I thought. After all, I'm a police officer and I'm on the other side of the law, so you have to learn that first!"

The practicing began.

Tommy played the bank clerk, Robin and Batman stormed into the living room from the kitchen and shouted their lines over and over again.

They also practiced retreating in a controlled manner, with Ernest tripping over the carpet twice while walking backwards and almost knocking Robin over. They then decided to leave the bench forwards rather than backwards.

After several attempts, they thought they had got it perfect. The next step was discussed. The *timing*! Here too, a few inconsistencies had to be ironed out. At the end of a long evening of discussion, the final raid plan was finalized.

Ernest summarized everything once again. "We pack the costumes and the Colts in the trunk. Then we drive to EDEKA-Korner. Willy and I will buy a little something. Tommy, you wait in the car. After shopping, we drop you off in front of Antonio's pizzeria. You hide in the bushes opposite the pizzeria. Meanwhile, we drive to the neighboring market town. We stop on the way and get changed. When we arrive in town, we park in the side street right next to the bank. Then we go in and carry out the robbery as planned. As soon as we're back in the car with the money, we send you the coded message that we've done the shopping. Then you go to Antonio and order the pizzas. A family pizza with extra cheese for me, please, and what would you like, Willy?"

Willy shrugged his shoulders. "I'm nervous. I don't know what kind of pizza to eat."

"Then why don't you have a Four Seasons pizza, you can't go wrong. If you're not hungry, I can help you," Ernest suggested.

"You already have the big family pizza," said Tommy.

"I'll have salami and pepperoni," Willy decided.

"Okay, that's not bad either," nodded Ernest. "And if you can't do it, I'll take care of the rest."

"What's the next step in the plan?" Tommy urged.

"We'll drive back, change again on the way and pick you up. You tell Antonio that we're at the EDEKA."

"A perfect plan!"

Tommy was not yet completely satisfied. "I still have one small objection."

"Like what?"

"If you're on the run, under stress and therefore can't send a message, I'll be sitting in these bushes for ages."

They thought about it. Willy had the perfect idea. "Guys, how about we keep the phone connection open all the time?"

"How?" the others wanted to know.

"We call Tommy before we storm into the bank. He can follow the robbery live on the phone, knows when we're back in the car and also when we're leaving."

"That could be mine. Brilliant!" praised Ernest. "That's exactly how we do it."

Everyone was satisfied. Everyone had played a part in the success of the perfect bank robbery. They were a team. They were better than the three musketeers, better than the three ??? and better than any other team in the world. They were three friends for life and stood up for each other.

The next morning, everything was as usual. Charles, the Frisian cockerel, crowed like a fool, Tommy opened the window, took a deep breath of manure-smelling country air and greeted Charles with: "Morning, Morning!", whereupon their talkative neighbor Alfons greeted him back. The mates shouted to Tommy to be quiet and Alfons laid fresh eggs outside the door because no one responded to his ringing and knocking.

Over breakfast, they went through the perfect plan for the bank robbery one last time. Everyone, including Tommy, knew what was important. All three of them were excited to no end, but everyone wanted to look *cool* in front of the others, so no one admitted to being ultra nervous.

The bag with the costumes and the two revolvers was packed. A cloth bag with a *WWF* panda print was to serve as a purse for the loot.

All three finally stood in front of the BMW.

"All right?" asked Willy.

Ernest held up his thumb. Tommy looked up and asked: "Did you see anything?"

Astonished, Ernest replied: "No."

"Then why are you pointing upwards?"

"I'm not pointing upwards, I'm making the sign for okay. And besides, what's supposed to be up there?"

"No idea. Maybe a dead bird."

Willy looked up. "What nonsense. Dead birds don't fly."

"But you're not sure. Otherwise you wouldn't have looked up."

Ernest had had enough. His nerves were strained to breaking point and he finally wanted to drive off to get the matter over with. He felt worse than before a dentist's appointment. "Quiet now. We'll discuss it another time. Otherwise it'll take as long as it did the other day when you claimed a plane broke down and another one towed it away."

Tommy put his hands on his hips. "It was like this. One plane was pulling another. So the one behind had broken down."

"Tommy, for the hundredth time. That was a glider. It is pulled upwards and released there so that it can sail."

"I'm not entirely sure about that. It could also be that it was left behind or didn't come down, so it had to be picked up. If you drag something up, you can drag it down again, it's as simple as that."

Willy and Ernest knew at that moment that their plan to park Tommy at Antonio's during the robbery was the right one.

"Come on, get in, we're off."

The three blackmailers were sitting in a Delivery van. "When I said we needed a new car with more volume, I meant that we should get a faster car, not a bigger car," grumbled the old man, squinting at the driver.

"Then you should have said we need a car with more displacement. For me, volume is the loading area, displacement is the engine!"

"One more line like that and you'll get a slap in the face."

The driver remained silent.

The youngest of them wanted to mediate. "Besides, this trolley was standing around looking really inviting. I would have loved to wait and look at the stupid faces of the people who unloaded the boxes and carried them into the house," he laughed. "How stupid of them to leave the keys in the door."

"And the driver is a special kind of fool. He's even got his wallet and papers in here," laughed the father, rummaging through the wallet. He lifted up a fifty, beaming with joy. "We can go shopping again!" Then he fell silent, thought about it and added: "This is a hire car."

The youngest pondered. "It doesn't belong to the people? Do we have to pay the fees now?" He caught some weird looks.

"Boy, you really aren't the brightest candle in the candlestick. We stole the box here. We're neither returning it nor paying anything. And the lettering on the side is the perfect camouflage. Everyone thinks we just borrowed the Delivery van."

The driver spoke up. "But the cops will find us quickly. They'll be looking for the car soon."

"You beginners," puffed the father. "We'll drive to this rental car company tonight and swap the license plates. No one will notice. Then we'll drive a rental car with license plates that aren't considered stolen."

All three of them laughed. "Dad, you're simply the best!"

"And soon we'll have big bucks. The three morons will pay. I can feel that. They're scared to death."

The driver laughed out loud. "The fat one was shaking more than a jelly."

They drove along the main street of the village.

"Look over there, there's Batman and Robin."

"What nonsense!"

Heads flew around.

"Indeed!"

The old man couldn't believe what he was seeing. "Pull over to the right. I have a hunch!"

The driver steered the Delivery van to the side of the road and stopped.

"Are these the real ones?"

"Stupid, they're not real," explained the brother.

"Is it carnival already?" came next.

"Shut up and watch out, boys. Today is our lucky day."

"So, is it carnival or not?" the youngest still wanted to know.

Gossip

"Ouch, why have I been slapped in the face again?"

"Because I said shut up!"

The other stared at the street. "Batman and Robin came out of the side street there. Do you think their Batmobile is there?"

The old man rubbed his hands together. "That could be good, my son. Drive in and stay there. We're going to make some real ashes today and then the three idiots will still put something on it." He laughed uproariously.

"If they're not the real thing, they don't have a Batmobile!"

A stern look from the father was enough.

As planned, they put on their costumes and drove on.

"We look pretty stupid. What will we say if the police stop us?" asked Willy.

"We put the masks on first before we get out. And if my future colleagues stop us, we just say that we've already bought the costumes for next carnival and are only wearing the clothes to try them on in case we have to exchange them if they're too big."

Willy looked at Ernest, whose costume was so tight that it threatened to burst. He wondered if his buddy was even breathing because it was stretched to breaking point.

"You're looking at me so skeptically. Do you think my Batman costume turned out a bit too big? Be honest!"

Willy shook his head in the negative. "It's definitely not too big," was his diplomatic reply.

"Thank goodness, I was worried it might be a bit too loose."

They parked. Both were visibly nervous. The *point of no return* was behind them. They had no other choice and had to get the money this way. Their lives were in danger. After weighing up all the facts, robbing the bank was the lesser risk.

Willy was so excited that his hands were shaking slightly. "Okay, we're going to do this thing now. First we'll put on the masks, then I'll call Tommy and plug in the cell phone without hanging up. That way he can hear everything."

Ernest was sweating again. "That's right. Then we get out and go to the bank. We storm in and shout: Robbery!"

They put on their masks and looked at themselves in the mirror, then at each other. They were satisfied.

"Just to be on the safe side. You call me Robin now and I'll call you Batman."

Ernest raised his thumb up again. "As agreed, Robin!"

"Batman, you secure with the Colt, I'll go to the bank clerk at the till and have the money put in the bag."

Ernest once again pointed out possible juice packs. "And remember to include the reference to the safety pack!"

Now Willy raised his thumb up. "Absolutely."

"Ready?"

"Done!"

Both nodded.

Willy said: "On the count of three!"

"You mean at three we get out or at two, and then we say three outside?"

"Ernest, we're going through with it now, so no discussions!"

"Okay!"

"One ... two ..."

"So are we getting out now or not until you've said three?"

"Three!", Willy blurted out, followed by an unmistakable: "Out!".

Batman and Robin left the BMW. They had both reached the limits of what was bearable. They looked around, suitably antsy and conspicuous. The side street was deserted. They hurried forward and turned right. Ernest was already limp at the junction. "Robin, not quite so fast," he panted. "We'll need the energy if we make a run for it after the raid!"

Robin waited. When Batman was close behind him again, they both continued at normal walking speed towards the bank branch. The excitement was enormous. Batman was sweating profusely under his costume. Robin could feel his knees getting weak and shaky. The two men dressed as superheroes didn't notice the delivery van that pulled over to the side of the road behind them and stopped. Nor had they noticed that they were being watched by the occupants of the stolen van.

Batman and Robin were standing right in front of the bank. The vestibule was empty. There were no customers at the statement printer or the ATM. Both drew their Colts and stormed off at the same time. The doorway was too narrow. They wedged themselves in.

"Robin, I'll go first so I can secure the back, then you charge ahead. That makes more of an impression because I look pretty bombastic as Batman!" gasped Ernest.

"Good, then you go first!"

Robin broke free from the door frame, took a step back and let Batman go first. He opened the nearest glass door and scurried through. Robin followed him. They were now standing in the bank office. An elderly lady was sitting with the branch manager in one of the two glass-walled offices, receiving advice. A young mother and her child were being served at one of the three customer counters. The little boy laughed and shouted: "Look mommy, Batman and Robin!"

Batman stopped at the entrance, panting heavily. Robin walked to the middle of the store. From here he had a good view of everything.

He stopped and shouted loudly: "Money up! Give me your hands! This is a robbery!"

Stunned looks from those present.

"He means hands up!" corrected Batman.

Robin turned around. "Of course that's what I mean!"

"Are you there with the Batmobile?" the child wanted to know.

Robin looked for the checkout counter. Nothing! He became even more nervous than he already was. "Crap! Where's the till?" he whined.

Batman replied to the child. "Of course! We're always speeding around in the Batmobile. By the way, you don't need to be afraid. We're the good guys. We're just taking out some money in a funny way to help someone."

"That's really funny," laughed the child.

Batman approached the bank employee who had served the child's mother. "Give the child a balloon and a lollipop. Or don't you have any freebies?"

"Do-you," trembled the frightened bank employee, reached under the counter and heard the warning words from the voluminous bank robber. "Don't raise the alarm, otherwise it will be dangerous here!"

"No alarm," she repeated and dug out a few balloons to give to the little boy.

"Thank you Batman!"

"Gladly!"

Robin opened the door to the counseling office. "Where's the stupid cash register?"

"Young man, there hasn't been a till here for two years. You're not from around here, are you?" the old lady replied relatively calmly, while the store manager slowly slipped off his chair and crawled under the desk.

Robin bent down and looked him in the eye. "Hello? Have you lost something?" he asked politely.

The old lady simply said: "Yes, his courage! And I advise you not to look up my skirt, otherwise I'll get uncomfortable!"

Robin stood up straight again. The bank employee crawled out from under the desk and sat back down on the office chair. In a somewhat shaky voice, he said, "My contact lens fell on the floor. I was looking for it." He tried to wring a smile out of his face.

The old lady simply said: "Well, well, a contact lens wearer. That's interesting."

Robin asked, "Where's the money?"

The branch manager cleared his throat and said: "We only have the money that's in the ATM. But there's a time lock on it. If you want me to open it, we'll have to wait a few minutes. That takes time!"

"Isn't there a safe here or something?"

"No."

Robin cursed: "Damn it!", turned to Batman and shouted. "They don't have a till, just a time lock on the ATM. What do we do?"

"We're only taking money that's lying around loose! We have to hurry."

Robin turned back to the store manager. "You've heard it. Go on! All the money in there, but no Safty Pack!"

"There's no money lying around here. Just whatever the woman wants to deposit."

"Young man, that's my money," the old lady scolded.

"Deposit it and take the receipt, then the money will be in your account and I'll take it from the bank," Robin replied.

The old lady grinned maliciously and addressed the store manager. "You've heard it. Give me a receipt."

The branch manager put the two hundred euro bills scribbled on with a ballpoint pen into the WWF bag, left the office, typed something into a machine and gave the customer a receipt. "Here. You have now officially deposited the money."

Satisfied, the old lady nodded, slipped the receipt into her handbag and said: "Mr. Bank Robber, you can carry on."

"Thank you," Robin replied and withdrew.

"Get out of here Batman! I've got everything we could get!"

Batman and Robin left the bank. They walked quickly to the side street and were just about to get into the BMW when a delivery van pulled up next to them and two familiar figures jumped out. One of them pointed a gun at them.

"Get in and ratchet up!"

Batman and Robin raised their hands in amazement. They felt bad and helpless. As if they had been caught red-handed by the principal in one of the worst school pranks. The sliding door was pushed open. Involuntarily and half pushed in, they got in.

"Sit down and don't make a sound! And give me the bag, it's mine now," laughed the old man, addressing the guy with the gun. "You get in the back. If they make a sound, you'll kill them!"

One of the kidnappers got in. He was still pointing his gun at Batman and Robin. The old man put the bank robbers' two decorative revolvers in the WWF bag, saw the meagre loot from the robbery and cursed loudly: "200 euros? Tell me, are you too stupid to rob a bank?"

"There is no cash desk. They only have the money in the machine and it has a time lock!"

A siren could be heard from afar.

"Cops approaching," shouted the driver.

The old man stared angrily at Batman and Robin. "Then the ransom will soon be due for you!"

The sliding door was slammed shut. The Delivery van started to move.

Ernest began to chatter. "Tommy, we're being kidnapped right now!"

"Shut up!" the kidnapper scolded. "You're not supposed to talk!"

"Tommy, can you hear us? The blackmailers from the parking lot have just kidnapped us. We're sitting in a van, being threatened and they've got all the loot too."

The kidnapper became suspicious. "Why are you talking so awkwardly to your buddy? He's sitting next to you. And why are you asking if he can hear you?"

"200 euros. You've got all the loot amounting to 200 euros," said Robin.

The hostage-taker saw the light. He gradually realized that something was wrong. "You're talking to someone. Now I'll check it out! Radios and phones out! But now, or I'll have to kill you!"

Both took the renewed threat seriously and immediately complied with the request. They reluctantly handed over the cell phone. The conversation was over.

Tommy was sitting in the bushes, shaking with excitement. His buddies' voices sounded a bit muffled, but he could understand everything. His two friends were brave, cool and clever. Of course, he also had to do his job correctly, then they would be out of trouble. A butterfly fluttered around. Tommy was distracted for a moment. He looked at the magnificent insect. "Peacock butterfly, how are you?" he grinned. "Today is a glorious day for fluttering around."

A glorious day. He suddenly returned to reality. The day they would solve their problems. *I hope I can manage the pizza order. Man, I'm nervous*, he admitted to himself.

The joy of soon having solved the dilemma with the blackmailers receded. He heard something about problems and that there was no cash register.

A bank without a till? What's going on there?

Tensely, he pressed his ear to the cell phone. He understood that Batman and Robin had made some loot after all and escaped from the bank. He was a little relieved. The panting sounded as if they were running fast. His body began to shake. Adrenaline raced through his bloodstream. *My mission is coming up!* Tommy stood up, looked around to see if anyone had seen him, and stepped out onto the road. *When they get in the car and drive off, I'll go to the pizzeria. I stay casual and order a family pizza with extra cheese, a salami pizza with pepperoni and for me? Hm, what am I actually going to have? At first I wanted the four seasons, but it's such a nice day that I decide to go for the vegetarian pizza with lots of garlic.*

Tommy was heading towards the entrance of the Italian restaurant when he became suspicious. *Something was wrong!* He could hear several voices. Had *they been caught by the police? Oh dear!*

The amateur gardener became frightened. He kept looking around to make sure. There were no police to be seen. Now he was contacted directly on his cell phone. He could clearly hear Ernest's voice. It sounded completely different to usual and the tone was similar to when he came into the pizzeria and told them about the attempted kidnapping. "Tommy, we're being kidnapped right now!"

Again, it flashed through him.

Tommy listened spellbound to the abduction. He immediately realized that this was definitely worse than an arrest. The blackmailers now not only had the loot from the bank robbery, but also Batman and Robin, alias Ernest and Willy, as hostages. Tommy suspected what would follow. He stood in front of the entrance to the pizzeria and pondered. He knew that he had been ordered to order pizza to provide an alibi. But his two buddies wouldn't show up. So he would be in need of an explanation. He needed to be astute. Tommy made a decision. He didn't go to Antonio's, but went home to wait.

I walk cross-country, then nobody will see me. It could be that the blackmailers are looking for me. Besides, I can think best in nature.

The journey didn't take too long and the last section of the route was extremely bumpy. Ernest had tried to memorize important details of the route. He knew this trick from one of the *96 Hours films* starring *Liam Neeson.* However, it had worked better in the movie than for him. Ernest decided to hone this tactic. The van stopped. The sliding door was pushed open. The old man's grim face peered in. "Was something wrong?" he asked.

"Dude, yeah! They secretly phoned a Tommy and told him they were being kidnapped. Of course, I totally checked it out and immediately took their cell phone. Good, right!" the young gangster boasted.

The old man eyed Batman and Robin. "You two seem very clever. I can tell you one thing, if your friend doesn't move over quickly with the coal, you'll be stuck in this quarry forever!"

"You've already got all the loot!" replied Willy.

The old man didn't seem to like the answer. He reacted gruffly. "Shut up, you clown!"

Ernest shook his head in the negative. "That's not a clown costume, that's Robin. He's Batman's sidekick," he tried to explain politely, but only got a "Shut up, fatso!", whereupon Batman looked at his buddy Robin and whispered to him: "You could have told me that the

Batman costume is a bit bulky. I don't like it when I look a bit corpulent."

The kidnapper with the gun was visibly annoyed, pointed the barrel of the revolver at Ernest and cocked the hammer. "Shut up, my .... er ... he said! Now get out of here!"

The mechanical click made the two hostages flinch.

"Don't shoot! We'll do anything you want," Willys said, who was beginning to feel ridiculous in his Robin costume.

"Don't worry, guys. These are just costumes. We're not the real Batman and Robin. You don't need to threaten us," Ernest huffed.

They got up somewhat awkwardly, with Willy having to help Ernest because his cape had got caught on one of the Delivery van's floor hooks. When they finally got out, the kidnapper jumped out of the van with the gun. "I know you're not the real heroes! I'm not stupid!"

"I just meant because we look so real!" Ernest added.

Willy poked him in the side, took off the eye mask and whispered: "Don't tease him." He squinted at the kidnapper. "They're serious."

Ernest put his index finger to his lips. "I am silent as the grave." Then he took off the mask too. "Phew, I was sweating under there like an ox working in the fields. Where are we here anyway?"

The old kidnapper turned bright red with rage, took a deep breath and shouted: "Shut up!"

That had done the trick. Ernest remained silent. He recalled his police mind, as he called it, and tried to memorize as many details as possible.

They were in the disused quarry, which was located in the vast area away from their village. The steep walls around them bore witness to decades of rock extraction, both deep and wide. Tons of rock had been blasted away, crushed and transported away to be used somewhere as a gravel road, bulk material or as a mass raw material. What was left behind was a rutted landscape reminiscent of a canyon and the perfect backdrop for a Wild West open-air spectacle.

The machines had been standing still for a long time; no heavily laden truck had left this site for years. No excavator was emptying its full shovel onto a conveyor belt, and no workers were waiting for the siren that warned of the blasting of rock faces.

Bare and steep rock faces towered over the partly overgrown access road. The grounds were surrounded by a man-high wire fence with rolls of barbed wire attached to the top edge to prevent unauthorized entry. The large entrance gate was wide open.

Ernest's brain rattled. *The area offers them a first-class hideout. You won't find anyone here. They have definitely broken down the gate and taken up residence there.*

The former office building looked in need of renovation, but not in danger of collapsing. A few window panes were shattered, the entrances boarded up. Except for one. And that was exactly where Ernest and Willy were led.

Tommy was extremely dejected and full of fear as he marched off. Who had kidnapped his friends and why? Lost in thought, he left the market town behind him, left the main road and strolled along a dusty country lane. Bees buzzed and flew from flower to flower in the lush meadows. A red kite circled in search of prey and cows stood in a fenced-off pasture, chewing grass, following him with their big brown eyes and depositing their cow pats, which were swarmed with hundreds of flies the next moment. Pure nature! Wonderful country life. In itself a paradise for the hobby gardener. But this time Tommy couldn't enjoy it. He felt more helpless than ever before in his life.

Damn, we shouldn't have done that!

When he finally arrived home, he sat down in the living room, stared at the wall and waited.

The branch manager of the bank had a real flow of words as he described the robbery to the police officer. In his mind, he could already see himself on the 8 p.m. news. The press would be besieging his house, he would become famous overnight. Secretly, he was expecting a transfer to the head office and a meteoric rise within the bank. "... then I told him that there was nothing to get here and that," he lowered his voice a little to appear even more striking, "if they were thinking of taking us hostage to extort a ransom, they should let the customers and my employees go. I would volunteer to be the sole hostage. You know, my motto was to save lives."

The officer noted everything down. "And the description again. What did the two perpetrators look like?"

A reporter from the Kreisblatt arrived. The branch manager knew him briefly. He waved to the press representative and tried to look as serious as possible. "They were wearing carnival costumes. Superheroes, ha, don't make me laugh. I had already thought of a plan to overpower them both, but as there were customers in the bank, their safety came first, of course. That's why I talked them down in a purely de-escalating manner, which ultimately persuaded them to flee without the loot."

"You liars," raged the old lady who had just joined them. "Those gangsters almost stole my 200 euros. Fortunately, the slim one of them suggested I deposit the money first. I have a receipt."

"Oh yes," the store manager improved. "200 euros. How could I have forgotten that? I wanted to distract the two robbers and get the customer to safety, so ..."

A second police officer came along. "The employee showed me the footage from the surveillance camera. Poor quality. You can see that the perpetrators were wearing the costumes of Batman and Robin, and then there's another shot where you can see someone disappearing under a desk and coming out again."

The reporter took notes and the store manager began to sweat. "That was the moment I wanted to raise the alarm, but this stupid office chair was so slippery that I slipped off."

The old lady ranted again. "So you didn't lose a contact lens after all?"

The store manager was already dripping with sweat. He turned to the reporter. "You don't need to write that."

The police officer asked: "Were the two perpetrators masked in the costumes of Batman and Robin?"

The store manager gave the old lady a dirty look. "The contact lens was a ruse, because if I'd said I wanted to raise the alarm, he might have gone crazy ..."

"They were scared!"

"Well, stop it now. Those two were extremely dangerous. I was afraid for your life, not mine!"

The policeman urged. "The description please!"

The child said: "They were nice. I especially liked Batman. He said that the woman should give me balloons."

The policeman swiveled his head from left to right like in a tennis match. "What now? Nice or dangerous?"

"Nice!"

"Very dangerous!"

"They came in the Batmobile! That's what they told me."

Exasperated, the officer went to the patrol car, picked up the radio and put out a wanted notice. "We're looking for Batman and Robin. They've probably fled in the Batmobile and are armed."

Secretly, he thought: *"My colleagues will make fun of me for this radio message until I retire!*

A passer-by had stopped next to the patrol car. "I think I saw something there that might interest them."

The policeman took off his cap, wiped his forehead and asked. "But not Superman, by any chance, who was behind the wheel of the Batmobile while Spiderman cleared the escape route, was he?"

"No, but I saw the two guys get into a Delivery van. There was someone else there. But he wasn't disguised. I saw three men in total. The two masked men and an older man. He took the bag with the loot from the robbery. Of course, I didn't know at the time that there had been a robbery, otherwise I would have looked more closely."

"That's finally a good clue. Why did you notice the men?"

"I was on the balcony watering my flowers. I looked down, not that I was pouring water on anyone's head. That's when I saw them briefly. The men weren't standing directly under my balcony, so I carried on watering my flowers."

"Didn't that seem strange to you?"

"Because of the costumes? No! I thought they were going to a children's birthday party or something like that."

That was plausible. The policeman made a note of the statement and asked further questions. "Can you describe the Delivery van in more detail?"

"No, unfortunately not and I didn't notice the license plate number either. I just noticed that the car had a rental car company sign on the side."

The policeman picked up the microphone on the radio again and completed the manhunt.

Ernest and Willy sat tied to chairs with ropes in the former kitchenette of the office building. The room was small. The furnishings consisted of a dining table and a kitchenette with a sink, fridge, stove and wall cupboards. Everything was just as run-down as the building itself. Old, shabby, but apparently still functional. Then, of course, there was a worn corner bench and the two chairs they were sitting on.

There were tons of empty tins lying around in one corner. Ravioli, chilli con carne, pasta with meatballs.

"They can't cook," Ernest realized immediately.

"Be quiet, they can probably hear us."

"Of course," replied Ernest, who was now whispering.

Silence for a minute. Then Willy asked. "What are they planning to do with us?"

"They wanted to grab the loot from the bank robbery and also extort the ransom. They're really nasty guys!"

"And how did they find us? I mean, how did they know about this bank robbery?"

Ernest shrugged his shoulders. "I have no idea. Either they bugged me without me noticing, or they were watching us, but I would definitely have noticed. I'm a professional," he looked at Willy to see if he had understood the word *professional*, "or it was just pure coincidence."

The old man came in, followed by the one with the gun. The slightly more intelligent kidnapper, who had been driving the Delivery van, hid the stolen van behind the office building. At least that's what Ernest assumed, because he could see out of the window from his seat and see that the guy had got into the van and was slowly driving away.

While the youngest sat down on the corner bench, his father stood in front of Ernest and Willy and looked at both of them. "You look really pathetic. Do you know how big your haul was?"

"Hi, hi," laughed the son.

Without waiting for an answer, the old man continued. "Two hundred measly euros! You're risking five years in prison for two hundred bucks! You really are as stupid as oatmeal."

Ernest wanted to justify himself. "There was no cash in the bank."

The old man mocked them: "You didn't spy out the property, but marched in there dressed like two carnival princes and waved your toy guns around. No wonder you didn't get more money out of it. I wouldn't have walked out of there with less than 50,000 euros. They keep them in every bank. They really took the piss out of you!"

Ernest swallowed, Willy looked down at the floor in dismay.

"Now I'll tell you something. I'll call your buddy right away. He'll make the 100,000 euros available by the day after tomorrow and for every day he delays, another 10,000 euros will be added. If he still hasn't paid within a week, I'll send you to another bank and you'll both rob it for me. That means one of you. If he doesn't do it, you can choose three graves at the cemetery!"

Ernest and Willy felt extremely queasy.

"Great, Dad," the son cheered.

The old man turned around. He shouted angrily at his son. "Harvey, you shouldn't keep calling me Daddy! Take an example from your brother!"

"Harry isn't even here!"

"You shall not reveal our names!"

"I didn't say we were called Hansen."

The father closed his eyes for a moment, muttered: "What have I done to deserve this?" and turned to the two hostages. "Now you know who we are. The infamous Hansen gang!"

"Who?" asked Willy.

He shook his head in the negative. "Hansen gang? Never heard of it."

The old man scratched the back of his head. "Never heard of us? Well, you can tell we've landed here in the Bavarian provinces. You really are still living in the last century."

Harvey stood up. "That's the famous Hubert Hansen!" he pointed at his father. "The most notorious criminal who ever roamed the country. We are outlaws! We're dangerous and soon to be filthy rich."

"We're not interested in that much information," Ernest blocked out. "If you don't know anything, you can't say anything."

Old Hansen came closer, bent down and looked deep into Ernest's eyes. The weather-beaten and unshaven face did not look very well-groomed. In addition, an unpleasant smell wafted into Ernest's nose. He grimaced in disgust.

"You must think you're really clever, friend. I advise you to be very careful. If, and I emphasize, *if* we release you after the ransom has been paid, I don't want to read about us in the newspapers. What we said about ourselves was only meant for you."

"That's right," Harvey interjected and added: "Why is that, Papsi?"

Hubert Hansen stood up straight again. "Because these two, who look like they've escaped from a puppet theater, should know that we're dangerous. That means that if they talk to the cops, we'll come back and make short work of them."

At that moment, Willy wondered whether it wouldn't have been better not to have gone to the bar where he had met Ernest and Tommy. He also wondered how his life would have turned out then. When he saw himself lying homeless under a bridge in his mind, he still didn't think the current situation was much better, but at least they still had a trump card up their sleeve. Tommy.

However, the longer Willy thought about this trump card, the more uncomfortable he felt. *No, Tommy is not a trump card. I think it's going to be very difficult for us. And if the police actually find us and free us, we'd still be wearing the clothes from the bank robbery and would have to serve a few years in prison for it.*

The thought gave him goose bumps. He didn't want to go to prison and meet the Hansen gang or, even worse, perhaps be locked up in a cell with them.

At the same time, Ernest mentally searched through all the Hollywood films he had seen to find the right words. He couldn't threaten the kidnappers like a James Bond would have done. He couldn't act like Arnold Schwarzenegger either, although he was probably quite similar in character, at least when Ernest started the training, the plan of which he had been working on for a good two years. Finally he said: "You'll get your money and we won't say a word. And you know what, we'll add the money from the bank robbery on top. As a bonus, so to speak."

Old Hansen looked at Ernest in astonishment. Harvey, on the other hand, clapped his hands. "Did you hear that, Papsi? We'll get the money, and we can keep the loot from the bank robbery too."

Hubert Hansen tried not to get upset. "Son, you cook us something to eat now and I'll call the buddy of those two clowns."

"Batman and Robin," Ernest improved. "They're superheroes, not clowns."

Hubert Hansen left the room shaking his head.

"Dad, do the hostages get any of our food?"

Ernest beat him to the answer. "You'll have to. If we starve to death, there will be no ransom!"

That made sense to Harvey. "Good, then I'll cook for you."

Ernest was satisfied. "As a hostage, my energy consumption is pretty high. A little extra for me, please."

From outside came a: "Yes, give them something."

Harvey opened one of the kitchen cupboards. It was full of tins. "We're having Serbian bean soup today."

Tommy was desperate. Again and again, he went through all the possibilities of how he could help his friends. In the end, he was left with three options. He could go to the police, call Uncle Eddie or tell Grandma Huber everything. His cell phone was ready to hand. He ruled out Uncle Eddie first. He didn't have his phone number.

"That leaves two options," he muttered to himself.

Suddenly his cell phone began to vibrate and the ringtone he had assigned to Ernest could be heard. *Somewhere over the Rainbow*, the version by the overweight Hawaiian singer *Israel Kamakawiwo'ole*. The performer reminded him of Ernest and his character. Tommy hummed along to the melody and didn't answer at first because he liked the song so much. Then he pressed the *accept call button*.

"Ernest! Thank goodness! I was already worried!" he gushed.

Silence.

"Ernest?" asked Tommy.

"Shut up!" a terribly rough-sounding voice rang out. "We've got your two buddies in our power, the two who wanted to rob a bank in masquerade costume, get it?"

"Yes, I did."

"You know who we are?"

"Of course, the blackmailers who tried to kidnap Ernest in the parking lot."

"Well recognized, smart guy. Then listen carefully! You're going to get the 100,000 euros we asked for. By the day after tomorrow. The sum will increase by 10,000 euros every day if you don't pay on time. If you can't find the money, you'll get the two carnival princes back slice by slice from next week. After that, we'll pay you a visit. Have you understood that?"

"Yes, 100,000 euros!"

"Very good. We'll call you tomorrow and tell you when and how the money will be handed over. And I'd like to hear from you then that you have the ashes."

"Ashes? What ashes?"

"Well the money, you fool!"

"Coal? Ashes? What should I get now? Coal or ash?"

"Plasticine, of course!"

"You want me to buy 100,000 euros worth of dough? How am I supposed to transport it?"

A gasp followed by a "No!" could be heard. The caller shouted so loudly that Tommy had to hold the cell phone away from his ear. "You're getting money. Cash! 100,000 euros! See you the day after tomorrow. We'll get back to you tomorrow. Was that clear and concise?"

"Uh, money after all!"

"Money, of course! Oh man, what a bunch of whistles you are!"

"Why you? I'm alone."

The caller was going crazy. "You get the money, I'll get back to you tomorrow. Then we'll discuss the handover."

"Say that right away!"

Silence.

The caller had hung up. Tommy was shocked. Now he knew who had kidnapped his two friends. The three guys from the supermarket. Tommy was shaking. He was alternately hot and cold. He was afraid for his friends, afraid for their lives and also for his own. For the first time, he was facing a major task alone and had to make a very important decision.

Tommy took a deep breath and reminded himself to stay calm. He instinctively crossed out his second option, which had been to call the police. He knew what to do. Tommy got up and prepared to visit Grandma Huber. He would tell her everything, leave nothing out and hoped very much that his old friend had a solution to the problem.

Chapter 4
When grandma smokes a pipe

Grandma Huber felt great. Since taking these medicinal herbs, her health improved rapidly. Her visits to the doctor decreased, her mood lifted and she was back in the midst of life with full strength and joy.

Her labor was no longer needed on the modern farm. New types of open stable housing, efficient milking machines and a large fleet of agricultural machinery made her son's everyday life easier and reduced her help to a minimum. This in turn created freedom.

It had also become really modern in the household. Electric vacuum cleaning robots drove around all by themselves. Modern dishwashers, washing machines and tumble dryers also reduced the amount of housework and suddenly she had time. A lot of time.

Among other things, this was invested in the dusty and much neglected ladies' regulars' table. Since then, she has met regularly with her old school friends at least once a week in the pub.

At the beginning, they were still funny and in a good mood, but as time went on, the topics changed and it was no longer about the latest fashion or general gossip, but about illnesses of all kinds. Suddenly, each of them had everything from minor ailments to seemingly serious illnesses. They had not only found a new meeting place with their visits to the doctor, but also a new hobby. The country doctor's waiting room filled up faster in the morning than the bar in the village pub when there was free beer. The aim was to outdo each other with illnesses.

In the end, Grandma Huber had convinced herself that she was old and ill. She also needed a walking stick as her rheumatism-ridden body no longer functioned properly.

She also needed a small cocktail of pills for breakfast in the morning to get her going. They avoided the dance events in the village pub that used to be so popular and limited themselves to a cup of coffee, albeit decaffeinated, when they met at the regulars' table.

In short, Grandma Huber admitted to herself one day that she was old. She felt worn out and frail and could no longer imagine life without medication. Her everyday life was gray, dreary and full of pain in her joints. In other words, the wait for death had begun.

One fine day, something like action came to their tranquil village. A huge contingent of police had arrived and arrested the tenants of the property opposite her farmhouse. Four weeks later, three likeable lads moved into Mrs. Müller-Meier's house. One was far too overweight, the second was constantly tinkering with cars and was otherwise extremely industrious and the third was in the garden every day, planting beds and taking care of this and that.

Then came the day that brought spring back into her life. When she struck up a conversation with a young man called Tommy on a walk, he offered her a few medicinal herbs out of nowhere to relieve her rheumatism. Hopeful, but with due skepticism, she tried the natural medicine. It went *boom*. The stuff worked. She could smoke it in her pipe, draw on a rolled cigarette or use it as a baking mix in cakes and cookies. Since then, she called Tommy her herb boy.

It was inevitable that her friends got wind of this.

"This smart young guy," she had said to Anna Schwinghofer and Klara Korner, "has got the hang of it. Of course there's some marijuana in there, but the main part consists of various herbs."

"That's forbidden," said Anna.

"What a criminal gang!" scolded Mrs. Korner. "How could you ..."

"Well," Grandma Huber grinned maliciously. It was exactly that sardonic grin that her two friends knew all too well. After all, they had been friends since their kindergarten days. And so they both knew that this look from Grandma Huber meant something. Something important. Something they absolutely had to know. Especially when a sentence began with *naja*.

"You have a secret," Klara advised.

"Speak up," urged Anna.

Grandma Huber took a deep breath. "Pay attention and listen," she began. "Tommy is a good boy and he means well with what he grows, mixes and gives me for a measly euro."

"One euro," came the surprised reply.

Grandma Huber waved her off. "That's a gift. And besides, ladies, what does the term *forbidden mean*? It's complete nonsense. Just look at us. What have we got to lose? Nothing! We're old and we've even lost our sense of humor. Each of us has been to the cemetery at least three or four times and thought about whether an urn or a coffin should be our final resting place."

Oppressive silence, astonished looks.

"So Elisabeth," Anna Schwinghofer said. The fact that she addressed Grandma Huber by her first name was a clear sign of protest. Grandma Huber was never called by her first name, people always called her *Grandma Huber*. Whether friend or stranger.

The old farmer's wife took it in her stride and raised her index finger admonishingly. "Have you noticed that I no longer need a walking stick?"

That had worked. Her friends knew that Grandma Huber could hardly take more than twenty steps without a walking stick. Astonishment was replaced by perplexity, which in turn encouraged whispering and finally led to the question: "You walked all the way from the farm to here without a walking stick?"

Nodding and that sardonic grin again. "Not only that. I do gymnastics every morning. And I surf."

Her friends stared at Grandma Huber with wide eyes. "You surf?" asked one of them. "Now you're pulling our leg," commented the other. "You can't surf here. We don't have a lake. Besides, I've never seen you with a surfboard before."

Grandma Huber laughed out loud. "You silly women," she said jokingly. "I don't surf the water, I surf the internet. I'm a modern woman in my prime now." To prove her physical fitness, she stood up and did three squats. Then she bent down, picked up a piece of fluff from the carpet and placed it on the table. "I'm feeling great. I may be old, but I'm full of zest for life. And that's since I started smoking Tommy's stuff. They're not criminals, they're three really likeable young men and Tommy is a first-class gardener. He knows all about plants. This boy has a big heart, is honest and when he grows a little hemp and sells his crop to me, I think that's anything but criminal. He is neither a drug dealer nor a pothead, junkie or whatever else those guys are called. He is and remains my good little herb boy who earns some pocket money for his valuable work. That's my opinion. What do you say to that, girls?"

That day, her friends decided to try some of Tommy's medicinal herbs too. The success was gigantic. Just two weeks later, Tommy became the most popular man in the whole village. Although his medicinal herbs were not entirely legal due to a certain ingredient, it was precisely this admixture that conjured up a good mood and new vitality in the old ladies' everyday lives. And compared to the expensive medicines, a *natural herb healing pack cost* just one euro.

Grandma Huber decided to smoke her daily pipe and opened the tobacco tin. As she stared into the void, she suddenly remembered that yesterday she had given the last portion to her friend Erna Schmachtinger, the police chief's mother. Erna was the last of the group of seven ladies to be initiated into the secret of medicinal herbs.

"We had to make sure that you would keep your mouth shut," the others had argued.

"As if I'd ever betrayed you," Erna pouted at first, but after the second cookie she was already laughing heartily. What's more, she could no longer feel her damaged knee. "The arthritis is gone."

"You haven't even told me that you've been to the doctor for arthritis."

"I don't need a doctor for that. I diagnosed it myself, but it doesn't matter now. I don't feel anything anymore. This stuff helps."

Grandma Huber closed the tobacco tin, took her purse and left the house. She strolled down the street, saw Faucet Charles, who was proudly looking after his chickens as usual and walking around in a suitably puffed-up manner, and was glad that Alfons was not in the garden. She didn't feel like talking to him at all.

She stopped in front of the garden door of the three buddies. For a moment, the cheerful pensioner admired Tommy's work. The path to the front door had been swept. No weeds were fighting their way between the cracks in the stone slabs or growing over the edge of the narrow path. All unwanted greenery had been neatly plucked away.

Colorful flower beds attracted butterflies, bees and bumblebees. A lemon butterfly fluttered close to her and flew off in the direction of the herb bed to her left. Behind it, elephant grass and bamboo towered high above her. Grandma Huber smiled, because she knew what was hiding behind the thickly sprouting greenery. She breathed in deeply. She could smell the subtle hint of cannabis, which latently masked the existing flair of dung heaps and manure. *Wonderful,* she thought. She noticed that the BMW was gone. *Hopefully Tommy is at home.* Her doubts were dispelled when the front door opened and Tommy appeared in the doorway. Grandma Huber had immediately noticed how bad her herb boy looked. His usually cheerful expression had disappeared. He looked desperate. Grandma Huber feared the worst. *Something big is coming,* she thought immediately.

Before she could say anything, Tommy started sobbing. "Grandma Huber," tears welled up in his eyes. His voice sounded brittle. "Something terrible has happened."

The old woman closed the garden door and went to the front door. There she put her right hand on Tommy's shoulder and said: "Let's go inside. I'll brew us some tea and then we'll talk about everything."

Grandma Huber was amazed at how clean and tidy the house was. Everything in the kitchen was also very tidy. She quickly found her way around and just minutes later she poured hot water from the kettle into two cups filled with teabags. She carried them into the living room, placed them on the table and sat down in the armchair. Tommy sat on the couch and shook like a leaf. He was scared. Grandma Huber's kind look had the same calming effect on him as her voice. "So, my dear friend, now tell me where the shoe pinches. What's bothering you so much that you're not feeling well? Did you have a fight?"

Tommy shook his head. "Much worse!"

"Don't let me pull everything out of your nose. If you want me to help you, you have to talk to me."

"But that must remain secret."

"Tommy, you and I are like business partners. We're already keeping a big secret. So you know you can trust me."

He took a deep breath and then began to tell the whole story. It just bubbled out of Tommy. He told how the three men had ambushed Ernest in the parking lot and tried to kidnap him, but failed because he didn't fit in their car. He told them that Ernest had drunk three grappas in a row, that a pizza with four pieces is just as big as a pizza with eight pieces and that Ernest's Uncle Eddie is stingier than Scrooge McDuck. Then he told them that they were being blackmailed and showed Grandma Huber the blackmail letter. The next thing he said was how hard they had tried to find the money and that they had almost hit the jackpot in the lottery. But unfortunately the numbers on the ticket were too mixed up and so they didn't win anything. And then came the part about the bank robbery, which was ingeniously planned and he was responsible for the perfect alibi. "I was able to follow the entire robbery live on my cell phone. Willy and Ernest fled the bank with the loot and were kidnapped by the blackmailers before they reached the Batmobile. They were threatened with a gun." He had tears in his eyes again. "And later this bad guy called me. He's keeping the loot from the bank robbery and wants me to hand over 100,000 euros the day after tomorrow, otherwise he'll send my buddies back in bits and pieces and come after me in the end. At first I thought it would take quite a long time because Ernest is so fat, but ..." tears were now rolling down my cheeks and seeping into the collar of my T-shirt.

Grandma Huber handed Tommy a handkerchief. "Wipe your tears and take a sip of tea." Her face looked petrified. "You really are a couple of stupid horndogs. Why didn't you come to me straight away?"

He shrugs his shoulders. The farmer's wife's presence did Tommy good. He felt lost. She sensed that the young man needed her help. It rattled inside her. Grandma Huber was angry and worried at the same time. She was ready to fight, she was ready to dig up the hatchet and show it to the blackmailers. They dared to come to her village and make a ruckus, they had better be careful who they messed with. They had to think clearly.

"This really is a mess," she said, "but there's a solution for everything!"

Tommy's face brightened a little. "Do you happen to have 100,000 euros lying around at home?" he asked in a tearful voice.

"No, but I'm currently thinking about a few possible solutions."

Hope began to spread. Tommy dabbed his eyes with his handkerchief, blew his nose and asked: "Does that mean you're going to help us?"

Grandma Huber stood up, put her fists on her hips and said in a determined voice. "Tommy, you're our herb boy. If the kidnappers killed you, we wouldn't have any medicine left. I don't know what would be more terrible. Your death, or not being able to smoke a pipe anymore."

He stared at the old woman in dismay. She winked at him. "I was joking."

"Phew," Tommy groaned with relief.

"I need my medicine, then my head works perfectly," grinned the old farmer's wife. "Remember, if Grandma smokes a bag, others can dress warmly! That's the end of the fun."

Tommy suddenly jumped up. The glimmer of hope solidified. The feeling of helplessness disappeared. Grandma Huber would be at their side and he had produced plenty of the *medicine* she needed. "I've prepared and packaged lots of portions. Just a moment, I'll get some up here. It's downstairs in the barn." He ran to the door, stopped and turned around again. "My other rescue plan was to go into business big with my herbal concoction, but my buddies thought the mob might object."

Grandma Huber simply said: "Well, with one euro per portion, you would have had to produce a lot to be able to scrape together the ransom money. We'll have to choose a different strategy. Now run and get me a pipe filling."

The first puff was blown out with relish. A blue-greyish cloud of vapor drifted towards the ceiling, caught and billowed like a wall of mist over the living room table. Grandma Huber enjoyed her unusual therapy. "Mmh, that's good! I can already feel my gray brain cells starting to work."

"Great," Tommy clapped his hands, went to the window and opened it to let the smoke out. The wall of fog still billowing under the ceiling spread out, moved towards the window and crept outside.

"I need a pad and paper!"

Tommy brought both.

"Now I want you to list all the details you can think of. What do you know about the kidnappers?"

Tommy tried to remember all the details. Grandma Huber took notes, took a puff from the pipe, felt the positive energy and was happy. "We'll show them who's in charge here. What a cheek, invading our village, grabbing a few innocent boys, turning them into criminals and threatening us!"

"Exactly!" Tommy agreed and demonstratively banged his fist on the table. He was amazed at himself and his fighting spirit.

Once all the data had been noted down, Grandma Huber looked at the piece of paper. She leaned back, took a puff from her pipe, let the herbs take effect and pondered over the available facts. You could see from her face how hard she was searching for a solution.

Finally, the old lady sat up straight. "We can't do this alone, I have to get my ladies from the regulars' table on board."

"But they're not allowed to tell anyone else!"

The pensioner grinned. "They're all your customers. They are also trustworthy and will keep quiet."

Tommy agreed. Besides, it didn't matter anyway. The situation could hardly get any worse. "Do you have a plan?"

"I think so, but it's not ready yet. Let's get the troops together, discuss everything and throw all the ideas together. Where's your phone?"

Anna Schwinghofer, Klara Korner, Else Gruber, who had run a law firm with her husband until five years ago, Uschi Brennauer, Erna Schmachtinger and Rosi Platter, the widow of former print shop owner Gustav Platter, were called one after the other. All of the women came from this village, had been close friends with Grandma Huber since childhood, formed the now legendary regulars' table and were all, without exception, Tommy's customers. They were also his only customers.

The phone calls were all the same. The wording could have been copied and played back one-to-one.

Grandma Huber: "It's me! We have a problem. A real problem. Can you come?"

There was a loud exhalation that sounded something like: "Phew, now of all times. There's a show on TV right now and I've got a cake in the oven, plus I'm expecting company in an hour." But none of these excuses came. It remained a loud and clearly audible exhalation.

The caller replied: "You're triggering our ladies' emergency call?"

Grandma Huber: "Yes, red alert!"

The called party: "When and where to?"

Grandma Huber: "Right now, I'll wait with Tommy."

The called party: "Have we been found out?"

Grandma Huber: "Worse!"

The called party: "Has someone died?"

Grandma Huber: "Not yet!"

The called party: "Who will die?"

Grandma Huber: "If we don't solve the problem, Tommy could get caught!"

The called party: "We'll solve the problem! I'll be there in fifteen minutes!"

Grandma Huber reached all six ladies. So they were complete. Tommy's neighbor was confident. "The cavalry is coming. That's a declaration of war on the kidnappers. We'll take care of your problem from now on. We're more powerful than *The Magnificent Seven!* Do you still have apples, flour, sugar and eggs in the house?"

Tommy nods. "It should all be there."

"Then of course I'll need some of that good baking mix, you know," she winked and went into the kitchen. "I need to bake a really quick cake. One with lots of pepper," she winked.

Tommy knew what she meant.

Klara Korner called her sister-in-law, who replaced her in the EDEKA store shortly afterwards. She took off her white coat and hung it up on the coat rack. Before the robust store owner left the office, she called two other members of the regulars' table.

"You know about this?"

"Yes! Ladies' emergency call! Red alert! Our supplier is in danger!"

"Right!"

"You're picking us up?"

"That's right! I'm off!"

"I'm ready!"

Then she left her store, went out to the parking lot, got into her car and picked up Rosi Platter and Else Gruber one after the other.

Uschi Brennauer drove herself. Anna Schwinghofer and Erna Schmachtinger had come on foot and by bike respectively. The living room filled up and the background noise from the old ladies increased steadily.

While the regulars were on their way, Grandma Huber had gathered everything in the kitchen for a quick cake batter and was baking. Tommy had fetched the ingredients for the special *flavor* from the barn.

By the time all the ladies had gathered in the living room, the smell of herbal apple pie was already wonderful.

"Ladies, the cake will take a good 30 minutes to cool down. That's enough time to bring you up to date and discuss a battle plan."

Klara addressed her friend with a serious expression. "You triggered the ladies' emergency call with a red alert. What happened that we had to leave everything behind?"

"In a moment," replied Grandma Huber and disappeared into the kitchen once again.

Tommy came in with a tray. "Coffee?"

Seven times came: "Yes."

While the sugar bowl and the milk jug made the rounds, Grandma Huber took off her apron in the kitchen and followed Tommy into the living room. She put her hands on her hips, looked at her best friends and said: "Girls, I'll get straight to the point! Three nasty gangsters have kidnapped Willy and Ernest! Tommy is being blackmailed! Everyone's life is in danger and so of course we're also in danger of losing our medicine!"

Frozen faces. Only slowly did the heads of the regulars move to the left and right in shock, only to end in a murmur. This quickly turned into whispering, which in turn turned into intense speculation, which ended with a loud "Quiet!".

Everyone stared at Grandma Huber again. "Listen here. Tommy is going to tell you all about what happened."

All eyes were on Tommy, who felt comfortable among his customers, but still strange in his position as a victim. He felt hot and cold. "Al-al-also," he stuttered.

"Stay calm, boy. Imagine we're sitting in the village pub and you're telling us about a movie you saw at the cinema," Else Gruber suggested.

She knew how to combat nervousness. At a number of court hearings, some loudmouths on the street had suddenly become meek and taciturn. And many of her clients were afraid to speak. She was practiced in taking away their fear and excitement.

Her tip was good. Tommy closed his eyes and repeated the whole story he had already told Grandma Huber. He didn't leave out a single detail and when he had finished, Klara Korner slapped her thighs angrily. "Those scoundrels. I knew straight away that something was wrong with them. The whole gang was in my store and almost bought up my entire stock of tins," she said, describing the three men.

The cake was ready before Klara's elaborate description and was divided into fourteen pieces. Tommy didn't like cake. He didn't feel like eating. At least not for anything sweet, whereupon Grandma Huber prepared an omelette for him and put it down with the unmistakable words: "Eat, otherwise you won't be able to think, let alone fight!"

Tommy didn't dare to argue. He took the fork and poked around on the plate. All seven women watched him. He felt as if he had seven grandmothers who were all looking after him.

"Eat, boy!" came the next clear request.

Tommy pushed the first fork listlessly into his mouth and chewed. His expression changed as the taste explosions began. "Mmm, that's great," he said and pushed the next fork into his mouth.

"I added some cheese, a few cubes of salami and seasoned everything with a touch of chili."

"Efft, legga," he groaned with his mouth full and barely intelligible.

"Great!"

"Thank God!"

"I'm relieved."

"You have to write that recipe down for me!"

They stared greedily at the cake. Grandma Huber relieved them with the words. "Ladies, now it's apple pie with a twist."

The ladies took a bite. Plates clattered, the clatter of forks could be heard and one praise trumped the next. First there was silence, then they whispered, started to giggle and suddenly they all showed euphoric combativeness. They were best friends, they were a team and they didn't want to lose anyone. Their herb boy!

Else Gruber was the first to speak. "We have to put a stop to these nasty fellows and free Tommy's roommate."

Erna Schmachtinger cleared her throat: "Should I tell my son ..."

Almost at the same time, a "No!" came six times.

Erna nodded. "That's what I thought."

The Gruberin, as Else's nickname was, explained briefly. "Our little business with Tommy and his herb garden must not be exposed. If your son has the slightest suspicion about this, there will be no more cakes, cookies, pipes or the cute little bags we smoke in front of the regulars' table."

Everyone agreed. Erna confirmed: "Of course my son won't find out anything and therefore won't set foot on this property. You can count on that!"

Rosi Platter took a sip of coffee. Images of roasted beans raced through her mind. The Coke man from the advertisement smiled at her and she felt inclined to wave at him. She smiled as she abruptly returned to reality. "Wow, girls, that second piece of cake really gets my imagination going. Do you know who I just saw in my mind's eye?" Without waiting for a reaction, she immediately followed up with the answer: "The coke man."

Klara was delighted. "A handsome man."

Tommy grimaced. "I don't know the guy. Who is he?"

"Just some advertising fudge," explained Grandma Huber and turned to her friends. "We have a problem to solve here. Concentrate, girls!"

Rosi Platter couldn't get the big grin off her face when she thought about the Coke man, but her mind was working normally again. "Could the kidnappers be from the drug scene?" she asked.

Anna Schwinghofer got in touch: "That's possible. Maybe they thought that our Tommy had taken over his previous tenants' business. After all, they're in jail for drug offenses."

Else Gruber shook her head. "I don't think so. The kidnappers would have mentioned that. Instead, they refer to Ernest's rich uncle in their demand. I rule out any connection to the drug mafia. Besides, how would they know anything about Tommy's little miracle plant field? You can't see it from the street."

Uschi Brennauer put it in a nutshell. "Girls, we now know that there are three kidnappers and that they are demanding 100,000 euros. What happens next? Speculation won't help us, we need facts and a good plan!"

Like Rosi before her, Klara Korner also took a sip of coffee, put her cup down and looked around. "Let's do some bookkeeping. Let's write down what we know. That's the credit side. Then let's write down what these nasty scoundrels are demanding, that's the debit side!"

"A bank robbery. Mei o mei," moaned Erna Schmachtinger. "Will we get it under control again?"

Else Gruber reassured her. "We'll worry about that once we've freed Ernest and Willy. As I said, let's look at the facts first. Pay attention!"

The ladies and Tommy listened attentively to the retired lawyer. "Three kidnappers have Ernest and Willy in their power. Our two friends were kidnapped after a bank robbery. We still have to evaluate other available facts in order to get more clarity. Next we'll have the blackmail letter," she paused, looked at Grandma Huber and winked: "Your apple pie with a twist is sheer madness. I feel great. I could tear out trees." Gruber pumped both fists in the air. In her mind, the eloquent woman was in the courtroom, making a rambling plea. She squinted at her plate, grabbed the last piece of cake and popped it into her mouth. "Girls," she smacked her lips full of euphoria, "we can do this!"

Anna Schwinghofer reached a little awkwardly for her lumbar vertebrae, felt around a little with her fingers and beamed. "My back pain is gone. If those crooks threaten my herb boy..." she didn't finish the sentence. This partial statement was groundbreaking.

This went on in turn until Else Gruber took the floor again. "Back to our case! Let's start with the internal inquiry. Which of you are on board and who is keeping quiet? We demonstrated unity earlier, but if we actually get going, it could be dangerous! So, girls, who's in?"

"Fight!" said Grandma Huber, raising her clenched fist.

"My health comes first! Without herbal medicine, I'd be sitting at the doctor's for hours again. I don't want that anymore. I'm also in favor of the fight!" Erna Schmachtinger joined in and everyone else joined in at the same time.

Gruber was satisfied. "Good, then we're agreed. Step two," she looked at Klara Korner. "Klara is right. We need a structured overview. She called it debit and credit, I call it pros and cons." Her gaze moved on to Tommy. "Write it down!"

Tommy picked up his pad and pen. "I can't write very well, but I'm ready!"

Grandma Huber put her hand on Tommy's shoulder. "You could have told me that long ago. When this is over, I'll give you private lessons."

This individual offer of help to eliminate one of his weaknesses was another energy boost for Tommy. He confidently began to write down what Else Gruber dictated. About half an hour later, the former lawyer skimmed over the facts, took off her reading glasses, looked around and said in a determined voice: "Long story short. We need the ransom! If anything, a handover would be the only weak point in this dangerous game."

A general shake of the head. "I can maybe raise three or four thousand euros quickly, the rest is invested," said the first of the ladies.

"Stop!" Else Gruber interjected with a grin but firmly, raising her hand with an outstretched index finger to emphasize the seriousness of her objection. "It's commendable that you're prepared to sacrifice your savings, but I have no intention of handing over our hard-earned money to this lot."

"But what?" came from Uschi Brennauer, slightly surprised.

Each of the ladies was familiar with the superior look on her friend's face. Gruber had a flash of inspiration, an idea or, to put it another way, a joker up her sleeve. She always had the same look on her face when she had at least three jokers or five aces in her hand in a game of canasta. And as much as this look annoyed her opponents when playing cards, the pensioners welcomed it at that moment. That was what they needed: Jokers and aces. To put it better: a promising plan, which the Gruber seemed to have. Her eyes rested on Rosi Platter. Although resting was probably a very reserved way of putting it. She stared at Rosi so penetratingly that she began to shift nervously back and forth. "Tell me, Rosi, how long has your old print shop been idle?"

The question came as a relief. Rosi had already feared that she had not been able to tolerate the apple pie with whistle and her face was covered in a rash. This was due to her allergy to pomaceous fruit. But so far, it hadn't been a problem with cooked or baked fruit. So it was all about the factory. Rosi didn't have to think long and had the answer ready straight away. "That's almost three years. After my husband died, I wanted to sell the company, but I haven't managed it yet. After all, that was our life."

"And the machines?"

"Everything is still there. Why? Should I deposit the company as collateral with the bank and we'll borrow the ransom? It won't be worth much. To get back into the business these days, you'd have to invest heavily. Our technology works, but it's outdated."

Else Gruber's expression changed slightly. It was the look of a winner. It was comparable to the finale of a big Hollywood courtroom drama in which the supposedly weak good guys win and the bad big guys lose. "No, not banking. I have a much better idea. We'll copy a few hundred so we have different serial numbers and print the ransom ourselves in your old factory!"

Erna Schmachtiger warned in horror: "That's counterfeiting. I know from my son that you go to prison for a long time for that. That's a crime!"

Gruber shook her head. "Yes and no! We don't put this money into circulation! Not directly," she added. "Erna, think about it. What do we do with the counterfeit money? We don't spend it, we use it to ransom Tommy's friends. It's not us who have the problem with the counterfeit money, it's the blackmailers."

"Drug offenses, bank robberies, counterfeiting. If anyone catches us, we'll spend the rest of our lives in prison," Klara interjected.

The lawyer waved her off. "Rubbish! Who's going to find out? The kidnappers? If they get caught, they'll hardly say that the money came from a kidnapping."

Rosi Platter ended the discussion by reaching into her handbag, pulling out her purse and slamming a hundred euro bill on the table.

"Bingo! I've got a hundred. My old machines are ready to go and as far as I can remember, there's some really good paper in my old stock," she grinned mischievously, just like Else Gruber before her.

Grandma Huber also agreed. "Does anyone have any other ideas on how we can raise 100,000 euros in this short time?"

None of the drugged-up ladies could come up with a better suggestion. So it was a done deal. They would make the ransom of 100,000 euros themselves.

Grandma Huber felt full of energy. The initially smoked bag filling in her pipe and the two pieces of cake took full effect. The pensioner jumped to her feet full of enthusiasm. "Let's get straight to work."

Rosi Platter also stood up. "Our friend is right. It takes a while to get the machines started. As soon as we're happy with the quality of the copies, we have to print them on paper, check the quality again and then cut them to size."

Uschi Brennauer also stood up. "The bills will look brand new and therefore smooth. We have to treat them somehow and make them look old. Maybe we'll crumple them up. Ladies, that's manual labor."

"Dude! What are you like?" Tommy, who had been listening in silence and spellbound the whole time, said in amazement.

"If you're going to use words like that, it means: Old people!" Anna Schwinghofer tried to instruct him.

"Nah, it's called age! That's what you say these days when you're surprised!" Klara Korner clarified.

"Ahh, I see," Anna confirmed and shook her head: "Dude, I wouldn't have thought that."

Tommy and the belligerent group of women entered the old print shop through a side entrance. The air was dry and dusty. Even after three years of standstill, it still smelled of various chemicals. The large skylight windows were so dirty that the printing and cutting machines were shrouded in dim light. Rosi flicked a light switch. Neon tubes flickered before their cold, artificial light was cast over everything.

"They could be cleaned again," Anna Schwinghofer noticed as she looked at the skylights.

Gruber asked: "Where can I open the windows? It's a bit stuffy in here."

Rosi ignored both remarks. Instead, she slipped back into the role of boss. She blossomed. "Grandma Huber, you cover the second machine from the right. Tommy, you'll find the cleaning trolley in the next room at the end of the hall. It has everything we need. Bring it here, please. Anna, Klara, Erna and Uschi, can you help Tommy and get everything ready? Else and I will go to the warehouse and get some chemicals and the right paper."

"The windows!" Else Gruber repeated.

Rosi pointed to the right. "Right at the back of the wall. You have to pull down the levers with the red handles and the skylights will open."

Gruber saw the levers and went to them. Each of them was connected to a long rod that led upwards and was nothing more than the extended arm of a window tilt handle. She flipped the first lever down and was amazed at how easily the linkage could be moved. The lawyer's widow had expected more resistance. One by one, she opened the fanlight windows. Fresh air flowed into the hall. When all the levers were folded down, she followed Rosi Platter into the warehouse.

"Sharp command," Tommy grinned and marched off to carry out the order he had received. "The blackmailers will be in for a surprise."

Another of the stoned grannies had discovered loudspeakers in the hall and followed the cables. She found the old stereo system in the office and switched it on. The reception was clear and distinct, the station perfect. The voice of a presenter could be heard from the hall. "... and I would like to welcome my listeners to a new edition of the Schlager-Oldie-Parade. In the next hour, we'll be playing all the hits from the 50s, 60s and 70s. Let's start with a threesome. You are now listening to Freddy Quinn with *Heimweh (Homesick)*, followed by Jürgen Marcus' hit *Eine neue Liebe ist wie ein neues Leben (A new love is like a new life)* and the finale of our opening threesome is Connie Francis with *Schöner fremder Mann (pretty strange guy)*."

The ladies hummed along to the first song and began to dance rhythmically to the second, swinging brooms and dusters and singing along loudly to the chorus. And when Connie Francis' hit came on,

Grandma Huber stood out as a solo singer. She belted out the song into the broomstick that served as her microphone.

The warehouse was about the same size as the hall. Twenty meters long and ten meters wide. The four rows of shelves held leftover stocks of chemicals, oils and various paints. There were also spare parts for the machines and various types of paper. Rosi grabbed one of the three trolleys standing around, pushed it into the first aisle of shelves and searched for a particular chemical. She stopped, put on her glasses and said: "This one! Twice!"

At the end of the aisle, Rosi looked at the full trolley and was satisfied. "That's all we need. I was worried that I didn't have the right colors in stock. Then I would have had to mix. But everything is perfect as it is."

"And the paper?" Else asked, tilting her head to one side and listening. "Really good music."

Rosi also heard the sound that was rocking the hall and tapped her right foot to the beat. "That's right, really good music. These women are crazy," she laughed. "They should be cleaning, not partying."

The print shop owner pushed the trolley to the door and parked it there. A glance into the hall followed. Anna Schwinghofer whirled around with the broom while Uschi Brennauer dusted the large printing press in time. Rosi would have loved to storm into the hall, open a bottle of champagne and celebrate, but they had a job to do. They had to counterfeit money. So she gave up champagne and dancing and grabbed a second trolley instead. She pushed it into another aisle of shelves and walked about halfway down. She stopped, took a good look at the stored paper and grabbed it. "It should work with this one. I'll take three different thicknesses of paper."

Gruber began to read the inscriptions, but quickly gave up, as all the designations consisted of combinations of various numbers and letters. "How difficult is it to copy banknotes?" she asked her friend. So far, like all the other ladies, she had never committed a crime. And all of a sudden, according to the law, she was a drug user, a counterfeiter and a member of a criminal organization, commonly known as a gang. In her mind's eye, she saw herself standing in line at the food counter in an orange suit, just like in the American prison TV series. A woman, tattooed from top to bottom and looking extremely masculine, slapped an indefinable porridge onto her plate with a ladle and winked at her. Else got goose bumps. Rosi's laughter catapulted her back to reality. She was relieved.

"They are copied quickly. It's all about the right paper and the security features. It's almost impossible to achieve the quality of a genuine bill."

"Do the blackmailers realize that we are deceiving them?"

Rosi frowned thoughtfully. You could just see her thinking. "Because we can only produce a limited quality of banknote here," she replied, "they will notice sooner or later. We have to manage to achieve a quality that looks genuine at first glance. In other words, it won't be noticeable when the hostages are shown it."

"This is a hugely stressful situation. If we create additional artificial stress, we increase the pressure and they may not realize it. That can really work. Let's get to work!"

Neither of them could believe their eyes as they pushed the loaded carts into the hall. *The Smurfs' song* by *Vader Abraham was playing on* the radio. Tommy mimed the role of the singer. Anna, Grandma Huber, Uschi and Klara sang the part of the Smurfs.

"Tell me, where are you from ..."
"From Smurfland, please ..."
"Does everyone there look like you ..."
"Yes, we look just like us ..."
"Shall I teach you a song ..."
"Yes, we want to sing to you ..."
"I know a song with a nice chorus ..."
"Please play it for us once ..."
"The flute smurf starts ... so sing along ..."
"La la lalalalalalalalala la la lalalalalalalala ..."

"Stooooop," Rosi's voice thundered through the hall.
The choir suddenly fell silent, only Tommy continued to sing.
"And now the second voice ..."

Then he felt funny and fell silent too, while the next verse boomed out of the speakers. Tommy clapped his hands and applauded. "Girls, we have to do the singing professionally. We're going to be famous!"

Rosi's look was serious. "Guys, either we try to make 100,000 euros of counterfeit money now or we start a girl group. What do you suggest?"

Uschi Brennauer cleared her throat. "You're still allowed to sing."

"She's right! Let's get to work. We're not here for pleasure," Grandma Huber caught herself, still swaying slightly to the beat. "But Tommy's idea isn't so bad," she murmured and winked at him.

The time had finally come. The excitement was enormous when the first of five different one hundred euro bills was placed on the copying field. The whole group stood around the huge copying machine. Rosi inserted a sheet of paper and closed the tray. "That was a bad purchase back then. Our production manager had mistyped the line. Fortunately, the delivery wasn't too big, because this stuff was expensive." She pointed to the trolley with the papers. "I didn't think I'd need it again one day."

Her finger moved to a button. "Attention ... ready ... go!" The button was pressed. A soft buzzing could be heard. A light flickered back and forth along the edges under the tray. Then it rattled and a sheet of paper was ejected and immediately returned to the machine.

"There's a mistake!" Tommy shouted excitedly and tried to hold the sheet of paper.

Rosi slapped his hand and scolded him: "Hands off! We'll copy the front and back!"

Tommy pulled his hands back in shock. "Sorry!"

The sheet was spat out. Rosi took it, held it up to the bright neon light and examined the copy. Astonished looks followed her.

"Wow, dude! It works!" the herb boy exclaimed.

Rosi took a pair of scissors and cut out a bill, then she took a real hundred, closed her eyes and let them both move back and forth between her fingers. Finally, she crumpled up the copy.

"No, what are you doing?" Anna Schwinghofer interjected.

"Too bad. We need the other paper. This one stands out immediately."

Klara Korner tore open another pack of copy paper, handed Rosi a sheet and the whole procedure was repeated. Again, everyone stared first at the output tray, then at Rosi's hands, then at the copy of the banknote. This time she rubbed a little longer and passed both bills to Klara. "Feel you. You always have a lot of money in your hands in your store."

The businesswoman closed her eyes. "Well, if I examine it closely, it stands out. If all hell broke loose and the bill was a little more worn, it might pass."

"I think so too," confirmed Rosi.

"Give me that," said Grandma Huber and grabbed the real and the fake hundred. She put on her glasses and held both bills up to the light. "Good copies, but when I check them, I'll know which one is fake."

"And if you don't check it?" asked Tommy.

Grandma Huber pulled her lips together and let out a "Hm?".

Else Gruber took the floor. "You have to remember that exchanging hostages for money is an exceptional situation. It's incredibly stressful. If the money looks real, the handover will work, I'm sure of it."

"And if not?" asked Erna Schmachtinger.

Grandma Huber clenched her right hand into a fist and stretched it upwards. "Then we'll have to get physical."

All heads flew around and stared at her.

"What are you looking at? We're old, but not sick and certainly not dead. We can fight!"

The farmer's wife was still being stared at in silence.

"T-they're armed," Tommy stammered.

"Grandma Huber is just thinking out loud about an emergency solution. And that's good. We have to be prepared for anything," Gruber interjected.

"We'll definitely arm ourselves!" the pugnacious farmer's wife added.

Consent. Under no circumstances should they trust the criminals and think about a smooth handover, and they should not be too careless in their approach. A little rearmament would certainly do no harm.

Rosi Platter got to the heart of the matter. "Girls, we're doing the whole thing now. Let us know at home that you won't be home much in the near future. We'll get pizza from Antonio and work late into the night. We have to copy 100,000 euros with different bills, cut them to size, make them look old and put some kind of band on them. Then we have to wrap the counterfeit money."

"I have enough old briefcases at home," said Else Gruber.

"Where's the phone? I'm calling home," said Anna Schwinghofer.

"I'll take the pizza orders," grinned Tommy, who felt completely safe and secure in the company of the old ladies. "And if someone drives me to pick up the pizzas later, I'll make a little detour home and pick up a few herb mixes for you."

"Yay!" they cheered.

"My dears, before we get to work here, let's also consider the other matter," Erna Schmachtinger interrupted the cheerful, confident composure.

"What other thing?" came the question.

"The bank robbery!"

Gruber tapped her forehead with the flat of her hand. "Jesus, you're brilliant, Erna. We really must iron that out."

Tommy swallowed nervously. His Adam's apple moved up and down several times, clearly visible. He had a guilty conscience. "What's there to smooth out?" he asked rather meekly.

Erna put her hands on her hips and gave the herb boy an unmistakable look. "That was no prank! If you can be proven to have committed the robbery, you will do time! It doesn't matter how much loot you made or what your motives were for pulling it off. A robbery is still a robbery! You don't need to have studied to know that!"

That was clear. Gruber echoed the same sentiment. "For an armed robbery, if the court is lenient, you'll get between four and eight years in prison."

Tommy turned white as a sheet.

Erna changed her bitter expression. "But as a fan of almost every detective series and as the mother of a policeman, I already have an idea."

For a moment, she was the center of attention. The ladies and Tommy in particular were curious. "What are you up to? Can you help us?" he asked hopefully. He was feeling pretty bad again at the moment. The young man was going through rollercoasters of emotions.

Erna asked Tommy: "Your buddies didn't go there on foot."

The Batmobile, he remembered. "No, of course not. They took Willys's BMW. That's the getaway vehicle."

"That's extremely important information." She paused for a moment and then added emphatically: "And you said they were kidnapped immediately after the attack."

"That's right," Tommy nodded in agreement. "I could overhear that on my cell phone."

"So your BMW is still parked near the bank. That's a lead," she explained, raising her index finger in warning. "We have to find the car and get it out of there."

Tommy didn't understand what was so dangerous about a parked vehicle. "Why do we have to do this?"

"It's a small place. If a strange car is parked for a long time, people get suspicious and call the police. I know enough stories like that from my son."

Else immediately realized how explosive the problem was and knew that they had to do something quickly.

Klara was also aware of this. "We'll drive right past there! We'll park the BMW before we get the pizza."

Else supported her friend's plan. "That's a good plan. Tommy, do you have a spare key at home?"

The herb boy didn't have to think long. Ernest had a pronounced obsession with order. Everything always had to be in its place, hanging or standing. The answer came like a shot from a pistol: "The key is in the key box!"

Else was relieved. "Bingo! When the BMW is back at your house, there'll be one less lane."

"You're the best!" Tommy's heart sank. None of his friends could be replaced. He loved them all.

Gruber raised her hand again and said in a monotone voice: "By the way, just so you don't forget! Counterfeiting money is just as much a crime as robbery. You'll get a few years in jail for that too."

Grandma Huber answered spontaneously. "But only if you get caught."

Rosi added: "Our plan is good and we will win in the end. We just have to stay one step ahead of both our opponents and the police and destroy all the evidence in the end!"

Else Gruber was satisfied. "That's exactly what I wanted to hear. Let's get going. We'll get the BMW, some herbs and pizza!"

Once again, unity was demonstrated. All seven women and Tommy formed a circle. Everyone put their arm on their neighbor's shoulders. Grandma Huber took the floor.

"Who are we?"

"The regulars' table women!" came the chorus.

Tommy shouted along, but felt a bit stupid because he was a man. So he added. "I'm the regulars' table man."

Grandma Huber: "Our motto!"

"All for one, one for all!"

And Tommy added. "... and one."

With the call: "Let's go girls!", everyone let go and clapped their hands. They were a team, they were a group and they helped together.

Three of the pensioners and Tommy drove off while the others continued to deal with the counterfeit money.

A long, hard night lay ahead of them.

Chapter 5
Don't mess with grannies

While Tommy and the cool grannies were busy counterfeiting money, Ernest and Willy had completely different problems to deal with. Night had fallen and their butts were aching from sitting around on the chairs.

"Can we move around a bit?" asked Willy. "I'm already getting calluses on my backside. It's very uncomfortable when you're tied to a chair for hours on end."

Harvey Hansen, who was engrossed in a comic book, did not react. Ernest cleared his throat. "Hm ... hm ..."

Now the youngest kidnapper lifted his head slightly and squinted at the two kidnap victims. "Is what?"

Ernest nodded briefly and, as always, his cheeks flushed slightly. "My friend asked if we could move around a bit."

Harvey frowned. Batman's head was still, but his cheeks were moving. *Crazy*, he thought. "Ey, why do you want to move?"

"Because it's uncomfortable. Aren't you listening to us?"

Harvey looked at the prisoners and said: "Sure, if it's good for you, why not. You can swivel your heads back and forth. That's a good exercise. It worked for Batman just now." As soon as he said it, he went back to staring at his comic.

Ernest let out an audible gasp. "My buddy said, like, traipsing around or something."

Harvey was visibly annoyed. "Dude, you're annoying. This is the fourth time I've started with the same speech bubble. Do you know how exhausting that is? By the time I've read this, I can't remember what happened before. The book is exciting without end. Donald has just fallen into a pit and can't get out for the life of him! So don't bother me!" He formed a pistol with his hand by holding his thumb up and extending his index finger, aiming at the two hostages in turn. "Otherwise ... bang!"

"That's okay," came from Willy. "No problem."

Harvey tried to read on. Ernest began to whistle.

"Hey dude! That's totally annoying! Stop warbling around so stupidly!"

Ernest fell silent. "I'm bored. Can't you read aloud?"

"Dude! Now you really want to tease me!"

The door opened. Hubert Hansen and his older son Harry entered the room. The old man grumbled: "Is there any stress?"

Harvey played the cool guy. "I've got everything under control, Dad. The two fools wanted to move and then they wanted me to read them something. But not with me. I was tough as nails," he gushed proudly.

"Not quite," Ernest interjected. "You gave us permission to move our heads!"

Harvey became angry. "Hey, dude! That's my last warning!" he shouted, rising up and standing menacingly in front of the kidnap victims.

Harry pushed his brother aside and pulled out a knife. Ernest and Willy got scared. Ernest wanted to have a calming effect on the criminal and rummaged through his knowledge of movie quotes. *Empty! Damn, what can I say? I can't think of anything.*

Willy beat him to it. "That's all right. We don't have to move. We've already really got used to this sitting position."

The kidnapper bent down. Ernest closed his eyes and expected a stab with the knife, but instead Harry cut the cable ties on his feet and hands. "Up you go!"

They both stood up, rubbed their wrists and said, "Thank you!"

Ernest gave Harvey a sardonic look. "You see, we're allowed to move after all."

Willy, meanwhile, approached Harry. "Are we free now?"

In the background, old Hansen began to laugh out loud. "Ha ... ha ... free! You're real comedians. Your buddy still has to get the money. Tomorrow we'll do the handover! 100,000 flakes against you! Otherwise you'll be handed back one slice at a time!"

"I think that ...", Ernest began in a snippy undertone, received a thoughtful nudge in the side from Willy and therefore broke off the sentence. Instead, he choked out an "It's okay".

Harry pointed the knife towards the door. "Go after my dad. We've set up your camp for the night! And don't do anything stupid!"

They were led through the corridor and finally stood in front of a metal fire door. Father Hansen opened it. "Get in here!"

The storage room was not large. Maybe 10 or 12 square meters. A bare 100-watt light bulb hung lonely from the ceiling and provided cold, harsh light. The window was barely the size of a soccer and strangled any thoughts of escape before they even arose.

The room was completely empty except for one piece of furniture. This was an inflatable double bed in the middle of the room.

"You can sleep here! One of us always keeps watch outside the door. In case you get the absurd idea of trying to escape," grumbled old Hansen, grinning maliciously and pointing to the window, "you won't fit through there."

"It smells bad in here," Ernest wrinkled his nose. "What was stored here? Romadur or some other stinky cheese?"

"Shut up and go inside!"

"That's right," shouted Harvey Hansen, who had also gone along, pulled out his revolver and raised it threateningly. "Shut up, otherwise it'll go off! And you could remember one thing! I'm not going to read you anything!"

Ernest reluctantly entered the room. "What if I have to go out at night? I mean, there were beans and ..."

"Put it in there!" came the dry reply. Hubert Hansen pointed to a bucket standing next to the bed.

Ernest didn't feel well at all, Willy looked at him. "If you have to go again, go now!"

The heavyweight tried to look rather pitiful and rubbed his stomach. "You'll have to let me do that. I won't be long either!"

All three Hansens looked at each other questioningly.

Ernest added: "I read that once, by the way. If you don't allow me to go to the toilet, I'll be punished mercilessly with the maximum penalty of torture!"

Harvey frowned again. "Is that true, Dad?"

Harry said: "Could be! I once saw a report about an American prison where a female warden was convicted of torture."

The old man hissed: "We're gangsters, not brutes! You can go to the loo again, but quickly!" Then he looked at Harvey. "You go with the fat one and Harry will look after the other one!"

Harvey turned white as a sheet. "Why me?"

Ernest said: "I'm not fat. The beans are bloating my belly enormously. That's an optical illusion!"

The old man rolled his eyes and swung a flat hand in exasperation. Harvey instinctively backed away and calmed him down. "It's all right, Dad! I'm going with you."

Ernest was taken to the toilet. When the order-loving young man saw the state of the toilet, he retched. "This is extremely dirty."

"You can also go for the bucket ..."

Ernest raised his hand and interrupted. "It's all right! It's not that bad."

"Then get started!"

Ernest plucked off some toilet paper and placed it over the toilet seat as a protective cushion. Then he turned to Harvey. "You're still there. I can't do it with someone watching."

The kidnapper grimaced. "Do you think I'm enjoying this?"

"I really can't. I'm not going to let anyone watch me do my business!"

"Then you don't have to be right!"

"Yes!"

"Then do it!"

"Turn around!"

"Yo, dude!"

Everyone knows the infamous saying: *every little bean makes a little sound!* It works stronger for one person and weaker for another. Ernest is one of those people who cannot digest the polysaccharides contained in beans particularly well, so that, to put it simply, they turn into hydrogen sulphide in the final stage of the digestive process, which is partly responsible for flatulence and leaves the body in the form of flatulence. In short, Ernest was struggling enormously with himself and the course of nature and had to find relief by farting. He secretly hoped that this would be quiet, but it didn't work. "Sorry," he said quietly and blushed as a huge fart escaped from him, clearly audible and, above all, smellable.

Harvey wrinkled his nose as the foul-smelling chemical mixture spread around the room. He reacted promptly. "Okay, I'll go out the door. But don't do anything stupid!"

Ernest was relieved. "No. I promise!"

Willy was sitting on the inflatable guest bed when Ernest came back into the room a little later, his face visibly relaxed. The door was closed and locked from the outside.

"Boy, I feel like I've been reborn," Ernest beamed.

Willy just shrugged his shoulders.

"What's going on?" asked the heavyweight in the Batman costume, looking around. "Don't tell me they're locking us up without provisions. Hang on, I'll complain right away."

Before Ernest could turn around and bang on the door with his fist clenched, he heard his buddy's resigned voice.

"Escape is really out of the question! We are absolutely trapped."

Ernest went to the bed and sat down next to Willy. The inflatable double bed gave way and Ernest sank in deeply, while Willy was literally catapulted upwards. Sitting in this extreme inclined position, the heavyweight shook his head dismissively. "Poor quality or too little air? What do you think?"

Willy was initially inclined to reply that this was not due to the lack of air or the quality of the guest bed, but that Ernest's estimated live weight of 160 kilograms was the cause. In order not to cause any unnecessary stress, he let it go and instead pressed out a lethargic: "It doesn't matter", followed by: "It's been a long, hard and not very successful day. Let's go to sleep. Maybe tomorrow we'll think of a solution to our problem."

Ernest yawned and stood up. Willy made a small jump upwards along with the unburdened bed. Ernest stretched, took off the Batman cape and said: "Good idea. I've suddenly become tired. A little sleep will do me good now."

Willy lay down on his side of the bed. When Ernest also lay down, he sank in deeply again. This time, however, along his entire length. As a result, Willy's side of the bed was pushed up and he rolled onto Ernest. "Shit!" he groaned, completely surprised and annoyed at the same time.

Ernest was startled when Willy plopped against him. "Ouch! Tell me, can't you stay on your side?"

Willy took an audible deep breath in and out. He suppressed the urge to shout out loud and tried to stay calm inside and find a balance between understanding, facts and anger. *Don't get upset,* he thought. *Ohmmmmm, find your inner center.*

Ernest demonstratively turned from his back to his side, pushing the bed to its limits. The air displaced by his weight was transferred to Willy's side in waves with every movement Ernest made. He felt as if he were sitting in a small rowing boat in the middle of the sea, caught in a hurricane-like storm with high waves.

Ohmmmm, find your inner center.

Finding the inner center. Where had he read this nonsense? Or was it a report on television? It didn't matter, it didn't work for him. There was no inner center. Next to him was a mountain of flesh and in front of him was the insurmountably high latex wall of the air bed. Willy knew at that moment that it was impossible to spend the night on this bed with his buddy.

Ernest lifted one leg, changed his position again and was now lying in the embryo position.

Willy rocked back and forth with his neighbor's every movement, alternately slapping against the latex wall and Ernest's back, and remained there when he stopped moving. Ernest mumbled, "Stay on your side, Willy," and began to snore lightly.

"Tell me, are you snoring?" asked Willy in horror.

No answer. Instead, Willy thought someone had started the sputtering engine of an ancient tractor. He stared at the ceiling with his eyes wide open. He was dog-tired, but sleep was out of the question. At some point he gave up. Willy struggled up the latex wall to get up. Then he grabbed the cape from the costume, spread it out on the floor and lay down on it.

"It's going to be a tough night!"

Grandma Huber closed the brown briefcase. "That's it! There's 100,000 euros of counterfeit money in here. Printed, crumpled and packed. Ladies and Tommy, we were great!"

They had been working long hours. Rosi Platter was in her element when the printing and cutting machines were running. She supervised all the tasks. Each of them, and of course Tommy too, completed their assigned job with precision.

Grandma Huber and her protégé added the sheets of paper one by one. "You can't push them in as a pack. They are so thin that the machine would pull in two or three sheets at a time," Rosi explained.

Klara and Anna Schwinghofer cut the bills out of the sheets of paper, Erna and Uschi crumpled them up and gave the counterfeit money a certain authenticity. Else Gruber checked the quality, counted and bundled the bills.

"Actually, I thought we'd have a pipe and a glass of champagne after work, but I'm tired beyond belief. Let's go home, girls. We need to be fit tomorrow," Rosi suggested and yawned.

Grandma Huber agreed immediately. "Off to bed! Tomorrow we'll show the kidnappers who's in charge here in the village and give them a good spanking!"

They had done it and made the impossible possible. They had a briefcase full of bundles of banknotes. It was counterfeit money, but that was only of secondary importance at the moment. Satisfied and still full of enthusiasm, the friends and Tommy said goodbye for the rest of the night and met up again in a few hours.

The breakfast table was set. Toast, raw ham, a steaming pot of white beans in tomato sauce. Willy saw four empty cans next to the stove. *Heinz Original Beans in Tomato Sauce*, he read. They were served with instant coffee.

"What are you staring at?" asked Harvey, who was playing with the butt of the revolver again, occasionally stroking the hammer of the gun with his thumb.

Willy secretly hoped that the kidnapper would shoot his own balls off. "Beans again?" he pressed out. He hadn't slept well and his back was aching. Having to spend the night on the rock-hard floor was one thing, but being subjected to Ernest's snoring was another. Willy was dead tired, felt exhausted and was therefore extremely irritable. He would definitely not survive another night like this. There were only two ways to escape this torture. Either escape or Tommy would pay the ransom. Willy categorically ruled out option three, a rescue by the police, as this was tantamount to prison. And the idea that he would have to spend a few years in a cramped cell with Ernest or one of the Hansen family would be tantamount to lifelong torture.

"Dude! Beans are healthy. They also come with toast," Harvey Hansen told him. "You get first-class treatment here. Hey, don't go on grumbling, or I'll punch a hole in your earlobe!"

Ernest warbled comfortably to himself in anticipation of a hearty breakfast. "... weekend and sunshine and then alone with you in the forest ..."

Harvey got into his stride. He turned to his enormously obese hostage. "Fat bastard, stop singing that garbage. It gives you ear cancer."

Ernest fell silent in horror. That was a huge affront! He was seething terribly. There was no way he was going to take that lying down. Not so early in the morning! "Firstly, who's fat here? Secondly, there's no such thing as ear cancer. That's utter nonsense! So both of those things are complete nonsense! And thirdly, it's a hit song from the 1930s and therefore a cultural asset. That's why Max Raabe staged it again."

The mood became more irritable.

"Did you just say I'm stupid, dude?"

Ernest stood up. "Did you say I was fat, you leek?"

Harvey pulled out his revolver. "That's enough! You won't get anything to eat for this."

Ernest turned bright red. Now he was completely furious. Nothing to eat and being insulted to boot. Some small, underexposed kidnapper wanted to deprive him of his delicious breakfast. He alternately looked at the gun and into the kidnapper's eyes.

Willy tried to mediate. "Nobody has said anything bad to anyone here. Why don't you calm down?"

The barrel of the revolver moved over to Willy, who immediately fell silent. "Shut up! I think you're both trying to get a rise out of me so you can overpower me, but I'm not stupid!"

Ernest sat down again. "No food, no ransom. End of the announcement! You can explain that to your father!"

Harvey was taken aback. "What nonsense!"

Willy noticed young Hansen's uncertainty. "Where he's right, he's right. No food, no ransom. The condition for paying the ransom is that we are treated well and given enough to eat."

"You two clown types are taking the piss," came the rather unsettled reply.

Ernest sensed his chance to get a sumptuous breakfast after all. "No. That's part of the deal. We're being treated like real hostages here. And like..." he thought about saying something clever. "Well, according to the Geneva Conventions, we're entitled to three meals ..." he thought about it and improved, "er ... five meals a day. If that's not respected, there's no business. We also have to be served. Just like in a restaurant. Otherwise it would be slavery. You get a few extra years on top for that!"

Willy interjected. "And of course there's a ransom deduction for tying us up. That means if you tie us up again, you'll get less money."

Harvey looked at Willy and Ernest in turn. The barrel of the gun swiveled in each case. "I don't believe it!"

"Then we'll have no choice but to tell your father everything, and of course we'll tell our buddy everything too and then," Ernest made a whirling motion with both arms, "the ransom money will be gone. Then everything will have been for nothing and guess who your father will blame? Certainly not us. We're just two hostages waiting for breakfast."

When the other two Hansens came into the kitchen, Ernest dipped the last piece of toast into the remaining sauce on his plate, wiped it all up and popped it into his mouth. "Mmm, that was a delicious breakfast," he said barely intelligibly.

It smelled of beans in tomato sauce and coffee. The two kidnap victims were obviously in high spirits as they ate their breakfast, while Harvey Hansen stood by and watched them. Willy pushed the empty coffee cup towards the kidnapper. "I'll have another cup."

Harvey nodded. "With milk and two sugars again?"

"Yes, with pleasure."

Father Hansen stared spellbound at the scene unfolding before him and couldn't believe what he was seeing. His son was serving the prisoners. The old man's stomach was churning. He was hungry and wanted breakfast. But instead of finding a table generously laid for him, Batman and Robin grinned at him while his son played head waiter. Stunned and almost boiling over with rage, he shouted: "What the hell is going on here?"

Harvey stood in front of his father with a swelling chest. "You can be proud of me. After the Geneva conversions ..."

"Conventions," Willy improved.

Harvey turned briefly to the prisoner and hissed: "Dude, I'm not in school here. When I say conservations or something like that, everyone knows what I mean, got it?"

Willy leaned back, grinned and replied: "It's okay. You're the boss!"

That had an effect. Harvey turned back to his father. "Well, I've made sure that the ransom won't be cut. We'll collect the full amount! And if the cops actually catch us, which of course I don't think they will, we won't be charged with slavery!"

Harry Hansen pushed past his father, went to the table and took a look in the pot. "Empty!"

His brother grinned. "The fat one, er ... Batman, was hungry. The other one didn't eat as much."

Harry pulled down the corners of his mouth. "That was my breakfast!"

Hubert Hansen discovered the empty toast wrapper. "Where's all the bread?"

"One here only had two disks," he pointed at Willy, "but the other one ..."

"Th-th-that was almost full," stuttered old Hansen in amazement. "You ate all the toast and beans?" he threw at Ernest.

He nodded. "The bread was very tasty with Heinz tomato beans. I love them. If I'd had one or three fried eggs with it, it would have been the icing on the cake, of course." Ernest frowned, looked thoughtfully at the stove and concluded: "And if you had toasted the bread, but like this..."

"Schnauuuuuuuzeeeee!" Hubert Hansen shouted angrily. His head was turning so red that he was afraid he was going to burst. "Take her back into the room, lock the door and sit in front of it! Immediately!"

The order was carried out immediately without objection. Harvey was not aware of any guilt, but he knew that any further words would result in a slap in the face.

Harry looked at the table. Empty plates, empty wrappers, a sip of coffee left in each cup. The gangster's stomach growled. He was also extremely angry. "Everything gone. Our lovely breakfast. Dad, they've eaten everything!"

The old man went to the kitchen cupboard, opened the door and stared inside. "Ravioli, green bean pot or lentils? What are we having for breakfast?"

"Ravioli for breakfast," growled Harry. "The two clowns will pay bitterly for that!"

Hubert Hansen took a can out of the cupboard and put it down. Then he reached for the can opener lying around, put it to work and turned it. He poured the contents of the opened can into the empty bean pot without rinsing it out first. "Tomato sauce is tomato sauce. That fits," he commented.

"Dad, I'm really angry!"

The old man's gaze was piercingly nasty. He grinned grimly. "We're going to give them a good licking for this, son."

Harry Hansen's face brightened again. "Do you already have a plan?"

Hubert Hansen stirred the meal in the pot. "I've got it!"

Curiosity shot up in Harry. "Oh, Dad, don't be so secretive now. Tell me how we're going to do it."

The head of the family gang put his wooden spoon aside. "I put pressure on the buddy of those two jerks."

"How?"

The tomato sauce began to bubble. Hubert had to stir it again to prevent it from burning. "I'll text him now and tell him we want the money in two hours. Delivery location to follow!"

Harry beamed. "Do you think he has the money?"

"Good idea," Hubert thought. "Better if I ask him for the money. Let him answer me. Then I'll do the handover. I'll rush him from one place to another. If there are any cops involved, we'll notice."

Harry pointed to the door. "And the two plums? Are we taking them to the handover?"

"No. We'll leave them here. If the money works out, we'll grab the money, get Harvey and set her free. Or better still. We'll get Harvey, then we'll leave and an hour later we'll write to him and tell him where we're holding them."

Harry clapped his hands. "Perfect. Then we have a head start." Suddenly his face darkened. "Dad, what are we going to do if he doesn't have the money?"

The old man didn't bat an eyelid as he replied: "Then we'll send him a very effective warning."

Harry felt a chill run down his spine. He knew what his father meant without saying it. He really was a brilliant and tough gangster boss.

Hubert took one last look in the pot. "Breakfast is ready. Let's eat in peace, then I'll write the news."

After a short sleep and a quick shower, the whole crew had gathered again in Tommy's living room. The table was sumptuously laid and it smelled of coffee, eggs with bacon and a special cake that looked like an ordinary bundt cake, but had that special *zing* thanks to the addition of Tommy's herbs. It smelled aromatically sweet, paired with a Mediterranean touch.

There were hard and soft-boiled eggs, wholemeal rolls, wheat rolls, potato rolls, two different types of bread, a liquid and a creamy, spreadable honey and five different types of jam. Each of the old ladies had brought something. There was even a current daily newspaper on the table. The Gruber woman had it under her arm when she arrived. "I get it delivered and I haven't had time to read it today."

Cups and dishes rattled. The friends talked about this and that, but not about the main topic that had brought them together in the first place. The rescue of Tommy's kidnapped friends. He was a little irritated. After yesterday's counterfeiting operation, he had fallen asleep without a care in the world despite the kidnapping of his flatmates and had woken up smiling to Charles' cock-a-doodle-doo. Now he was hell-bent on finding out what the next steps of the self-made task force were.

"The eggs are brightly colored. Easter is long gone," grinned Grandma Huber, who had already puffed on half a pipe on the way here to get fit.

"I get the eggs from Alfons. He breeds different chicken breeds."

"Yes, yes, good Alfons," grinned Grandma Huber. "He's very talkative, but a good-hearted guy."

"Is the yolk also colored?" asked Erna Schmachtinger and laughed. "Oops, I think I can still feel the herbs from yesterday."

"Tommy, you have to work hard growing and storing so that we can get through the winter," warned Klara. "If you need a greenhouse, you can use mine. I don't need it any more."

"My son is investigating the bank robbery with the police. I overheard him on the phone to the criminal investigation department this morning. A neighbor of the bank got in touch again. He wanted to report something else. My son said on the phone that it was a blind lead and the neighbor just wanted to make himself important, but they'll still question him and listen to what he has to say."

"You have to keep at it," said Klara. "We need all the information we can get."

Erna winked. "No problem at all. I'll take care of it."

Else Gruber tapped her spoon against her cup.

pling-pling-pling

The talking stopped. When silence had returned, she began to speak: "Ladies and gentlemen, I've been thinking the whole time about how we should go about handing over the money and I had a brilliant idea before I went to sleep last night. It could work. Listen to me."

Tommy was excited. He still had the words of the kidnapper in his ear, who had threatened to send his friends back piece by piece. His mood fluctuated between fear for Ernest and Willy and euphoria about the rescue plan.

The lawyer was astute and showed it. She put herself in the blackmailers' shoes and tried to copy their way of thinking. "The gangsters will direct us to a place where they see themselves at an advantage. We'll prevent that, of course, and take matters into our own hands."

"Isn't that a little optimistic?" Erna interjected. "People like that don't usually argue. They give clear instructions!"

Else answered in the negative. "Not if we play it wisely. We just have to play poker well and not do it like..."

Klara interrupted her friend and euphorically completed the sentence. "... make it look like commanding!"

"Don't interrupt the Gruberin," said Grandma Huber, who was just as excited about Else Gruber's plan as everyone else.

Klara put her hand over her mouth, a little startled. "Sorry! It just slipped out. I'm already quiet."

Else continued. "So Tommy and girls, watch out! As soon as these crooks call, we'll quietly and secretly take control. They won't notice that we're taking over."

Uschi was glowing with enthusiasm. "Finally something going on in this town. How do we do it? What's the first step?"

Else savored her monologue. She felt fantastic. "The first thing we demand is a sign of life from our friends!"

Tommy beamed. For the first time, someone other than himself had consciously referred to Ernest and Willy as friends. Despite the terrible situation, he was overcome with an indescribable feeling of happiness for a few seconds. They, the three young men, who had only ever had bad luck in their lives and had gone from one misfortune to the next, had found friends. Friends who were prepared to fight for them. Tommy slipped into his own world of thoughts. He could hear Else's voice, but her words didn't come through. Her mouth was moving, words were spilling out, the other women seemed to be very enthusiastic, but Tommy was unaware of the plan. It was the same when he was at school. The teachers talked and talked and he watched a bird in the tree outside. Just as the teachers had brought him back to reality back then, Grandma Huber interrupted his digressions. He was back and returned to reality. Of course, it was the same here as back then. Everyone was staring at him. He cleared his throat. "Hm ... hm."

"Tell me, boy! What do you think? Could it work?"

Tommy felt caught out. "I ... uh, well, what can I say? I think ... well ... hm ...", he stammered and when his cell phone vibrated briefly, he was glad for the distraction. "Wait a minute," he said and pulled the cell phone out of his pocket. He glanced at it and turned white as a sheet. "It's a text message from the blackmailers!"

Suddenly there was silence. Grandma Huber patted Tommy's shoulder lightly. "You look pale. Is everything all right?"

He picked up his coffee cup, took a sip and put it back. Grandma Huber handed Tommy a piece of Gugelhupf. "Eat some of this, it'll do you good!"

The herb boy broke off a piece of cake, popped it into his mouth and chewed on it listlessly. The flavors unfolded on the palate. Sweet and tart mingled. The Mediterranean tang emerged. He liked it. Very much so. He swallowed the resulting gruel, swallowed the next piece of cake and felt his strength return. "Tastes really good". He was astonished. "This stuff really works," he grinned.

"Of course it works. I can't walk again without a stick for no reason. But now to the text message. You wanted to read it out."

Tommy raised his cell phone slightly and read out. "Watch out, you leek. Today is payday. I hope you've got the money. I expect an answer in ten minutes, otherwise...!" Tommy looked around the room. "That's where the message stops. He doesn't write anything else. Do you think his battery is flat or has he accidentally pressed the send button?"

Else Gruber denied it and smiled at Tommy's almost endearing simplicity. Nevertheless, she was also angry. "What does this blackmailer fart think he's doing? He demands money, puts you under time pressure, insults you and at the same time threatens you with an unspoken evil by not finishing the sentence. Well wait, we'll strike back in kind! He wants a mental duel? He can have it. I don't normally fight unarmed people, but in this case I'll make an exception!"

Everyone laughed, only Tommy was taken aback. "You want to challenge him to a duel? Do you think he'd do that?"

Grandma Huber, who was still sitting next to Tommy, patted him on the shoulder again. "Boy, you're a little confused. What Gruber means is that we're responding to his text message with gusto, turning the tables and making the gang dance to our tune. And if I know my girlfriend, she's already got a text ready!"

Else grabbed Tommy's cell phone and was already typing the first words. "You bet I have," she said. "From now on, we play by our rules!"

The noise level in the living room of the small house dropped to almost zero. You could hear every single letter being typed. Else Gruber was in her element. She had written many justifications over the course of her career and she felt as if she was pulling out all the stops of her knowledge. She had to squeeze a lot of power into a few words and even fewer lines and then make sure that someone with a low IQ understood everything clearly. It was an art.

Grandma Huber pressed her hand firmly against Tommy's shoulder in excitement. Klara Korner didn't dare put the coffee cup back on the saucer and held it in her hand. Uschi Brennauer urgently needed to go to the toilet, but refrained from doing so and remembered what her old primary school teacher used to say when a child called to go to the loo: "Keep working for now, it's break time in a few minutes anyway!"

When Else Gruber pressed the send button within the ten-minute time limit and leaned back with her familiar superior look, it was done. The contact had been made, the challenge had been announced. There was no turning back.

Gruber took a deep breath to read out what she had answered in a confident voice. "If I'm a leek, are you a complete vegetable soup? I have the money. Without a sign of life from my friends, however, you won't get a penny! I expect an answer within the next ten minutes! Otherwise the deal is off."

Silence.

Grandma Huber was the first to catch it. "That was pretty cheeky. Do you think that was clever? We shouldn't tease the kidnappers too much."

Else made a disparaging gesture with her hand. "I know these guys well enough. They think they're incredibly cool. You'll find more brains in a yellow sausage than in the heads of such wannabe mafiosi."

Pling, it sounded from Tommy's cell phone, followed by a vibration
- *brrrt*

"You see, there's already an answer," grinned Gruber and read out. "Don't be cheeky, you soft pear, otherwise you'll get an earful from the fat man."

Else typed in the answer: "I have 100,000 euros here. With every further insult, I reduce the ransom by 10,000 euros. I'm not arguing. Either we have a deal or we don't!"

Send. Tense looks.

Pling - brrrrrrt

"Show me the money, then you'll get the sign of life!"

Else clapped her hands. "Now we've got them. It's 1:0 for us!"

Tommy was at a loss. "How do we do it with the money?"

Else gave a few quick instructions. A minute later, the opened suitcase of money was on the table. Next to it was the latest daily newspaper. She took a photo with her cell phone and sent it via MMS. She immediately typed in a text. "Here's the money. Now I want to make a phone call to my friends, otherwise I'll be gone with the money!"

Send.

"I can't wait to see how he reacts," whispered Grandma Huber.

Else pulled a pen and a notebook out of her handbag. She jotted something down, tore out the note and gave it to Tommy. "If he calls and actually lets you talk to them on the phone, *tell* your friends. They'll know then that we're planning something to get them out."

Tommy took the note and read it. "But that's not true at all. Uncle Eddie didn't pay the money and he's not married to Klara and we don't have an Aunt Else or a Grandma Huber either."

"Tooorsten!" came the women's chorus.

The herb boy pinched his lips together. "Checked. It's a trick."

Hubert Hansen hammered his fist angrily on the table. The dirty breakfast dishes bounced up and rattled. "What does this village idiot think he's doing? He calls us vegetable soup!"

Harry pulled out his knife and waved it around wildly. "Dad, I'll flatten him! Nobody calls us vegetable soup!"

"And he wants a sign of life from these two clowns."

Harry shrugged his shoulders. "So what if it is? We don't care! He can demand whatever he wants. We're the boss!"

"I'm going to show that soft head," the old man murmured and sent his reply, only to become even angrier shortly afterwards. By the end of the short chat, Hubert Hansen had turned bright red with rage. "Now the little shit is threatening to cut the money. I wouldn't put it past him to run off with the money."

"That would be really nasty, yo. He can't do that." Panic set in. Harry slid the knife back in. "How do we know he even has the money, Dad? Maybe he's bluffing."

The old man grinned superiorly. "He's got the money. I asked for proof. Look here." He showed his son the photo with the suitcase full of banknotes and the latest newspaper. "Before that bastard runs off with my ashes, he'll get his stupid phone call. But only with one of the two clowns. Get me the fat one!"

Five minutes later, Hubert Hansen pressed the call symbol on the display of his smartphone under Tommy's saved mobile phone number, switched the loudspeaker to *listen in* and held the phone to Ernest's ear. "One wrong word and Harry will give you a new hairstyle with his knife!" he breathed to the hostage in no uncertain terms.

Ernest tried to appear relaxed, even though he was extremely excited, and just chatted away. Talking helped him to reduce the tension. "I've just had my hair cut. Ears free, two centimetres above the shirt collar at the back. I used to think I wore my hair shoulder-length, but I need a short haircut, you know, I'm going po..." he almost blabbed and stopped just in time. Of course, he couldn't tell his kidnappers that he was as good as at the police station. Just a few more formalities, a little diet and they would hire him. In a flash, he changed the last word to: "Po letter carrier. You need a good short hairstyle for that!"

Hansen tapped his forehead with his index finger. "They've all been snorting too much manure here."

The call was answered. "This is Tommy!"

The old man warned again: "Now you can chat with one of the clowns. You have 30 seconds! Just like the telephone joker on *Who Wants to Be a Millionaire*! And not a wrong word!"

Ernest gushed. "Hello Tommy. He means Batman and Robin, of course, we don't wear clown costumes."

"Are you all right?"

"Breakfast was okay. I'm curious to see what's for lunch."

Tommy read out Else's words. "Don't worry about the ransom. Uncle Eddie and Aunt Klara gave me the money. Our Grandma Huber has also put in some. She'll be visiting us soon with her sisters ..."

Hubert Hansen took the cell phone away and interrupted Tommy. "That was the sign of life. I'll send you a text message to hand over the money. Don't do anything stupid! You know what will happen if you don't!" Then he ended the call. Ernest was taken back to the storeroom. He was slightly irritated. His friend's words echoed through his head again and again. *What was going on?*

Tommy was relieved. "You're alive!"

Else was triumphant. "The kidnappers have taken the bait. The sight of the suitcase of money must have convinced them. Their greed for money has blinded them. Now we have to prepare the handover! I want to lure them to a very specific place!"

"Where to?"

"Do you remember where we trapped the boys back then?"

"My God, that was ages ago. When was that again?" Grandma Huber pondered.

Else helped. "More than 60 years ago!"

The women were reminded of a magnificent victory over the boys from the village, but that was another story.

"A brilliant place," Grandma Huber agreed immediately.

A semi-paved road led to the location in question. To the east of it were the cow pastures, to the west a wooded area, to which a path branched off. What you couldn't see from the road was that there was a small ravine not far behind the first row of trees, through which a stream meandered. The natural obstacle was not particularly wide, but you still had to cross a bridge to get over the ravine. This bridge was wooden and rotten and therefore closed. The local council had been arguing for weeks about whether to replace it with a steel structure or a wooden bridge again.

Else explained: "If we suggest this place as a drop-off point, it may seem ideal to the kidnappers. They will look at the aerial photo on

Google Maps or something similar and think they have three escape directions to choose from."

Tommy listened attentively, but didn't understand what Gruber was getting at.

"Grandma Huber and Anna, you grab tractors from your farms, position yourselves inconspicuously by the pastures and close the route as soon as the gangsters have driven onto the road towards the forest."

Grandma Huber was delighted. "The cow pasture there belongs to us. Our young breeding bulls are standing there right now. They don't like strangers," she laughed, stretched out her index fingers, put them to her forehead to mimic horns and mooed. "The bulls spear everything on their territory! I hope these gangsters try to escape across the pasture."

"And I'll get two wicker baskets from the store. We'll disguise ourselves as mushroom pickers," Klara suggested.

Uschi was delighted. "But first I'll get some tools from the petrol station. We'll remove the barrier on the wooden bridge," she winked. "Let them escape over the bridge," she added, imitating a fall with her hands. She whistled as she did so.

Tommy's plan became clearer and clearer. The kidnappers were to be lured into a trap.

More final details of the lawyer's plan followed. Each of those present was assigned a task. At the end, Else leaned back. "Now we'll wait for the next text message and enjoy the Gugelhupf in the meantime."

Everyone grabbed it. It didn't take long for the expected news to arrive.

Pling

"Hand it over at 3 p.m. in the parking lot next to the highway entrance to Munich. You come alone and give me the money. Then I'll release your friends. No cops!"

"Wait a minute, kiddo," said Else, typing the answer. "I don't have a driver's license! How am I supposed to get there? If someone drives me, there'll be confidants."

Break. The tension grew.

Pling

"Take a bike!"

Else typed the answer. "I can't ride a bike. Never had one!"

She laughed heartily as she sent the text message. "I can really feel him boiling with rage! And now comes my proposal."

"I can walk to the EDEKA parking lot. So that nobody sees me, I walk along the forest, where the fork in the road is, which hardly anyone knows. I can do that by 3 pm. Alternatively, we can postpone the handover until later, then I'll go to this highway ramp. But that will be in the evening. It's a long way!"

Hubert Hansen was furious. "Of all people, we have to get the guy without a driver's license as a negotiating partner!"

"If he doesn't have a driver's license, let him take a cab, Dad!"

"Idiot! We don't need any more confidants!"

Hansen thought about it and the second message arrived. Hubert read it and grinned maliciously. He had a flash of inspiration. At the same time, he opened Google Maps. He replied shortly afterwards. "All right. But at 1 pm!"

Harry couldn't hold back his curiosity. "All right, Dad? Did he bite?"

Hubert Hansen was proud of himself and his genius. "Of course he did."

The transfer point seemed to be in a good location. In the vast prairie of Bavaria, you were safely alone and you could smell bulls a kilometer away. The spot was well chosen. Nevertheless, caution was required. "Of course, we set off immediately and scouted the location. The time window is small, the advantages are ours.

"And the hostages?"

"What about them?"

"Aren't we taking them with us?"

The old man laughed uproariously. "Are you stupid? Of course I'm not. They're our life insurance. We'll leave them here, of course. If everything goes well with the money, we'll bunk off and send a text message telling them where the idiots are."

Harry beamed. "Dad, you're a genius!" Then he pondered, scratched the back of his head and added: "And Harvey? He's with the hostages, guarding them."

"We'll pick it up first, of course."

Harry laughed now. "Of course you did. I could have thought of that on my own."

"Girls, hurry up. We have to be in position before the gangsters arrive. They'll be there early to scout out the location," Else urged them. The old ladies left their base of operations, the living room of the men's shared flat, to rearm. Tommy was the only one holding the fort. He waited with his briefcase full of counterfeit money for further instructions.

Grandma Huber hadn't felt so energetic and strong for a long time. She had slipped into the checked blouse, put on the denim dungarees that she had only worn twice in her life and was amazed at how well they still fit. "I've got a really great figure in them. I need to wear them more often," she said as she looked at herself in the large mirror in the closet. She decided to wear her brown lace-up boots with them and finally put on a straw sun hat. Pure *country look*! Satisfied, she opened the right-hand cupboard door, pushed a few jackets aside and reached for her father's old shotgun. Then she opened one of the bottom drawers and pulled out a pack of ammunition. After reaching into the box, she slipped a handful of cartridges into the pocket of her jeans.

That should be enough.

The box of ammunition then went back into the drawer. A few minutes later, her son's frozen lunch was defrosting in the sink. She wrote on a piece of paper:

I'm traveling with the Fendt. You can heat up Sunday's sauerbraten in the microwave. See you later, mom.

She wondered whether her eldest would ever find a wife. Her daughter lived in the district town with her husband and three grandchildren, and her youngest son was studying in Munich. *Well, at least my older son is a farmer with heart and soul!* She wondered whether *Bauer sucht Frau* would be something for him, but dismissed the idea again. Now she had another task to solve and went outside. The tractor was ready and the trailer was hitched up.

Grandma Huber climbed up and stowed the shotgun. Full of zest for action, the farmer's wife put her pipe in her mouth, lit it, started the engine of the ancient tractor, which had more years on it than she did, and chugged off. Thick clouds of steam billowed out of the pipe and the exhaust pipe. The old lady in the fashionable *country look was* happy and ready for battle.

"Snip," said Uschi and cut the barrier tape.

At the same time, Klara had sawn through the last two intact planks of the bridge walkway. "No one will come over here," she said and put the handy saw in one of the two baskets. "Now we can hide in the bushes and if anyone sees us, we can pretend we're picking mushrooms."

Uschi grabbed the remains of the barrier tape and stowed them in the basket too. She spread a tea towel over it. "We absolutely have to put the tape back on after the action, so that nothing else happens."

"But of course we will," her friend replied.

"Where are you going with the tractor?" Anna Schwinghofer's husband wanted to know.

"Over to the Hubers' pasture. Grandma Huber and I have plans," came the reply. She put the old flail and a pitchfork on the small trailer and climbed on.

"And lunch?"

"There's still some left over from yesterday. You can warm it up."

As Anna drove out of the yard, her husband just shook his head. "Ever since those women started taking their new herbal medicine, they've gone completely mad," he muttered and went into the kitchen.

Rosi and Else were also armed. Else had slipped her blank-firing revolver into her handbag, while Rosi proudly displayed a hunting rifle with a telescopic sight. Her husband had been a keen hunter for decades and the widow was free to choose from the arsenal of weapons he had left behind.

"Maybe we need good aim," she explained to the lawyer, who was more than surprised. "Not at people, but to shoot tires flat or something like that."

"A very good idea," said Else and followed Rosi into the large garage. Three vehicles were parked next to each other. A sporty Mercedes, a practical estate car and an older Land Rover. "Which car do we take?"

"The old off-road vehicle that we used to take hunting. We can get through anywhere with it."

Else got in on the passenger side and fastened her seatbelt. "There are binoculars here. We could do with those too."

Rosi started the engine. The garage door opened automatically by remote control. The cell phones vibrated as the first messages arrived in their regulars' chat.

"They're on guard," Else commented.

"Very good! What is our mission?" asked Rosi.

Else pushed her cell phone back into her pocket. "We're observing and protecting Tommy and, of course, the briefcase with the counterfeit money. Once we've freed the hostages, we have to get the briefcase with the counterfeit bills back to destroy them. If there's no more counterfeit money, then no counterfeiting ever took place," she winked.

"I see," came the reply with a grin.

Rosi was not used to the off-road vehicle. Accordingly, she shifted into first gear uncertainly and pressed a little too hard on the gas pedal. The monstrous vehicle sped out of the garage and onto the road with enormous momentum, accompanied by squealing tires. A cyclist swerved onto a patch of grass, cursing loudly, braked and crashed.

Else clung to the seat. Her face was white as a sheet. "Whew, that was close. Can you drive a bit more carefully?"

Rosi laughed. "That's fun." A glance in the rear-view mirror followed. The cyclist had stood up and was shouting the worst swear words at them with a clenched fist. Rosi's only comment: "No harm done. Besides, the guy's not from around here."

The color slowly returned to Else's face. "Those weren't kind words the guy shouted after us."

They both looked at each other briefly, giggled and then laughed out loud. The vehicle lurched a little.

"Concentrate on the traffic now," said Else.

Rosi switched on the radio. A fitting classic was playing. *Highway to Hell* by AC/DC blared out of the Bose loudspeakers in top sound quality. Both women immediately joined in and sang along to the chorus. Although their English pronunciation had a rough Bavarian flavor.

On the other hand, news could be heard from the cheap radio speakers of the Fiat Panda. The monotonous and tinny-sounding voice of a bored presenter had a soporific effect on Harry. "Dad, can I change the channel? I want to listen to music."

"No!"

"Why not?"

"Firstly, the radio is full of crap and secondly, as a professional you always have to be informed."

Harry was just about to list a few arguments against the annoying and deadly boring news channel when his father turned up the volume.

"... we are repeating a police wanted notice. Two masked bank robbers are wanted. They were wearing costumes of the comic book heroes Batman and Robin ..."

"You see, boy. Always be informed!" Hubert was feeling great. He was on the verge of the biggest coup of his criminal career.

Both listened to the report.

"... possibly the perpetrators are in a white van from the company ... we are repeating once more ..."

Harry banged angrily against the steering wheel with the flat of his hand. "Damn, how do they know that? Those guys drove to the bank in their own car."

Hubert gave his son a reproachful look. "Did you at least hide the van well?"

The driver's features brightened a little. "Sure!"

"I mean really good! They'll probably be looking for it with helicopters. If they discover the car in the old quarry, we're screwed!"

Harry was really beaming. "You can count on me, Pops. Nobody will see the van. It's in the big hall. I'm not stupid."

The old man was relieved. "At least you did that right." He tapped around on the display of his smartphone. "The network here really sucks," he grumbled, lifting the phone in different directions. "Ah, here we go," he grumbled after a while and used GPS to find their position on Google Maps. "Stop!"

Harry stepped on the brake pedal, startled. The small car started to lurch. Hubert hit his head against the window. The cell phone slipped out of his hands, crashed against the dashboard and fell into the footwell.

The Panda came to a standstill with screeching tires.

"You fool!" old Hansen grumbled, unbuckled his seatbelt and bent down to fumble awkwardly for his cell phone in the footwell.

"What's wrong, Pop? Did I miss something?"

With a bright red head, Hubert Hansen gasped angrily: "No! You didn't!"

"Why would I..."

Hubert interrupted his son and hissed: "First I had reception, then no more!"

Old Hansen caught the cell phone and sat down normally again. His head was still bright red. "Go on, drive back. But slowly! And when I tell you to stop, stop slowly! Got it?"

Harry had understood. He put the car in reverse and drove off. As soon as the Panda started rolling, his father began swearing so loudly and crudely that Harry spontaneously hit the brakes again. Hubert, who was still not wearing his seatbelt, slammed forward and hit his head on the dashboard.

"Ouch!"

Harry knew what would follow. He instinctively raised his hands to protect himself. Hubert was furious. "That'll give you a set of hot ears! The phone is broken. The screen is coal black. How are we supposed to find this stupid drop-off point now? I'll hit you ..."

Tüt ... tüüüüt

Loud honking that sounded like a rusty foghorn. The loud engine of a tractor chugged along beside him. A farmer's wife with a pipe in the corner of her mouth sat at the wheel and glared at them. "Is there a problem?" asked Grandma Huber, making an effort to speak in an extreme Bavarian dialect. She guessed who the two guys in the car were. Tommy had told her about the small car that Ernest hadn't been able to fit into during the first kidnapping attempt. And the description was right. Ugly with a horse face.

Harry rolled down the side window. "Uh, no thanks."

The farmer's wife followed up. "Two roasted skulls. Hob's eich va-laffa?"

The two men didn't understand a word. They both stared help-lessly at Grandma Huber for a moment. Harry shook his head and replied: "Yes, we have wonderful weather today", thinking that this ans-wer probably made the most sense.

Hubert got out, put on a slimy, friendly grin and asked: "Where's the way to the little wood? I've heard it's a nice place to go for a walk."

"Haa? What? Wohi' woits?" Grandma Huber exclaimed, took a puff from her pipe and had a great time. She would tell her friends later.

Hubert cleared his throat. "There must be a forest here."

Grandma Huber shrugged her shoulders. "Zum Woid woit's?"

Old Hansen was in despair. "What on earth is that language? I could fly off the handle. Only fools around me," he whispered, then put on his smarmy smile again. "Sorry. I didn't understand them exactly. We're looking for the forest. There must be a nice little wood near here that you can hike through to the next idyllic little village."

"Ah," said Grandma Huber in response, raising her head accord-ingly, nodding and smiling. A general sign that she had understood the question. "Next right and only straight ahead. Two kilometers. You can follow me. I have to milk cows there," she replied, albeit with only mi-nimal dialect and therefore in easily understandable German. Without waiting for a response, Grandma Huber nodded in greeting, laughed and chugged off in her vehicle.

Hubert Hansen got in. "They all have a big bang here."

Harry, on the other hand, raised his head proudly. "Dad, I think I've got the hang of it. At first I hardly understood the old lady, but by the end I could understand everything perfectly. I think I've just learned Bavarian!"

Hubert closed his eyes for a moment and wondered why the intel-ligence had given his two sons a wide berth. "Just follow her!"

Grandma Huber pulled out her cell phone and called Else.

Her friend was in an audibly good mood when she took the call. "What's going on?" Else giggled. Grandma Huber could hear Rosi singing in the background. The notes were shrill and loud. Nevertheless, she recognized the song. *Highway to Hell*. That was the melody of her Shrove Tuesday morning go-home song. After the annual Rosenmontags-Kappenabend in the Village-mug-Inn, they would bawl after a night of revelry: *The way home is too bright for me ...*

Grandma Huber smiled. "Are you all right?" she asked.

Else sounded normal. "Yes! We only listen to good music!"

Without further ado, Grandma Huber immediately got to the bottom of the phone call. "They're behind me!"

"Who?" came the slightly unsettled reply.

"The kidnappers! In the car!"

"Sure?"

"Quite!"

A brief silence. Else followed up: "Are Ernest and Willy there?"

"No. There are just two rather unsympathetic guys in the car."

Grandma Huber heard Else tell Rosi that she should stop singing. She then asked in a serious voice: "What kind of car?"

"Fiat Panda!"

"Where are you?"

"Two kilometers before the finish. They don't seem to know their way around and have asked me for directions. I'm going ahead of them now. I told them that I have to milk cows in the pasture near the forest," Grandma Huber laughed. "Anyway, I'm only driving at walking pace. They breathe in the extreme exhaust fumes from my old Fendt and don't dare overtake."

"All right. We'll be in position in a minute. I'll inform the others."

"What about Ernest and Willy?" asked Grandma Huber. "We had planned a handover. What should we do?"

Else was highly concentrated. "If you say they're not with the kidnappers, they must still be with the third guy."

"Let's hope nothing has happened to them. In any case, we have to be careful that they don't leave us!"

Else's answer came quickly. "No! Without the hostages, they wouldn't get any money. I think they want to be extremely clever, but they don't know who they're dealing with."

"What should I do?"

"Take your time! Drive as slowly as possible. I'll warn the others!"

"All right! Over!"

"Over!"

Grandma Huber shifted down a gear and crept ahead of the two hijackers at walking pace. "Don't mess with grannies," she muttered quietly, grinning and accelerating hard with every gear change, emitting thick clouds of exhaust fogging up the Fiat Panda.

The Hansens drove through several clouds of exhaust fumes and were constantly coughing. When they breathed in, the smoke stung their lungs. Harry was furious. "The old woman wants to poison us!"

"Ugh," his father gasped and rolled down the side window a little, drawing even more exhaust fumes into the car.

"I'm overtaking the old box now!"

The old man vetoed it. "Leave it, otherwise we'll get lost."

Harry stopped. "Then at least we'll follow at a greater distance. No pig can stand that!"

Hubert Hansen had now rolled the window all the way down and stuck his head out of the car as the clouds of exhaust fumes had dissipated. He sucked in a lungful of fresh air. "Don't lose sight of her!"

Tommy repeated his new instructions for the third time. He was on his way to the handover location and was not only extremely nervous, but also a real bundle of anxiety. He was shaking all over when Else told him on the phone that Ernest and Willy were not with the kidnappers. "I'll tell them they won't get the money," he huffed.

"No! You say you have the money and open the suitcase. Let them see the bills. But at a distance."

"Okay, I'll open the suitcase at a distance and give them the money when I see my friends."

The lawyer heard the fear in Tommy's voice. "Calm down and listen to me very carefully."

The herb boy would have liked to throw the smartphone away, throw the case after it and run away. But he couldn't do that. He had to concentrate. "I don't think I can do it. I'm sorry, but I can't do it."

Else became calmer and calmer. Her voice sounded caring. "You don't need to worry at all. Nothing can happen. We're all on site and have everything under control. We control the entire handover. Do you understand? You're not alone!"

The small miracle happened, the spark was ignited. "I'm really not alone?"

"No! You just can't see us. We are cloaked."

"But you're here," came another uncertain voice.

Gruber confirmed. "I'm watching you right now. You walk along the path and you'll soon reach the pasture with the young bulls from Grandma Huber's farm."

Tommy was amazed. He looked around and spotted the young bulls. "That's right."

"You can see a tractor with a trailer on your right."

Tommy turned to his right. "Yes, I can see him."

"That's Anna Schwinghofer. She'll be blocking the road with the tractor later! The rest of us are also spread out around you. You don't need to be afraid."

Tommy felt better now, much better. The certainty that he was not alone boosted his self-confidence. Now he was ready to follow Else's instructions. He had the briefcase with the counterfeit money in his hand. His best friends needed him and all of Grandma Huber's regulars were here. They had his back. Nothing could go wrong.

"What should I do?"

Else was reassured. She had managed to get Tommy back on track. "You know the path into the forest?"

"Sure."

"Good, this is the drop-off point. If you see the blackmailer, keep your distance. He'll want to see the money. You can open the suitcase and show it to him. Then close it again and change the code on the lock."

"Okay."

"Next, ask about Ernest and Willy."

"But they're not there."

"Exactly! We need to know where they are."

"Ah, I see!"

"Always keep that guy at a distance."

"What should I do if he wants the money?"

Else thought about it. "In an emergency, you can give him the suitcase. You can't plan it down to the smallest detail. Besides, I'm watching you and will react accordingly."

"So I don't have to do anything else?"

"No. We'll do the rest. Can you manage that?"

Tommy was satisfied. He had understood what he had to do. And he was no longer afraid. At least not as much as before. "Don't worry! I'll manage!" he said at the end of the conversation and walked on with a proudly swollen chest.

Chapter 6
When cops hunt and acquaintances of acquaintances meet acquaintances

Willy and Ernest were desperate. The situation they found themselves in was extremely precarious. They were locked up, an armed man was sitting outside the door and their buddy Tommy was supposed to pay a ransom of 100,000 euros for them, which Uncle Eddie had allegedly provided. Plus the strange reference to some unknown aunt. None of it made any sense. The only thing that was clear was that something was going on out there and they were sitting here locked up and helplessly idle.

"Has the money already been handed over?" asked Willy.

"Never!" Ernest literally shouted. He nervously paced up and down the twelve square meter room. "There's something fishy about this! Very rotten, in fact! Uncle Eddie wouldn't even give five cents for our release. So that can only mean that Tommy has a plan."

"Tommy? Never!" Willy remarked.

"Not him, but Grandma Huber," Ernest countered, but also immediately expressed his concerns. "If the kidnappers notice anything, there'll be a big bang and I'm afraid that either Tommy or both of us will be in the line of fire."

Willy sat on the inflatable bed and became increasingly restless. He realized that Tommy was a good gardener. Over. Over. That was as good as it got. Her buddy was otherwise completely talentless. Without exception. Tommy could even burn water. Whatever her boyfriend tried to do was doomed to failure. Except gardening, of course. Here he had a golden hand. "I'm seriously worried."

Ernest stopped. He saw how sad Willy was and sat down next to his buddy on the bed. Ernest sank down, Willy was lifted up and now towered over Ernest by two heads. He waited for the bed to burst again, but miraculously the valves were still able to withstand the enormous pressure. Yesterday he had been upset about it, today he didn't care.

He had also gotten used to these ridiculous costumes. Batman and Robin. He was fully aware that they would become the biggest laughing stock in Germany or even the world when this all came out. In his mind, Willy could already see the headline that would appear in the tabloids. *Batman and Robin - two super idiots rob a bank - loot 200 euros* or *Batman and Robin - taken hostage after bank robbery.*

He felt Ernest's hand on his shoulder. "You don't have to worry about either of us. I'll protect you."

Willy stared at his buddy. Ernest was a good-hearted guy. "I'm not worried about us, I'm worried about Tommy. If I've heard correctly, two of the Hansens have gone away. The young guy who made us breakfast and is always playing with his gun should be sitting outside the door."

Ernest frowned thoughtfully, stood up awkwardly and Willy slumped down. "You're right. Tommy and his girlfriends are walking into disaster. We have to help them."

Willy put his hands over his head. "What do you mean? We're locked in here! Have you forgotten that? You ... you ... you Batman wannabe!"

Ernest, who had started walking up and down again, stopped instantly. "Brilliant! You're simply brilliant."

Willy no longer understood the world. He had just insulted Ernest halfway. Why did he think that was brilliant? Willy began to doubt Ernest's sanity and wondered if it was some kind of camp fever.

Ernest looked absolutely sure of himself. "We wear the costumes of superheroes and act like superheroes!"

Willy didn't believe what he was hearing. He cautiously asked. "What do you want to do?"

Ernest began to whisper. "We're breaking out!"

Willy hadn't understood him because of the whispering, but he whispered too. "What did you say? I can't understand you because you're whispering too quietly."

Ernest moved very close to Willy and leaned forward. His lips were close to Willy's ear. "We're breaking out!"

Willy was surprised. He looked around the room. The window was far too small and an armed man was sitting in front of the door. "I'd love to, but how are you going to do that?" he said incredulously.

Ernest picked up his Batman cape, which was still lying on the floor, and gestured towards the door. "We'll get him to open the door and come in, then I'll put the cape on him and we'll overpower him."

Willy stared at Ernest. "You only overlooked one small detail in your plan."

"Like what?"

"He's armed."

Ernest waved him off with a smile. "We simply act with lightning speed!"

Before Willy could come up with any more arguments against Ernest's plan, he knocked on the door and shouted: "Guard! I have to go to the bathroom urgently!"

The answer sounded muffled. "No!"

Ernest didn't give up. "Yes, I really have to!"

Again the muffled voice of the kidnapper. "Take the bucket!"

"Boy, you don't want to violate the Geneva Conventions!"

Silence.

Ernest followed up. "You know I'll have to report it if you don't let me go to the toilet. We've had this discussion before."

Muffled reply. "Take the bucket and report me!"

Ernest clapped his right fist into the palm of his left hand in annoyance. "Crap!"

Willy intervened. If his buddy was already fighting for him and Tommy, he couldn't sit idly by. He called out loudly: "All right, then I hope you have fun cleaning later!"

Silence.

"Why?" it still sounded muffled, but a little louder than before.

Willy went to Ernest, who was standing next to the entrance in his cloak, and whispered to him. "He's up and standing in front of the door."

Harvey was upset. "Dude! I asked why?"

Willy grinned. His idea was working. "Because *we won't* be emptying and cleaning the bucket, *you will*. These are traces of us and, of course, incriminating evidence for the court proceedings."

Silence.

After a good minute, they heard Harvey Hansen's muffled voice again: "Empty it yourself!"

Ernest: "No!"

Willy: "Never!"

Ernest again: "Not on your life! How are you going to control that?"

Willy: "Your dad won't be happy at all. Who do you think he'll blame for this?"

Silence.

Harvey: "You're just trying to get me to unlock the door."

Ernest: "I just have to go to the loo!"

Willy: "I'll tell your dad!"

Harvey: "You're annoying!"

Ernest: "Then let me go to the toilet at last!"

Harvey: "Hey, dude! If this is a trap, I'm going to be pissed!"

Willy: "Listen, you leek, which one of us has the gun and still shits himself?"

Harvey became angry. He was also quite insecure. If the two prisoners were actually right and the bucket was considered evidence, his dad would be furious. Besides, the prisoner was right. He was the one with the gun and the two unarmed clowns couldn't do him any harm. What could possibly go wrong? The revolver was in his waistband. His right hand wandered over the pommel of the gun.

Ernest: "All right, then I'll take the bucket after all. It's my own fault!"

Harvey went crazy. "Wait a minute! I'm not afraid of you! I'm the boss here, not you!" he shouted. However, he wasn't quite finished thinking. "I just need some more time to think."

Ernest kept up the pressure. "Sorry. I don't have any more time."

"Hey, dude! Wait a minute. I'll let you go to the bathroom."

"Now!"

"In a few minutes!"

"Now or it's too late!"

"Okay, but I'm warning you. One stupid move and it goes bang!"

Ernest: "I just want to go to the loo, that's all. I'm not tired of living. After all, you've got a gun!"

Harvey was sure that they had understood. They knew he was dangerous. They knew he had a gun and they had respect for it.

Willy: "I go right behind the wall. When you unlock the door, you can see that I'm not doing anything. I'll stay there until you've locked the door again."

That sounded good. "I was just about to say something like that," Harvey shouted through the locked door. All he had to do was unlock it and, of course, draw his revolver. "Up against the wall with you!" he demanded, bending down to look through the keyhole. He recognized Willy against the wall. "Okay. I'll unlock the door. You stay against the wall, the other one can come out." Harvey dug the key out of his trouser pocket, slid it into the keyhole and turned it. Then he pushed the door handle down and gently pushed it open. It opened inwards. The revolver lay ready to fire in his right hand. "Stand still!" he warned Willy.

Ernest stood behind the door. His heart was beating wildly, his pulse pounding. Sweat was pouring from his forehead, his Batman shirt was turning dark on his back and under his armpits. He was excited and tried to breathe shallowly. Adrenaline raced through his bloodstream. Batman gripped his cape with both hands. He was determined to put it over the hostage-taker as soon as he was in the room. But he didn't come in. Milliseconds felt like minutes, seconds like hours. *Damn it, how am I supposed to throw the cloak over him now?*

"Where is the fat man?"

He just stopped at the door. That can't be true.

Willy rolled his eyes to give Ernest a sign, but his buddy didn't react.

Besides, I'm not fat! I'm strong, but not fat! What does this asparagus think he is? Ernest became angry. More adrenaline was released. His whole body was on the attack. He tried to think clearly. Ernest knew he had to act with lightning speed. This was his only chance to escape.

He heaved the cloak over the door, heard a "What are you doing?" and feared that the hostage-taker would fire at Willy. Furious and full of despair, he threw his estimated 160 kilos of fighting weight against the fire door. It slammed with full force against the hostage-taker, who was knocked out as if by a boxing knockout. As he fell, Harvey reflexively pulled both arms upwards. A shot rang out, the gun slipped from his hand, fell to the floor and skittered into the hallway.

"Willyiiiiii!" squealed Ernest, who suspected the worst after the shot was fired.

His friend stood against the wall, uninjured but pale as a sheet. "E-e-he really did shoot," stuttered Willy, pointing at Harvey Hansen.

Lime trickled from the ceiling. They both discovered the bullet hole. Their guard lay motionless on the floor.

"Is he dead?" asked Willy.

"You think so?"

"How could this happen?"

Ernest pondered. "Maybe a ricochet from the shot ... hm ..." he thought, then Harvey groaned. "No, he's not dead. And I don't see any blood either. I put him out of action with the door, so to speak." Ernest took advantage of the situation. "That was my plan too, by the way. I had to change my mind quickly," he added to appear cooler.

The Hansens had explored the grounds and discovered nothing out of the ordinary. All around them were fenced pastures and tall grass swaying in the balmy summer breeze, crickets chirping, bees flying from flower to flower, a red kite flying in search of mice. Somewhere, a few songbirds were chirping.

Back in the Fiat, the waiting began. The land around them was lush green, peaceful and deserted. At least almost.

"The old lady from earlier is standing with her cattle in the pasture. There's also a tractor at the far end if you continue along this path. But there's not a farmer to be seen for miles around," said Harry.

Hubert Hansen laughed. "I chose this time especially. They're all sitting together at the lunch table. Typical country bumpkins!"

"Except for that stupid old woman who tried to poison us with her dung. She should be reported directly to the police."

The incomprehensible dialect made Hubert uncomfortable again. "The way she was talking, she's one of those people who have lunch at eleven o'clock."

Harry grimaced slightly in disgust. "Lunch at breakfast time! Disgusting. No wonder they're all stupid here."

Old Hansen left the last sentence uncommented and looked at his wristwatch. "In five minutes, the third fool will arrive and hopefully bring our money with him."

"How does the handover actually work, Pop?"

Hubert got out of the car. "I'll go and meet him, you wait in the car. When I come back with the money, we're leaving!"

The car door slammed shut forcefully. Harry sat behind the wheel and watched his father. He strutted along the road like a harmless stroller.

Else and Rosi lay in the tall grass and watched both Tommy and the two kidnappers with binoculars. Klara and Uschi were watching the escape route from the bridge, while Anna and Grandma Huber were checking the access and escape routes. If necessary, they could block them with their tractors at a moment's notice.

After several repetitions, Tommy had memorized the instructions he had received from Else. Accordingly, he stopped about ten meters away from the criminal. The worst guy Tommy had ever come across stood in front of him and grinned nastily at him. The amateur gardener was afraid of this man. Terrible fear. He looked as if he would carry out all his threats. When Hubert tried to get closer, Tommy took a step back. "Stop! Stop!" he demanded in a somewhat brittle voice. His uncertainty was obvious.

"What's wrong, you comedian?" Hansen taunted him.

"Keep your distance, otherwise I'll be gone with the money!"

Hubert suspected that Tommy could run fast. *I may be very fast, but this guy looks like he could outrun me!* So as not to jeopardize the operation and scare off the man delivering the money, Hubert decided to keep the desired minimum distance. "Have you got the money?" The old man's eyes immediately wandered to the briefcase Tommy was carrying in his right hand.

Tommy went through his instructions. *Firstly, keep my distance and don't let him take me by surprise. That's what I did. Secondly, ask for my friends Ernest and Willy.* He stared at Hansen. Tommy would have liked to tell him that he was a really bad person, but he stuck to Else's words. "Where are my friends?"

"In a safe place. Now give me the damn money!"

Tommy took another step back. Hubert Hansen immediately raised his hands placatingly. "Slowly, slowly. Don't run away."

"Money against my friends. That was the deal!"

Hansen let his gaze wander over the area. He felt a little uneasy, but couldn't see anything conspicuous. "They're healthy, of course, and are waiting to be released. I'll arrange that as soon as I have the money," he said in a slimy, friendly voice. "After all, I still need a little insurance so I can run off with the cash."

"No friends, no money!"

"I just don't want to be ripped off, kid! That's why you're going to show me if the money is even in this suitcase!"

Tommy was unsettled. He was allowed to show the money, but not to hand it over. "Okay," he said. "You stay right there."

Hansen took another look around the entire site. His instincts warned him, but he could detect absolutely nothing suspicious. He had the gift of being able to smell bulls at a distance of 1,000 meters. There were no cops, he was sure of it. *Maybe it's because this old woman is jumping around in the pasture with her cattle,* he told himself. "Open up!"

"And my friends?"

"All right, I'll tell you how the deal works. You give me the money, then I'll drive to your buddies and set them free."

"No!"

Hubert was starting to get angry. This dumbass with the briefcase was starting to get on his nerves. "You're dealing with honorable professionals here."

"I want to talk to you on the phone."

Hubert put all his eggs in one basket. "All right, then don't. I'll tell your friends that you had the money but didn't want to buy them off. You alone are responsible for what happens to them." He turned around and slowly walked away.

Tommy shrugged his shoulders and hoped that Else could see this and intervene. This situation had not been planned. Nothing happened. *Think about it! What else did she say? If in doubt, I should give him the money. We'll catch them and get it back. I have to do that now!*

The soft click of the briefcase opening was music to Hansen's ears. When he heard another "Look here", he grinned maliciously, stopped and turned around. Hubert Hansen couldn't believe what he saw. This village idiot actually had a briefcase full of banknotes in his hand. The hundred-dollar bills were just shining out. On the face of it, everything looked perfect. "Take out a packet and lift it up!"

Tommy carried out the instructions. When the kidnapper saw the bundle of money underneath, he was satisfied. He walked up to the man delivering the money. Tommy closed the briefcase and twisted the combination. Then he put the briefcase on the floor and walked back. Else had told him to do that. This was to prevent Tommy from being overpowered and taken hostage when he handed over the money.

"Where are my friends?" he asked, walking backwards.

The kidnapper reached the suitcase. Greedily, he knelt down and wanted to open it to check the bills. When Hansen realized that the briefcase was locked, his true self emerged. The slimy friendliness was gone. "Tell me the combination right now, or you'll be in trouble!"

Tommy mentally repeated Else's other emergency instructions. *Stay cool when threatened and say the bomb!*

"By the way," Tommy groaned, "Ernest's uncle isn't just rich, he's also a creep. He has a bomb built in. If you open the suitcase by force, it explodes."

Hubert was startled. "You're bluffing!"

"Release my friends and I'll tell them the combination!"

Hubert laughed maliciously. "I know something better! Your friends will open the suitcase, then I'll let them go." A roar of laughter followed. Hansen marched back to the Fiat Panda with the briefcase.

Else had watched the handover with binoculars, Rosi through the scope of her late husband's hunting rifle. "That leftist bastard! We'll call the girls. Access!"

Both tapped the speed dials on their smartphones. Just moments later, the tractor engines roared. Anna and Grandma Huber headed purposefully for the access road.

Uschi and Klara lurked by the bridge and Rosi aimed through the scope at the tires of the Fiat Panda.

"Can you do that?" asked Else.

"My husband insisted that I learn to shoot. I never knew why, but now I'm grateful to him."

Else was reassured. "Then don't let them get away!"

"I don't intend to!" Rosi kept her aim and breathed in and out. *Stay calm, aim, shoot.*

Grandma Huber stopped. She grabbed the shotgun and jumped off the Fendt relatively quickly. She felt like she was in a western. The covered wagon trek was attacked and everyone had to reach for their weapons. The battle-ready woman tilted the barrel forward, reached into the pocket of her jeans and slipped two cartridges into the double-barrelled shotgun. She flipped the barrel up, cocked both cocks and fired. "Come here, you hoodlums!"

Hubert Hansen stopped. He looked around again. He felt uncomfortable, and he could rely on this feeling almost blindly.

No cops, but the whole thing stinks. Let's get out of here, he thought.

When he realized that both tractors were driving onto the dirt road at the same time and that it was closed, so to speak, he started to run. "Blimey, I knew something was wrong straight away!"

A shot rang out. Hansen threw himself to the ground. He expected a special police squad to rush in and arrest him. Seconds passed. It remained calm. Too calm. He raised his head. No action, no uniform boots rushing towards him, no loud shouting, not a single uniform to be seen, let alone emergency vehicles or a helicopter. So there were no police here either. The blackmailer regained hope. Had chance played a trick on him this time and the shot had come from the shotgun of a hunter who had just shot a deer nearby?

Nonsense! Run!

Hansen leapt upwards with astonishing agility and rushed on. Harry saw his father running towards him and wanted to start the engine. It stuttered, but didn't start. Hubert reached the small car, yanked open the passenger door, swung himself onto the seat and shouted in panic: "Drive off!"

The engine yodeled worse than a folk musician. The Hansens began to hate Bavaria. Hubert was extremely upset. He was sweating and getting goose bumps at the same time. Harry repeatedly banged the steering wheel. "Crap! Crap! Crap car!"

Another shot rang out. Hubert instinctively ducked down. "Are you too stupid to start the car?"

"Dad, it's a Fiat!" Harry defended himself.

The old man cursed and nervously drummed his fingers on the briefcase lying on his lap. "Errors in all parts. That's exactly what Fiat means!" he shouted and finally slapped the briefcase with the flat of his hand. "There's 100 mil in here! I've seen it with my own eyes! Start the car and step on the gas!"

The father's panic spread to his son. Harry needed two attempts to get the ignition key into the right position. The engine began to cough, howl and yodel again, then it ignited.

Wrommmmm

Harry had done it. "Yay," he cheered as the engine whirred steadily. They were able to escape. "Ferrari in anonymous camouflage! That's exactly what Fiat means!" he countered and drove off, only to stop again after exactly ten meters. He stared straight ahead and clutched the steering wheel desperately. "I don't believe it now!"

Grandma Huber's tractor was parked across the dirt road in front of them. The old farmer's wife, who had explained the way here in a language they could barely understand, was blocking the escape route. She was standing between the tractor and the trailer, pointing a shotgun at them.

Harry stared ahead, stunned. "And now?"

"Reverse gear!" his father hissed.

Rosi had the right tire of the Fiat in her sights. She breathed in, blew out about halfway and held her breath. Then the shooter crooked her right index finger.

Wumm

The shot rang out and the butt hit her shoulder, the projectile whirred towards the target, missed and dug itself into the ground away from the car tire. Small stones flew around.

"Gone!" commented Else, who was watching the kidnappers' getaway car with binoculars.

"I can see that too. There's something wrong with the sights."

"Don't talk, shoot again! The guy with the suitcase is right by the car!"

Rosi fired the repeater. Accompanied by a metallic click, a cartridge case was ejected and one was fed into the chamber. She fired again, this time aiming a little further to the left and repeating the procedure.

"Now he's in the car!"

Rosi was annoyed. "I can see that too. I'm not blind. What do you think it is?" She tapped her finger against the scope of the bolt-action rifle.

Else didn't respond to the comment, instead saying, "They're getting lost!"

Rosi took aim, remained calm, breathed shallowly and fired.

Wumm

This time, the projectile only just missed the tire. Again, some earth and small stones whirled away on all sides at the point of impact.

"That's better. Just correct it a little and you'll have it!"

Rosi remained calm. Her right hand heaved the chamber stem backwards and forwards again. The ejected cartridge case landed in the grass not far from the first one.

"The next shot is on target!"

Else didn't take her eyes off the kidnappers for a moment. "That's what he should do. They're already rolling!"

Rosi regretted that although she had learned to load and shoot back then, she had no idea about sights and adjusting the distance. *Never mind,* she thought, *I'll make up for it by correcting my aim!*

The Fiat had rolled off, but stopped again shortly afterwards. The brake lights came on, as did the reversing lights.

"They've discovered Grandma Huber's barrier and want to turn around," commented Else.

"Oh, fuck you," muttered Rosi, aiming right between the two rear wheels of the Fiat Panda and pulling the trigger.

Else could see that a piece of black rubber had literally been shredded off the right rear wheel. The car was leaning slightly and had become stuck due to the simultaneous turning maneuver.

"Score, sunk!" laughed the lawyer.

Rosi raised her hand. "Give me five!"

Both women clapped their hands.

"Come here, you zeros! I'll give you a load of buckshot!" the Hansens heard.

A tractor and trailer were parked across the road in front of them. This farmer's wife was standing between the tractor and the trailer, pointing a shotgun at them.

Harry grinned, as he still thought he had learned Bavarian. "I told you, Dad, I can speak this Bavarian dialect now. I understood everything the old lady called out. Shall I translate it for you?"

Hubert was almost in despair. "You cattle, you stupid one! She no longer speaks in dialect! She can articulate normally too! Get away from here! She's about to shoot."

Wham - crash - hiss

The echo of the shot had not yet faded when a rear tire went flat. Harry tried to turn around and drive on, but the rim with the flat tire ate into the ground.

"You're stuck! Damn it, dad! We're stuck!"

Hubert's face changed color almost every second from bright red with rage to chalky white with fear. Harry stared at his father spellbound. "Cool, how do you do that? It's like a chameleon."

Hubert did not respond. He had analyzed the situation they were in within a fraction of a second. "They've set a trap for us. We have to split up and pile in. You into the forest, I'll cross the meadow! Meet me at the quarry! Loooooos!"

Harry was still processing the words his father had quickly blurted out when he sprinted off. "Get away!" he said to himself, got out of the car too and ran in the direction of Grandma Huber. She fired a warning shot into the air.

Wumm

Harry braked, pulled a face as if he had bitten into a lemon, changed direction and ran towards the forest.

Hubert heard the shot and threw himself to the ground again. His head flew around quickly to see who had shot whom.

That was a warning shot! We were lucky.

He clutched the handle of the briefcase with his left hand, jumped up and reached the pasture fence. As he tried to push it down with his right hand to climb over it, his whole body tingled. Electricity! "Ouch!" he gasped. He bent down to slip through and grazed the live electric fence with one ear. He felt the electrical impulse flow through his body again and flinched.

"Ouch! Bloody hell!"

Then he put the briefcase over the live wire, pushed it down and climbed over the fence. He turned to Grandma Huber, raised his clenched fist threateningly and shouted: "You country bumpkins can't stop me! I'll talk to you later!"

Grandma Huber heard the words, climbed onto the Fendt, sat down on the seat, took her pipe out of the breast pocket of her dungarees and put it in her mouth. She felt great.

Better than in the movies, she laughed and waited. The exciting part was about to begin. *Wonderful, this day.* Grandma Huber was overcome with happiness as she waited for the show.

Hubert Hansen ran across the pasture. From a distance, it looked like an obstacle course. He hopped from left to right, stopped every now and then and took larger and smaller steps. Grandma Huber knew he was swearing, but couldn't hear it because of the distance.

Hubert was constantly trying to dodge the footpath mines in the form of cow pats. "Not my new Italian shoes," he moaned. "I have to watch out like hell!"

The *mooing* behind him didn't sound good at all. It wasn't the cozy mooing that you heard from time to time along the roadside when you were walking across Bavarian meadows and fields. Rather, it was comparable to the mooing and wild snorting from a Spanish bullfighting arena. The leader of the criminal family clan suspected the worst. He barely dared to turn around when he heard the trampling of heavy hooves that reminded him of a stampede.

"Noooo!" From now on, he didn't care whether his brand new Italian leather shoes stayed clean or not. Driven by mortal fear, Hubert Hansen rushed across the pasture. He no longer paid attention to the masses of cattle droppings lying around. The soles of his branded shoes ended up in dozens of cow pats. The young bulls' patties, some of them fresh, sometimes splashed around knee-high and soiled the fleeing man's clothes.

Muhhhh

The cattle increased their pace menacingly and followed him. Hansen pulled everything out of his body. His lungs pumped like crazy. His chest rose and fell with every breath. His left arm whirled wildly like the rotor of a helicopter, while his right arm with the briefcase swung back and forth like a rocking ship. He got a stitch in his side. Hansen clenched his teeth in pain. He had almost made it. The fence at the other end of this cursed, infested pasture was visible. He was ready to take the electric shocks. He was almost there. He turned around again. His eyes grew as big as soup plates. A living mountain of meat cast its huge shadow over him. The bull snorted wildly. Its huge skull was slightly lowered and only a few centimeters away from the fugitive's buttocks. Suddenly the animal rammed its skull into Hubert Hansen's backside. A loud scream preceded a somersault through the air. The fleeing blackmailer landed roughly in a cow patty covered in blowflies, rolled through more cow dung towards the pasture fence and finally came to a halt. His first glance was at the briefcase. He was still clutching it tightly in his right fist; it was undamaged. Hansen breathed a sigh of relief. His second glance was less pleasant. The cattle were facing him. The young bull that had rammed into him took aim at him, scraped his front hoof, lowered his skull and ran off. Driven by panic, Hubert leapt up, overcame the distance to the pasture fence in two strides, wincing at the electrical impulses and climbed over the wire, screaming in pain.

On the other side, he sat powerlessly on the ground, panting and not knowing which part of his body hurt the most.

The bulls had gathered at the pasture fence, staring at him and mooing. He felt as if they were laughing at him. At the far end, on the opposite side of the pasture, Grandma Huber was sitting on the trailer, holding her stomach with laughter. The wind carried the laughter over to him.

Hubert Hansen stood up, clenched his left hand into a fist, raised it upwards and shouted: "I've won!" He turned to the cops. "And you'll end up as goulash, roast beef and steaks!"

Muhhh

Hubert stepped back, startled. He wondered whether the thin electric wire really deterred the mighty animals and decided to continue his escape.

Harry reached the forest. He felt safer here. While the road was blocked with vehicles, everything seemed to be clear in the forest. "I'm a lucky man," he breathed out and ran towards the ravine.

Ratchet - noise

The sound of a plank bursting is particularly unpleasant when you are on a bridge and the planks under your feet are the only separation between your body and a deep ravine. If they burst slowly, you may still be able to save yourself on one side of the bridge or on an intact plank. However, if all the footboards burst together because they are not only old and rotten, as here on this bridge, but have also been sawn off, you have no chance.

Harry sank through a hole. He instinctively spread his arms, managed to cling to the railings on the left and right and hung over the ravine like a flag in the wind. He was in danger of falling into the depths. "H-H-H-Heeeelp!" he heard himself scream.

Two old ladies emerged from the bushes. Harry suspected nothing good. He wriggled in the hole with his arms outstretched. His strength was failing and he was in danger of falling into the depths. "Help," he repeated.

Klara Korner recognized him immediately. "That's one of the three guys who bought loads of tins from me in the store."

Uschi Brennauer put her hands on her hips and looked at Harry, who was desperately fighting against falling. "Yes, I think the guy has refueled with us once or twice."

"Help me, I can't hold on any longer," Harry whimpered.

Uschi moved closer.

"Be careful!" warned Klara.

"Get the rope."

Two fingers of the blackmailer's left hand slipped off the railing. Harry let out an "Ahh ...". "Quick .... please!"

Klara came with the rope. "It was a good idea of yours to bring the tow rope and some cable ties."

Harry's expression was fearful, panicked and worried at the same time. Uschi stood in front of him, looked at the fingers on Harry's right hand and said: "They're already slipping. Should we drop him and then pick him up at the bottom?"

Harry looked helpless. "P-please."

Klara looked calm. "Let's let him fidget a little longer. That takes strength. Then when we pull him out, he won't be able to fight back."

The little finger and the ring finger of his right hand slipped off. The criminal was only hanging on to the railing with his index finger and middle finger.

Uschi grinned. "Like the famous bavarian *Huberbuam*."

Klara responded. "The free climbers?"

"Yes, that's the one."

Harry could take no more. "Help," he croaked.

Uschi responded. "Klara, you hold me tight. I'll bend over and put the rope around his chest. If he grabs me, you pull me back and bang the hammer on his fingers!"

Harry closed his eyes. "Please! Quick!"

Uschi crawled on all fours to the hole, bent over slightly, skillfully swung the tow rope around the kidnapper's chest, deftly grabbed the other end and hooked it in. She called out to Klara: "We'll pull him out a bit, then he should stretch his hands out so we can tie him up with the cable ties."

Klara grabbed hold. "Friend, one stupid move and the hammer will come crashing down on your fins!" she warned, but her fear was unjustified. Harry was powerless. The hanging was too strenuous. Even if he had wanted to, he would not have been able to fight back. He was freed from his awkward position and tied up with cable ties and the tow rope.

Uschi and Klara then reported their success by cell phone and re-attached the barrier tape to the bridge, which was in danger of collapsing.

Despite all precautions, Hubert Hansen had escaped the trap. That was a defeat and possibly worsened the already dangerous situation for Ernest and Willy. He had also got hold of the money box, which didn't make things any better. The belligerent grannies and Tommy stood around their hostage. Else was the most skilled speaker and tried to question Harry Hansen accordingly.

"You don't stand a chance. Help us save our friends and I'll put in a good word for you in court."

The criminal raised an eyebrow, lowered it again and simply said: "My dad has the money and the hostages. You'll have to let me go sooner or later."

"I think we'll hand you over to the police," the woman from Gruber barked at him.

Harry remained calm. "If you'd brought the police on board, the cops would have been here long ago." He laughed maliciously. "But for some reason you wanted to do it without the cops. And I guess that's the way it's going to stay."

Klara became angry. "Let me have a go," she said, pushing herself forward and standing nose to nose with Harry. She could smell his foul breath. "We'll torture you," she threatened. "Sooner or later you'll tell us where you're hiding."

The prisoner's grin seemed impertinent. "You can save your breath. You can't crack me!"

Disgusted by the bad breath, Klara took a step back. "And you need to see a dentist too."

Harry started to whistle. He thought the game was funny. The old women and the simple-minded guy would never get him to talk. That was certain! They weren't opponents to him, they were victims. They just didn't know it yet.

The ladies' clique and Tommy retreated a few meters to confer with each other. Without knowing where the criminals were, they couldn't help Ernest and Willy.

"What if we do call the police?" asked Erna Schmachtinger. "I can talk to my son and explain everything to him."

"Then we're screwed! Everyone without exception!"

Perplexity spread.

"We're powerless," Else Gruber resigned after a few minutes.

Harry laughed uproariously. "Ha, ha, ha. You can cackle all you like, you old hens. You won't get anything out of me. And there's no point in torturing me. I'm pretty resistant to pain. Give it a try!"

Tommy's face suddenly brightened. "I know how to get him to talk. He just gave the tip himself."

All eyes turned to Tommy. The herb boy was really beaming. "Girls, we'll get him to my house and he'll go through hell there, believe me!"

Else raised her hand to object. "What are you up to? I'm prepared to do anything, but brute force is the last straw. We'll probably have to call the police."

"Unless it's self-defense," Grandma Huber interjected. "That's when you're allowed to hit someone!"

"Yes!"

"Sure!"

"Of course!" everyone agreed.

Tommy waved him off. "No violence." He frowned. "Or is it violence if we ask Alfons to look after this guy and have a little chat with him."

Klara threw her hands up over her head. "For God's sake!"

Uschi glanced at Harry and said: "Poor guy!"

"I already feel sorry for him!" Anna Schwinghofer agreed.

"We can't do that!" said Erna. "That's psychological terror. We'll definitely have to commit him to a psychiatric institution afterwards."

Harry stumbled and looked unsettled. "What can't you do?"

Five minutes later, he was sitting gagged and tied up on Grandma Huber's trailer. The image was strongly reminiscent of the bard *Troubadix*, who hung tied up in a tree in the same way at the end of every Asterix volume.

Tommy and Else were sitting opposite the prisoner. They were both smiling very confidently. Harry didn't like that at all. He feared that something was rolling towards him that he neither expected nor could assess. Pain would not be a problem. He would be able to withstand it. He was only afraid of his dad when he was grumpy and of the police.

The old fogies are definitely not calling the cops. What are they planning? Are they planning an exchange? Then dad will finish them off!

Whatever. He felt completely uncomfortable.

A little later, everyone met up at Tommy's. Harry was tied to an office chair and began to sweat. This cursed uncertainty was getting to him. He kept wondering what the grannies were up to and couldn't come up with anything.

Two women looked after Harry at a time, while the others fiddled around in one of the bedrooms. At some point it smelled of coffee. Grandma Huber finally came into the living room. The farmer's wife's sleeves were rolled up. "Ready! We can bring him over."

They rolled the chair with Harry into a room where the window was covered by a blanket. In front of it were piles of egg cartons. It was a simple attempt to make the room more or less soundproof, or to make it look that way. Harry took it in his stride.

The slamming of the front door could be heard. Footsteps followed.

Grandma Huber listened up. "They're here."

Uschi stood next to the criminal. "I hope we don't hear anything in the living room."

Harry felt slightly queasy. He wondered who they had brought in. Perhaps an interrogation specialist? Did these women have connections to the secret service? Nonsense. *They're clumsy yokels! How would they know a specialist?* He heard a man's voice. That was the only thing he heard, because this male voice was chattering non-stop. He didn't seem to have taken a single breath between the gushing waterfall of babbling words.

When Alfons entered the room, the criminal was amazed at how nice and polite the guy seemed. *This pipe is supposed to make me talk?* He laughed inwardly. *This is going to be fun. I'll be surprised.*

Tommy stood next to the guest and pointed to Harry. "Alfons, this is the man we told you about. He's interested in chickens. You can talk in peace. We'll bring you some coffee. And you know why he's tied up," Tommy winked. "But I'll take the gag off him now. Maybe he wants to tell us something. And if he gets abusive, just keep talking. You know he suffers from Touret syndrome."

Harry didn't understand a word of what was being said. He was glad to get rid of the gag. He wanted to endure what was about to happen completely calmly. He cleared his throat and said: "It's going to be a long day and a long night for you. I won't say a word! Talk is silver, silence is golden."

Alfons was delighted and his eyes shone as he took the cue. "Gold," he gushed. His head immediately rattled and he associated the word with his favorite subject, chickens. "Yes, you could describe chickens like that. They are the gold of agriculture," he began and sat down opposite the prisoner on a chair provided. There was coffee and cake on a small table, albeit one without a *whistle.*

With the first words from his neighbor, Tommy and the grannies immediately left the room. Harry was surprised, but took it in his stride.

"Gold used to be found less among farmers and more among the nobility. Speaking of nobility, did you know that I was once crowned chicken baron?" Without waiting for a response, Alfons chatted on. "That was sixteen, hm ... no, seventeen years ago. At the time, I was breeding *chabos*, which are the chickens that also have feathers on their legs. The eggs are cream-colored ..."

So it went on and on and on. Harry tried to switch off and ignore the chatter. The situation was comparable to the dripping of a tap. It doesn't bother you at first, but over time it becomes absolutely annoying. It was the same with Alfon's babbling. At some point, Harry broke his self-imposed silence and snapped at the constant speaker: "Shut up!"

Alfons took a sip of coffee and put the cup down again. "Shut up," he laughed. "That reminds me of a funny story that happened to an acquaintance of an acquaintance of someone I know briefly. Watch this. This acquaintance of my casual acquaintance's acquaintance knew someone by sight and something hilarious happened to this person, now pay attention, this person who knew the casual acquaintance of my acquaintance's acquaintance by sight. She was out with her dog. So the casual acquaintance of the acquaintance ..."

Harry thought he was going crazy. The word *acquaintance was* constantly echoing in his head. Like a chime, it *echoed* from left to right and from top to bottom. Over and over again. Without a break. He just couldn't follow this guy anymore. "Quiet!" he scolded.

Alfons laughed. "Quiet, yes, you've got me on a completely diffe-rent track. I'll tell you about that in a moment, after I've told you the story of the acquaintance, that is, the fugitive acquaintance, I mean the one who knew the fugitive acquaintance of the acquaintance of my ac-quaintance. But then I'll come straight back to our main topic, the story of the chicken baron and how I came to have the honor of being called that. Man, it's nice to meet someone with whom you can have such a delightfully rambling conversation."

"This isn't a conversation, it's a monologue," growled Harry.

"Monologue, oh my goodness, I can tell you stories." Alfons made a disparaging gesture and rolled his eyes. "I used to know a chicken bree-der, so he specialized in *dwarf Wyandottes.* These are these cute, small, trusting, black and white and extremely robust chickens that lay 180 eggs a year. So this breeder, oh, I remember it like it was yesterday, but it was ages ago. Well, he was wearing such light-colored pants at the time and," Alfons narrowed his eyes, frowned briefly and finally continued, "he could also know the acquaintance who had the acquaintance who had ..."

Harry collapsed. That was far more than he could bear. He longed for peace and quiet. The old women had to remove this pain in the ass. It was no use, he had to tell them. He had to reveal the hiding place, otherwise he would not survive this day unscathed. Another half hour and he would be ready for the psychiatric ward. Harry made a decision. "I'm talking! Do you understand me? I'll tell you everything you want to know! We're hiding in the quarry. Hello, can anyone hear me? We're in the quarry! Help! I'll say anything, just get this pain in the ass away."

"Nerve killer? Oh yes, I used to have a cockerel, so not Charles. Charles is a genuine *Friesian hen* and comes from the breed of another friend ..."

Harry hoped he would be rescued quickly. "Save me!" he added in a panic.

"Because you just said so, my friend, I once rescued a chicken from a difficult situation. That was when I was out with a friend. Well, not the friend who ..."

The door opened. Harry sat sobbing on the office chair. "I can't take it anymore. I'll say anything. Just spare me this blabbermouth," he whimpered.

Alfons took the last sip of coffee, put the empty cup down and smiled. "Since you just mentioned a chatterbox. I once took the train from Munich to Hamburg, man, I tell you, there was a lady on board who just couldn't keep her mouth shut. No matter what you said, she knew a story for everything. It's a sick thing, don't you think?"

Tommy tapped Alfons on the shoulder. "Thank you very much Alfons, we have to go then. Was the coffee good?"

"First class, Tommy. Thank you very much for the invitation. The two of us," he pointed to Harry, "had a wonderful time." He glanced at his watch. "For heaven's sake, I still have to go shopping." He looked at Harry and said, "You're one of me. We talk and talk and I completely forget to look at my watch."

Tommy tugged Alfons by the sleeve. "Come on."

They left the room. Of course, Alfons continued to talk without interruption. "Tommy, that was nice of you to invite me in for a coffee and a little chat. We should do that more often. The cake was delicious, by the way. Who baked it?"

Grandma Huber and Else entered the room and stood in front of the prisoner. "In the old quarry, then!" came from Grandma Huber, who put her hands on her hips to assume a slightly threatening stance.

Harry nodded.

The old lady asked. "Are our friends there too?"

Harry remained silent.

Grandma Huber turned around. "Tommy," she called, "is Alfons still here? I have a feeling our friend here would like to talk to him for another hour or two."

Harry opened his eyes wide and fidgeted back and forth on the chair. "No, no, no! I'm guaranteed to be dreaming today about acquaintances who have acquaintances."

Else knew that they had won. Triumphantly, she asked: "Our friends. Where are they?"

Harry thought for a split second about whether he should play dumb, but decided to tell the truth in view of the possibility of another encounter with the chicken baron. "The two clowns who are too stupid to rob a bank are also at my dad's quarry. We've locked them in a room." He paused for a moment. Then he added: "And they're fine. My brother even cooked them a big breakfast."

Else turned up the volume. "You tell us everything you know now! How do you get in, where exactly is the room and how is it guarded? If I doubt the veracity of your information for even a second, you'll spend the rest of the day and the entire night with Alfons. He's always up for a nice chat."

Harry's will was broken. "I never want to see this person again in my life. I'll tell you everything!"

Chapter 7
Mine - yours - to be

Every time Hubert Hansen imagined being rich, he had a very specific image in his head. He was sitting in a pool with a fat cigar and a glass of whiskey. It smelled of orchids and grilled beef steak. A string of flowers hung around his neck and his wife was lying next to him on a lounger in the shade of a coconut palm. Their two sons were cruising up and down the beach in their motorboat. The warm Caribbean wind carried their laughter across the hot sand to the pool.

Now he was rich. At least he had 100,000 euros on him. However, he was neither in a pool nor did it smell of orchids. He was drenched in sweat, covered in cow poo from head to toe and stank terribly. A few pieces of pita were still stuck to his hair, cheek, shirt, arms, trousers and expensive, brand-new Italian leather shoes. The wind did not carry the sound of a motorboat to his ears, but the buzzing of the flies he had attracted. In short, Hubert Hansen was a walking pile of dung and miserable.

One of his sons was guarding two morons dressed as comic book heroes, the other was on the run from a horde of crazy old women. His wife would be released from Munich Stadelheim women's prison in exactly one week and he had to get everything back under control by then.

His dream image of the Caribbean burst in his mind. "No palm trees, no beach, no cigar!" he muttered to himself. "My shoes are fucked, I've walked for miles in this heat through this fucking pampas and I'm being chased by swarms of flies!"

Hubert was furious beyond measure. Money doesn't stink, he was always told. He couldn't confirm that at the moment. Old Hansen was thinking of revenge. Ice-cold revenge. He would chase the two prisoners over dung heaps, dump manure on the old women's doorsteps and use some of the money to bribe the refuse collection workers to go on strike.

Let this cow town drown in its own wretched stench and waste!

The more pronounced and detailed his thoughts of revenge were, the more his mood improved. A stray dog came running towards him, stopped, sniffed and gave Hubert Hansen a wide berth.

The head of the Hansen clan longed for a shower. He finally had to get rid of that wretched stench. Hubert dreamed of a bubble bath. Of course, they first had to find a hotel and check in. At the quarry, the only option was to wash with cold water in the sink. Anger arose. Immense rage, which could only be cushioned by plans for revenge.

His backside ached with every step he took. That stupid bull had rammed his fat skull against his bottom. "I can't imagine if one of the horns ..." Hansen exclaimed as he reviewed his escape. Looking at it that way, he was extremely lucky. His backside would turn green and blue and he was guaranteed to have problems sitting for the next week or two, but that was all better than if one of the horns had impaled him.

"That stupid cow of a farmer's granny," he cursed, clutching the money case. His plan was set. As soon as he got to the quarry, they would pack up, wait for Harry and then leave. "Yes," he groaned as his final escape plan took shape. "Now I know how to get a little piece of revenge and we can bunk off in peace."

Malicious laughter followed.

Accompanied by several flies, the boss approached their hiding place. He thought of Harry and wondered where he was at the moment. Hubert had no doubt that his son had escaped from the farmers' wives.

I'm just worried that he's lost his way. His sense of direction isn't exactly the best, he thought. He instinctively pulled out his cell phone to see if his son had contacted him yet and stared at the black screen.

That's right! The thing is fucked. The defective cell phone went back into my pocket. *Harry will be in touch. Maybe he's called his brother in the meantime.*

At last he had reached the quarry's access gate. Hubert opened the chain on which the broken padlock was still dangling, pushed open the large gate, scurried through and pushed it back again. The swarm of flies circling around him seemed to have doubled in the last 500 meters. Hubert whirled his free hand around his head once every other step, whereupon countless flies of all sizes and colors buzzed up, buzzed around the living dung heap and sat down again.

As Hubert stood in front of the door of the old office building, he thought about how he could get rid of the swarm of flies.

Variant one. He tried to run away from them. He waved his arm around his head once, the flies buzzed up and Hubert ran off. No luck. Either the flies were as fast as arrows or he was as slow as an ass. After a meter at the latest, they were all there again.

Variant two followed. He took off his shirt, waved it in a circle around his head and approached the door relatively fly-free. As he was carrying the briefcase with the money in his left hand, he had to open the door with his right. At the same time, this stopped the shirt twirling. The flies immediately sat on him again.

Option three. Hubert placed the briefcase on the floor next to the door. His plan was to run the shirt rotor, open the door with his left hand and at the same time push the briefcase in with his foot to quickly close the door behind him.

Hubert began. The shirt circled around him. The flies buzzed away annoyed, his left hand went to the door handle, the door was pushed open, the suitcase was pushed in and the flies stayed outside, deterred by the swirling shirt.

Old Hansen was proud of himself. As soon as he stood in the hallway, however, the swarm of flies was already sitting on his cowpat patches again. Totally disappointed, Hubert raised his head. The fanlight window above the door was open. The flies followed the scent, or rather, the wretched stench that Hubert exuded. He gave up.

Just as he was about to call Harvey, the head of the family heard a loud thump and a shot. He flinched, startled. *Hopefully Harvey hadn't done anything stupid.*

At the same moment, Harvey's revolver skittered along the corridor and came to rest right at Hubert's feet. He bent down, picked up the gun and followed the sounds coming from the room where the two hostages were supposed to be locked up. Then he heard the prisoners talking. *They knocked my son out. Wait a minute!*

"Willy, it suddenly smells pretty bad here," said Ernest. "Do you think he's wet his pants?"

"That's possible." Willy lifted his nose slightly. "You're right. It stinks here. Maybe the toilet has overflowed. Come on, let's have a look."

They both entered the hallway and stood there transfixed. The dream of freedom suddenly froze, splintered and shattered into a thousand pieces. Hubert Hansen stood in front of them, surrounded by a swarm of flies. The kidnapper was covered in sweat and soiled from top to bottom with cow dung. He stank terribly. But the worst thing was that he was pointing Harvey's revolver at them.

"Hello," Ernest grinned politely. "Your son has been sick. We were just going to get him a glass of water. I'm sure it'll do him good," he babbled on. "You look like hell. A little slip? Can happen. Well, country life isn't for everyone."

Willy saw the serious expression on the old man's face, which made him feel rather queasy. He poked Ernest lightly in the side. "Shh! Quiet!"

Ernest giggled. "I'm ticklish after all." He spotted the briefcase and combined. "I see you've already received the ransom. Then we're ransomed, so to speak, and can go. Thank you very much for your hospitality." He turned to Willy. "Come on, let's go."

"Shut up!", roared Hansen so loudly that all the flies were startled into a flight and buzzed around wildly. "Back to the room!"

Harvey woke up from his faint and sat down. He looked around in disbelief, grabbed his head and said: "What was that? Wow! I think there's just been an earthquake or something like that. My eyes suddenly went black."

Hubert directed the two prisoners past Harvey and back into the room. "Come on, against the wall!"

They complied with the request. Hubert stood next to Harvey and held out his hand to his son. He pulled him up.

"Funny, everything's spinning now," said Harvey. Slowly, the memory returned. "You've overwhelmed me. You came at the right time." An unpleasant smell rose to his nose. "That's great! You could wash yourself again," he said and opened the hand he had given his father to pull him up. He smelled it and twisted the corners of his mouth. Then he exhaled loudly and exclaimed: "Phew! Disgusting!"

Hubert's head turned a deep red. His exhalation resembled that of the young bull before his attack. "Keep your mouth shut and don't talk to me about it!"

Harvey instinctively took a step backwards. Firstly, he was familiar with his old man's outbursts of anger. Secondly, he wanted to avoid touching his father in any way. Not only did he smell extremely bad of cow dung, he also looked very worn out. "Sorry," Harvey apologized. To change the subject, he asked about Harry, but he didn't get a normal response. Instead, old Hansen let off steam by accusing his youngest of being too stupid to look after two clowns locked in a room.

Harvey then decided it was better not to say anything more. His head was pretty sore anyway and when he stroked the most painful spot with the flat of his hand, he noticed that a fat bump had formed. Instead of getting into an argument with his father, which would end badly for him anyway, he changed the subject again. "What's next, Dad? I'm sure you already have a plan," he cajoled. "Thanks Dad, by the way, you really are the best. You're in the right place at the right time. You really have to teach me that. When I tell my mom, she'll definitely be super proud of you. You're the king! Yeah, dude! You are!"

That helped. Hubert's complexion returned to normal. "You think so?"

Harvey nodded in agreement. "Sure. Mom said, before she went to prison, that you should look after us, otherwise she'll set you on fire."

Hubert pushed out his chest. "My Hilde," he enthused. "She's a beautiful woman. You'll see, my boy, when we pick her up with the suitcase full of ashes, she'll be in a great mood."

Done. The old man is no longer angry. Harvey was satisfied.

"What's next, Daddy?"

"First I'll get changed, then we'll pack everything up and wait for Harry. Those old women wanted to set a trap for us. They even shot at us."

Harvey couldn't believe it. While he was almost dying of boredom here, his brother and father were getting some real action. "And you finished them off?" he asked, his eyes blazing with envy. "And Harry is just covering his tracks? Like in a detective story?"

Hubert slipped out of his shoes and shirt. He looked at the undershirt, saw that the damp pancakes had left stains here too and took it off. "Well, son, that's how we did it. Harry was the driver, I did the dangerous part. When I managed to grab the money case, I immediately ran to the getaway car. I was under heavy fire, but managed to dodge the targeted shots. I reached the Fiat, jumped in and we sped off. On our daring escape, we fell into another trap. A roadblock! Everything was closed! The shelling increased. Suddenly there were bangs everywhere. I really thought we wouldn't get out of there. It was like being at war."

Harvey was glued to his father's lips. "Wow, dude! Tell me, what happened then?"

Hubert continued to embellish his experience, heroically placing himself at the center of attention. "We got out of the car at the risk of our lives. I gave Harry precise instructions on how to get out safely. Then I took up the unequal fight."

"Really? How?"

"Quite simply. I grabbed the money case, drew attention to myself and used it to draw fire. Harry was able to escape effortlessly."

Harvey knew he would be at least as cool as his father. "And you? How did you get out of the trap?"

"As I mentioned, I was under heavy fire. There was banging and crashing everywhere. They thought I was trapped, because not only was there a roadblock, but they had blocked the only escape route I had left with power cables."

"Wow, this is getting worse and worse!"

"I almost got caught once. I could already feel the electric shock, but at that moment I relied on my athleticism and jumped over this life-threatening barrier like a hurdler, only to be immediately confronted by the next trap."

"Dude!" Harvey exclaimed. "That's more exciting than a *blockbuster* on the TV. What else did they use against you?"

"Wild bulls! You know those Spanish bullfights."

Harvey thought about it for a moment and finally nodded.

"I was up against a whole horde of these monster bulls and had to fight my way through. Sometimes I was on top, sometimes a bull. I grabbed the horns and fought like a lion. I got a bit dirty in this fight to the death. But I don't care. I won, as you can see."

Harvey soaked up every word from his father, who gave an extremely distorted account of the money handover and his escape. He was already looking forward to Harry's story. It wouldn't be as cool as his dad's, but it would certainly be very interesting.

While Hubert Hansen washed his hands, face and upper body with cold water as best he could, he continued to embellish his story. He used the numerous films he knew, stole their stories and incorporated them. Only when he stood in front of Harvey - still smelling bad, but at least with fresh clothes - did he finish the story with: "When I heard the shot, I immediately stormed into the building. And now we have all the money and still have the two clowns as hostages."

"You're an absolute pro, Dad!" Harvey beamed, ran his hand over the bump, which had grown enormously in the meantime, and asked: "And what's next?"

"I'll tell you in a minute," Hubert replied and picked up the briefcase that was still in the hallway. He cleaned it with a damp cloth and then placed it on the dining table in the small kitchen.

"Our future is in there. We'll pack up and as soon as Harry gets here, we'll be off to the Caribbean."

Harvey pointed to the door. "And the two prisoners?"

Hubert laughed. "We'll take them with us, of course. That's our pledge. As long as we have them under our control, these crazy farmer's wives will leave us alone."

"Are we going to fly to the Caribbean and take the hostages with us?"

"Fool! Of course not. We'll drive to the next town, steal a new car and park the van with the clowns. Then we'll call the cops."

"We voluntarily give ourselves up to them? Isn't that dangerous for us? I mean because of jail and all that."

Hubert's face regained some color. "Don't always ask such stupid questions. Of course we're not going to face the cops. On the contrary! We're handing the two clowns over to the cops."

The young Hansen scratched the back of his head questioningly. "I don't understand. They're our prisoners. Who are we supposed to rat them out to?"

Hubert thought about what had gone wrong with his sons' upbringing. He wanted to raise them to be respectable criminals who were capable of doing such things without him. He was almost despairing. "Have you forgotten?" he asked and followed up with the right answer. "They're bank robbers! The cops will be busy for a while and will send a large contingent there. That means we can disappear in peace."

Harvey clapped his hands with excitement. "Sure, now I understand. And the farmers' wives will then chase the cops to free the two clowns while we disappear with the suitcase full of money."

Hubert gave up. "Yes, it will be something like that!"

Grandma Huber and Else Gruber had worked out a battle plan and then presented it to their regulars. They were ready to carry out the final rescue operation to free the two roommates of their herb boy. Harry Hansen simply poured out the necessary information. A final health pipe did the rounds and those who didn't want to smoke nibbled on a small special cookie.

The liberation army of the older ladies was prepared for the general attack. They had decided to lock the captured blackmailer in Alfons' chicken coop. He had a great deal of respect for him, or rather for his monotonous power of speech. This was put to good use. "If you lied to us and we meet resistance, we won't make it back in time to get you out of here," they warned Harry.

Frightened looks. "What do you mean?"

"Quite simply. If we get held up and don't make it back here before feeding time, the next person to come in here will be none other than Alfons."

"I haven't concealed anything. You have to make it," Harry Hansen exclaimed in panic.

Else put her index finger to her mouth. "Shh," she breathed. "If Alfons hears the slightest noise, he'll storm straight into his henhouse. Is that what you want?"

"No," whispered Harry.

"Then I wouldn't call for help if I were you," recommended Gruber.

Harry Hansen nodded. His eyes widened at the word *Alfons*. Pure fear was in his eyes. "I won't make a sound. I promise! But please, please come back before this guy feeds his chickens!"

Else Gruber winked. "If everything goes smoothly, we'll make it."

Ten minutes later, Grandma Huber clapped her hands. "Mount up, girls! Here we go! We're on the attack!" She started the tractor's engine, elated and euphoric. The first time the old machine stuttered, the second time the engine coughed a little more and on the third attempt the vintage tractor started up. The engine hummed and chugged powerfully.

Tommy and Else took a seat on the emergency seats of the slightly rusted mudguards. Their companions climbed onto the trailer and made themselves comfortable. On Else's advice, Tommy had gathered some fresh clothes for his friends and packed them in a small travel bag. "They'll stand out like colorful dogs in their costumes," she had said.

If the women hadn't been armed to the teeth with a shotgun, a flail and two pitchforks, a tow rope, two pliers and a large screwdriver as well as Rosi's hunting rifle, you could have thought it was a fun company outing. Especially because Erna Schmachtinger sang the song: *Hoch auf dem gelben Wagen* and everyone sang along except Tommy, who had never heard the song before.

Tommy was surprised. "The car is green," he said to Grandma Huber, who was cranking the steering wheel vigorously. "Or at least it used to be green. The paint has already peeled off a bit."

Grandma Huber loved the tractor. "The old buddy here served us for decades. It's a *Fendt Farmer 1*, built in 1959, with an air-cooled two-cylinder four-stroke in-line direct injection diesel engine from MWM, type AKD 112 Z, with a displacement of 1810 cm³, overhead valves, triple-bearing crankshaft, recirculating pressure lubrication, Bosch injection system, MWM centrifugal governor and axial cooling fan. Its 25 hp allows it to run at almost 20 km/h. And my good old Fendt runs and runs and runs. It's allowed to lose a bit of color."

Erna's voice boomed: ".... I'm sitting in front with my brother-in-law. The horses trot forward, the horn blares merrily ..."

Grandma Huber was now singing along, swiftly shifted into the next gear and turned off the main road. She took a cross-country shortcut that led away from the paved road directly to the quarry.

Tommy didn't understand any of the technical stuff. He had already stopped thinking about the *air-cooled two-cylinder engine.* All that stuck in his mind was the *year of construction 1959,* to which he said: "Wow, 1959. Are you the same age?"

The farmer's wife stopped singing again and winked. "A lady never reveals her age."

Gruber laughed: "You're always as old as you feel and at the moment I feel 17!"

That was the cue for Erna. The song from the *yellow car* was over and a new hit was immediately sung: "17 years, blonde hair ..."

Text uncertainty spread. This was followed by "At 17 you still have dreams ...", but here too the choir failed after the first verse.

Tommy, who stuck his head into the moderate breeze and enjoyed the enchanting landscape, provided the next steep template for the oldie hit parade. "Are there only cow pastures here or are there also cornfields?"

Erna clapped her hands. "Girls, our song from Uncle Jürgen. Do you remember it? Back then ... in 1976, when it was a hit on the hits of the week?"

"Yaaaaaay," came the almost screeching and the whole crew began to sing.

"A bed in a cornfield, that's always free, because it's summer, and what's the big deal ..."

Two songs later, Grandma Huber stopped the Fendt. Gradually, the ladies' choir fell silent. They had reached the access road to the old quarry. The engine purred at idle, the tractor and trailer jerked slightly. Tommy's backside hurt a little, as the seat had virtually no padding and the road was more than bumpy. He wondered whether he should ride in the back of the trailer on the return journey.

Grandma Huber pointed ahead. "We are there. There's the old quarry!"

Everyone suddenly became serious. Erna stood up a little and peered forward. "I don't know, girls, shouldn't I rather take my son ..."

"No!" came from all sides.

She shrugged her shoulders. "All right, I was just saying."

Gruber observed the access road and the gate through the binoculars. "Nothing to see. The road is clear and the gate is closed."

"How do we want to proceed?" asked Klara.

Grandma Huber clenched one hand into a fist and stretched her arm upwards. "How should we proceed? We attack head-on and at full throttle! Attack! At arms girls, we'll storm the castle of these criminals and free our friends."

At the same time as the battle cry, Grandma Huber shifted into first gear, pressed on the gas pedal and got everything out of the old diesel engine. The pistons rattled, the classic car jerked, picked up speed and rolled towards the closed gate. A thick cloud of exhaust fumes was left behind, wafting in the shimmering summer air and only slowly dissipating. They were armed and ready to free their friends from captivity.

Tommy clung to the metal bracket. "The gate seems to be closed," he shouted to drown out the loud engine noise.

Else suspected what her friend was up to and clung on tightly. She turned around backwards. "Girls, hold on tight, we're ramming the gate!"

Tommy opened his eyes wide. "Grandma Huber, what are you up to?"

Top gear was engaged. The pugnacious farmer's wife held the steering wheel firmly in her hands. The accelerator pedal was depressed. Her gaze rested on the gate. "Steel frame, wire mesh, dilapidated concrete base. Ladies, we'll easily move it!"

Tommy heard cheers from the trailer. Erna Schmachtinger had probably taken a little too much of the herbs. She stood up and raised her clenched fists in the air. For a moment, she looked like the woman waving a flag during the French July Revolution of 1830 depicted in the painting by the painter Eugène Delacroix. Hardly anyone who is not an art enthusiast knows the painter's name. But everyone knows the painting.

The moderate breeze played a little with the police chief's mother's long gray hair. She opened her mouth and began to sing again: "Off to battle Torero!"

Klara grabbed one of the two pitchforks. Anna Schwinghofer reached for the old flail. "We'll pull your legs out from under you!" she shouted.

Tommy began to tremble. The most dangerous undertaking in his life so far was riding the chain carousel at the Munich Oktoberfest. He had gotten off the ride white as a sheet and vowed never to do anything so dangerous again.

He regarded bumper cars, let alone a rollercoaster or all the other rides, as lethal instruments of torture.

And of all people, he, the scaredy-cat par excellence, was sitting on the mudguard of an old tractor that was heading towards a locked gate at its top speed of 19.6 km/h in order to ram it. "Uh, shouldn't we discuss our tactics again," he hastily suggested, but no one seemed to have any concerns. There was no response. His objection was completely drowned out. "Okay, just an idea," he answered his own question, closing his eyes and clutching the mount so tightly that the whites of his knuckles stood out.

"Juhuuuuu!" cheered Grandma Huber. "Show me what you can do, my old Fendt!"

Tommy would have liked to jump off, but that seemed even more dangerous than ramming the gate. His heart was racing, his pulse pounding. Goose bumps covered his body. He was expecting a huge impact and expected to be thrown from the tractor. Were the women at the regulars' table just crazy or were they also tired of life?

I must have done something wrong with my herbal mixture, he thought.

His eyes were still closed, but he knew that there was about to be a terrible crash and rumble. The screeching and cheering of the women told him. It sounded like the funny screeching of crazy Oktoberfest visitors who were about to go into the loop on the rollercoaster. Tommy let himself be infected, opened his mouth and shouted loudly: "Aaaaaah!"

He even dared to blink, realized that the gate was within his grasp, felt a rather light push and heard a terrible clanging, rattling and grinding. The gate was lifted off its hinges and flung to the ground. It crunched under the wheels of the tractor as it rolled over it. Tommy's body was heaved up and down a little during the whole action. He opened his eyes. "We're through! We've made it!" he shouted and threw his arms up. "Yay! I'm a hero!"

Grandma Huber narrowed her eyes. "We're in there girls! Be extremely careful. As soon as I stop, we'll swarm out and storm the farm building. If that pipe of a kidnapper wasn't lying, Ernest and Willy are being held there."

She steered the Fendt towards the former office wing.

"Drive faster," Else demanded. "There's a white van parked in front of the house. I think they're trying to get out with it!"

Grandma Huber took aim at the van. "Tommy, hand me the shotgun."

The fear that he had overcome returned. Tommy looked at Grandma Huber, looked at the rifle, at the van and back at Grandma Huber. "What are you going to do with it?"

She laughed. "Ha, ha. I'm really enjoying this right now. Do you remember the old western movies? The coach races across the prairie, gets ambushed and the coachman and his co-driver shoot like crazy."

"Sure," Else replied.

"That's exactly how I feel!"

Tommy hesitated. "Shouldn't you keep both hands on the steering wheel?"

"Give me the shotgun!"

Else let out a warning cry: "Watch out!"

Tommy had already bent down to reach for the shotgun. He was super nervous and his hands were wet. When he tried to hand the shotgun to the driver, she abruptly slammed on the brakes. "Hold on, we're destroying the getaway car."

The Fendt lurched forward and smashed head-on into the van. The crash sound reminded Tommy of breaking plastic. On impact, he,

Grandma Huber and Else Gruber were lifted from their seats and landed roughly on their butts again.

"Ouch!"

"Wow!"

"Ahhhh!" were the comments.

The girls on the trailer let go of their weapons, screeched even louder than before and tried to find somewhere to hold on to. The shotgun slipped out of Tommy's hand, bounced once and fell off the tractor. "Shit!" he yelled.

Grandma Huber raised her fists in jubilation. "Yes! Mission accomplished!"

Hubert Hansen had changed his clothes. His gut feeling told him that they had to disappear. He could literally smell the impending danger. "Boy, let's pack up and get out of here. I don't trust this whole thing anymore."

Harvey was a little surprised. "Why is that, Dad? You said we were completely safe here."

Hubert went to the door. "Because your brother isn't here yet!" He opened the door and went outside. A reassuring glance followed. "The coast is still clear. I'll get the stolen car out of the hall, then we'll load up."

The packing was done quickly. All of the Hansens' belongings fitted into two travel bags. They each had three pairs of underpants, three T-shirts, two shirts, two pairs of socks and two pairs of pants. That was all they needed. At least while Mama Hansen was in prison.

When Harvey had finished packing, he stowed the bags in the van. Back in the office building, he asked. "But you said Harry was coming here. Why are we leaving first?"

Hubert Hansen was sitting in the kitchen. The briefcase with the money lay on the table. The criminal's fingers drummed melodically over the leather. "What if they've caught him and called the cops and they come here with special squads?"

Harvey scratched the back of his head questioningly. "Dude! That would have been really cool if those old grannies had caught him. Hey, dude, if those pensioners and the leek come here to free the fat guy and the other leek, I'm going to get really aggro! Dad, if the cops attack, we need a plan!"

Hubert stood up. "Don't worry, I'll take care of it! And take good care, you can learn something from me."

Harvey was just about to answer when he heard a loud engine noise. "What's that?"

They both went to the window. "I don't believe it," Hubert Hansen exclaimed. "The old women and the leek!"

Harvey stared spellbound at the scenario. "Dad, what are they doing? The old lady is forgetting to brake. Hey, she can't be ..."

At that moment, the Fendt rammed into the gate.

Crash - schepper

"Come on, boy, get the hostages. Tell them to raise their flippers and go out the door. Take the gun! And watch out!"

Crash - crunch

"My getaway car!" Hubert wailed as the Fendt crashed into the van. His plan burst like a soap bubble. Furious, he rushed for the door. He was followed by Harvey and the two hostages. The youngest Hansen pointed the revolver menacingly at Ernest and Willy, who raised their hands. They all stepped outside.

"That'll give me at least two big bruises on my backside," moaned Else and got off the tractor.

Tommy was glad that he was still alive. "Didn't you see the car?" he hissed at Grandma Huber, simultaneously angry, surprised and worried.

The girls on the trailer also grumbled, but immediately started giggling again due to the effects of the herbal medicine they had taken. They grabbed their weapons and dismounted.

Grandma Huber got off the tractor, walked to the front and looked at the damage. Then she put her hands on her hips and said: "Knocked out by Fendt on the first lap. My oldie is undamaged, the other one is a total loss. At least it's no longer roadworthy."

The man's grumpy voice sounded anything but friendly. "You again!" A long, indefinable curse followed, ending with: "... you destroyed my getaway car!".

"Weapons out and swarm out!" Grandma Huber ordered quickly, turned around and asked Tommy: "Where's my shotgun?"

He pointed to the back. "Somewhere there on the floor."

"Everyone put your hands up!" demanded Hubert Hansen.

A front of women had formed in front of him. All seven stood in a row, united and ready to fight. Klara and Erna held pitchforks in their hands. The tips pointed threateningly forwards. Anna held up the flail ready to strike. Uschi swung the tow rope in her hands, the metal end of which she regarded as a knightly morning star.

Rosi fired her hunting rifle, Else pulled out her shotgun and Grandma Huber clenched her fists because her shotgun was not within reach. Tommy just stood there, trembling with excitement.

"I'd suggest you put your hands up, you mafiosi!" Grandma Huber countered.

"You must have forgotten that I have Batman and Robin in my power," laughed Hansen, signaling to his son.

Harvey then pushed Ernest and Willy into the front row. Both were still holding their hands up. To emphasize the threat, the hostage-taker cocked the hammer of his revolver. The click sounded extremely threatening.

"And now? Still such a big mouth?" Hubert grins nastily.

Rosi lowered the barrel of the gun. Grandma Huber grumbled: "If I had my shotgun, I'd pull the trigger right now!"

"But you didn't, you crazy yokel!" replied Harvey.

"What am I?"

"A country bumpkin!" laughed Harvey.

"But that's rude," said Tommy.

Grandma Huber was seething with rage. That was downright insolent. She took a step forward. "Hang on, friend!"

Harvey fired a warning shot into the air.

Bang

The situation immediately froze. Even Hubert was startled. The barrel of the revolver pointed at Ernest and Willy again. "One more threat like that and I'll make Swiss cheese out of your friends!"

Ernest shook his head. "Swiss cheese has lots of holes. You have a revolver. It has six cartridges in the cylinder. You've already fired one. So you can shoot five more times. That's not enough for a Swiss cheese."

"Shut up!" hissed Hubert Hansen.

Ernest remained silent.

Else took the floor. The lawyer tried to defuse the fatal situation by talking. "I see we have a stalemate. You have our friends as hostages, we have your son as a hostage. Let's negotiate."

Harvey turned to his father. "Hey, they've got Harry, that's why he didn't come here."

Hubert gritted his teeth. "He betrayed our hiding place. They must have tortured him badly."

Else: "What is it? Are we negotiating?"

Hubert took a step forward. "You get Harry here immediately and release him. Then we'll leave with the money and a hostage. We'll release them as soon as we're safe."

Ernest and Willy glanced at each other. "As I really need to eat something, maybe you should go with me," said Ernest.

Willy shook his head. "I think it's better if you go with us, because you're ..." at first he wanted to say heavier and they would make slower progress, but then he decided on: "... because you think like a policeman and can outsmart them."

Ernest couldn't disagree. "There's something to it."

It was too much for Hubert. "We decide who our hostage is, not you."

"The money stays here!" shouted Else.

"Are you stupid? You want to rip us off," hissed Harvey.

Hubert thought about it. He remembered the warning that an explosive charge would supposedly go off when the suitcase was opened. "Wait a minute," he said. "Firstly, I'm setting the conditions here. Secondly, I want my son Harry here immediately and thirdly, you will now open the suitcase with the money so that I can put it in another bag. You think I've forgotten about the bomb?" he laughed maliciously. "Now, the fat man is going to open the suitcase," he ordered.

"Dad, if there's a bomb in there, all the money will be gone," warned Harvey.

"Don't worry, my boy. They're just bluffing!"

Harvey grinned. "You're so clever!"

Hubert put the briefcase on the ground. "That's the end of the fun! This Batman clown opens the briefcase and you put down your weapons or I'll get really nasty. And I don't have to tell you what that means, do I?"

No, he didn't have to. Perplexity spread through the ranks of the liberation army. Everyone reluctantly laid down their weapons.

Hubert took the revolver from his son's hand. "Now I'll tell you where to go." He pointed at the accident-damaged van. "That car is fucked. One of you chicks is going to bring my son here in a proper speedster. That'll be our new getaway car!"

Tommy summoned up all his courage. "That's not fair! You're a really bad person!"

Hubert went completely berserk. He pointed the barrel of the revolver at Tommy and cocked the hammer. "You pathetic leek dare to contradict me? You didn't follow my instructions from the start. Now you'll pay for it!"

Ernest recognized the danger. He was terrified, but he feared even more for his friend's life. He was seething inside, his stomach rebelled, his knees went weak. Tommy's life was in danger just because of him. He couldn't let that happen. For a brief moment, his self-reflection worked.

I'm fat, I'm a coward and I'm a loser. I often lie to myself and yet everyone sticks by me. Tommy and his girlfriends tried to free Willy and me and risked his life to do it. That's the best thing that's ever happened to me. These people like me and I like them. And now this criminal is threatening my friends.

Ernest closed his eyes for a few milliseconds. Something was going on inside him. It was as if someone had flipped a switch. *I don't dare, I don't want to, but I have to do it,* he admitted to himself and made a decision. He was wearing the Batman costume and he wanted to be a policeman, so he should act like one.

"I am Batman and you will not hurt my friend!" he shouted, clenching his hands into fists and swinging. His elbow accidentally hit the chin of Harvey Hansen, who was standing behind him. Harvey toppled over like a wet sack of cement and lay dazed. Ernest didn't even notice.

He only had Hubert Hansen in his field of vision. Everything else around him was completely blurred. The movement seemed rather clumsy and slow to everyone present, but Ernest himself felt as if he was flying through the air at lightning speed like Batman. He swung his fist forward and pushed his voluminous body forward. As he did so, he let out a long, loud cry: "Ahhhhhh!"

The rest was pure physics. $F = m \times a$, for anti-physicists: force = mass times acceleration. Ernest had a lot of mass. The acceleration was also reasonably okay and so a lot of force thundered towards Hubert Hansen.

He was completely perplexed. He hadn't expected any resistance from these two clowns. He turned around in a flash, saw his son lying knocked out on the ground, raised his revolver to aim at Ernest, but then his fist hit him right in the face. The force of the moving 160 kilos of live weight hit so hard that Hubert Hansen thought a sledgehammer had smashed into his head. Little angels danced, stars flickered, then someone switched off the light. It went dark. Hubert Hansen fell over like a felled tree.

"Knockout with one punch. You've got more power in your fist than my Fendt in ramming mode," cheered Grandma Huber.

Ernest gasped. He still couldn't believe it. He had struck for the first time in his life. In self-defense, of course, he told himself. His knees were still shaking. The shot from the revolver had missed. The heavyweight stared at his opponent in disbelief. "I hit him dead center," he stated. Then he looked at his fist. He opened it and shook his hand. "Ouch, that hurts. I'm afraid I won't be able to do any sport for a few weeks!"

Everyone clapped.

Else picked up her blank-firing revolver and fired a shot into the air out of sheer joy. A rocket whizzed into the sky and exploded. Purple, yellow, green and red stars danced around and burned up after their colorful display. "Oops, I must have loaded the star shells I always fire on New Year's Eve."

Everyone laughed.

"Batman! You're a real bull," praised Klara, walked over to Ernest, patted him on the shoulder and whispered in his ear: "And from now on, I'll give you the old doughnuts from the day before in the store."

Tommy was moved to tears. "You would have sacrificed yourself for me. You are a true friend!"

Willy cleared his throat. "You are all true friends. You fought together against this gang to free us. I am overwhelmed with happiness."

Erna was the first to hear the police siren. "I know that from my son," she huffed and ran to the tractor with the presence of mind. Ernest and Willy's clothes were still there. She grabbed them and waved her friends over. "Get changed! But now!"

The first of three patrol cars sped into the courtyard of the old quarry. Erna Schmachtinger's son got out and ran towards the group of people. "What's going on here?"

"Boy, we've got everything under control," Erna replied.

The policeman was more than surprised when he came face to face with his mother and her friends. "Mom? What are you doing here?"

The police chief's mother pointed to her son's uniform. "You should put these pants in the laundry. There's a stain on them from yesterday's lunch."

"Not now, Mom," the police chief replied quietly. He was a little embarrassed by this little rebuke.

"And you haven't shaved either."

"Mom, stop it now. You'd better explain to me what's going on. The emergency call center received a few calls today because shots were heard over by the forest. We were here with a few patrol cars but couldn't find anything. I was just about to call off the search when we saw the rocket fireworks in the sky." The police chief looked at the overall situation. "Your entire regulars' table is assembled. Now let's talk, what are you doing here?"

Else took over the explaining. "They are dangerous criminals. They had Ernest and Willy in their power," she began and told them about the kidnapping, blackmail and the money handover. She didn't mention the bank robbery and the counterfeiting. She also didn't say a word about why all the ladies at the regulars' table were so euphoric and funny.

At the end of the execution, the police chief was astonished. "If I didn't know you all from an early age, I'd think you were a bunch of crazy, stoned hippie girls from the 1960s."

Hubert Hansen came to. His head felt as if he had run into a moving bus. He had been handcuffed. He looked at a blue uniform and a not at all friendly face. *Police!* The professional criminal immediately adjusted to the new situation. The cop standing opposite him had something to say. There were lots of stars on his epaulettes. He was definitely the boss. "It's a good thing you're here, Mr. Constable," Hansen gushed, but was abruptly interrupted.

"Hubert Hansen. I'm arresting you. Hostage-taking, blackmail, bank robbery, car theft and many other offenses. That's enough for a long prison sentence for you and your sons."

Hansen mimicked the innocent and smiled. It was that malicious, slimy grin again. "Slow down, my friend, otherwise you'll make the biggest mistake of your life," he said, pointing at Ernest and Willy with both hands tied together. "Those two there are the bank robbers. They're in cahoots with the old women. They also kidnapped my son Harry and wanted to blackmail us. I scraped together all my savings and put them in this briefcase to pay the ransom."

Else Gruber pushed herself forward. "So you're seriously saying that this briefcase and all its contents belong to you?"

Hubert nodded. "Of course. Why don't you ask my son?"

Harvey nodded frantically. "That's our suitcase. Dad has all our money in there."

"I see," said the policeman. "Let me introduce myself briefly. My name is Schmachtinger. I'm the chief of police and I found the bank robbers' clothes in the van you stole. I was also able to find exactly two hundred euro bills in your wallet, which were taken from an old lady during the bank robbery."

Hubert laughed. "How do you know it's that old woman's money?"

"Quite simply, her grandson painted a little heart on each one! In addition, a witness identified this van, which had been reported stolen, as the getaway vehicle. And this witness saw an elderly gentleman take the bag with the loot while Batman and Robin got into this very vehicle."

"Bullshit!" replied Hubert Hansen. "I have so much money, I don't need to rob a bank."

"You mean the money in the briefcase?"

"Yes! My suitcase and my money!"

"Open it, please!" the policeman demanded.

Hubert became nervous. He still wasn't sure whether a booby trap had been installed. "It's better if you open the briefcase."

Tommy cleared his throat. "The combination is 123 321. That's what he told his son. I heard it."

Hubert confirmed it and felt extremely clever. "Yes, that's the combination."

The suitcase was opened. The policeman was amazed when he lifted the lid and stared at the bundles of money. "And this is really your suitcase and your money?"

"Absolutely. I swear it!"

"Well, then the charge is extended to possession of counterfeit money. These are all blossoms! Good color copies, but still recognizable as counterfeit money."

Hansen realized that he had been tricked. His face color changed from chalky pale to crimson red. "Noooooo! You've tricked me!" he squealed. "That's not my suitcase! It belongs to those stupid old grannies."

The chief of police made a hand gesture, whereupon two of his men grabbed Hubert by the arms. "Take him to the station. The evidence is clear. This gang will go to prison for many years."

A policeman radioed, came to his boss and said something to him. He then turned to the women's regulars' table. "My men have found and arrested the guy you locked up in Alfons' henhouse," he informed them and turned to his mother. "Mom, what did you actually do with him? I was told that he was completely frightened and distraught."

Erna grinned. "Nothing. He was just talking to Alfons."

The chief of police took note. "By the way, we also looked around Willy, Tommy and Ernest's house and found the blackmail letter there. The evidence against the Hansen gang is overwhelming."

The entire regulars' table and the three friends froze instantly. Only Grandma Huber remained relaxed. The moment of truth had arrived. Had the police discovered the hemp field?

"Did you find anything else? In the garden, for example?" Erna Schmachtinger asked with mixed feelings.

Shrugging his shoulders. "What were we supposed to find there?"

Relief and a smile. "That was just a question."

He turned to Tommy. "Nice garden, by the way. And apparently a good neighborhood. Farmer Huber was plowing up her little field when we were there. He told my colleagues that Grandma Huber had asked him to do it because she wanted to grow potatoes."

Everyone breathed a sigh of relief. Else put her hand on Grandma Huber's shoulder. "You are and always will be the best."

Grandma Huber leaned forward and whispered. "We should think about the herbs and get a doctor to prescribe them so we can buy them in a pharmacy. What do you think?"

"A good idea!"

The policeman looked at Ernest's stature and spoke to him. "You knocked Hansen down?"

Ernest raised his head proudly. "Yes. I'm almost a colleague, so to speak, and had to act to avoid something worse."

"You've done well. By the way, a reward of 10,000 euros has been offered for the capture of the Hansen gang. You've absolutely earned it all together."

Tommy jumped into the air. "We're rich!"

Willy dreamed of his workshop. "We've made it!"

The ladies shrieked. "This is going to be a mega trip to Malle!"

Later, when they were all sitting together on the Fendt and driving home, Tommy reached into his trouser pocket and pulled out a few plant seeds. "Look what else I found in the shed. Seeds for a Bolivian coca bush, do you think I should ..."

There was a chorus of "Noooooo!"

grandma smokes

©by Sophia Wallenda

Another book by M. J. Wallenda

Friends with a bite
and the curse of the vampire

ISBN: 9783759767462
Print Book: 13,99 EUR

324 pages

9783759774354
E-Book: 6,99 EUR

16-year-old James Allington moves with his parents to the supposedly quiet small town of Greenfield in Massachusetts/USA. As soon as he arrives, the teenager witnesses a crime and is gradually drawn into a swamp of mysterious events.

James finds out that he lives among vampires and werewolves. His new friends Riley, Kieran and Cassie are also harboring dark secrets. The teenagers must trust each other to banish an ancient curse or Riley will die. An unequal battle against a powerful opponent and against time begins.

The novel ***Friends with bite and the curse oft he vampire*** an extremely exciting fantasy adventure thriller with a bit of heart and a good dash of humor and offers great entertainment.

Books by W. T. Wallenda

Now in English – the German bestseller:

The Sniper from Stalingrad

ISBN: 978-3759720580

188 pages, 9,99 €.

*also available as an
E-Book 6,99 €*

Stalingrad, 1942 - 19-year-old Alfred Miller, a member of the 100th Panzer Division, comes to know and hate the cruel horrors of war during the fierce and costly battles for the "Red October" factory. Thanks to his marksmanship, he becomes a sniper.

After the encirclement of the 6th Army, the young Austrian wanders through the ruins of the dying city on the Volga during the coldest winter in years, both hunter and hunted. Hunger, cold, misery, death and fear are his constant companions.

The war hits hard and merciless every day. The soldiers are brutalized, the hope of salvation dies. Ultimately, there are only two ways to escape suffering and a grim fate: either get on one of the planes out of the cauldron, or die.

A true Story - without pathos, free of heroism and frighteningly close to reality.

ISBN: 978-3757845223

200 Pages, 11,99 €

E-Book: 6,99 €

"Sometimes I can still hear them screaming," Josef Altmann said more than 50 years after the Battle of Monte Cassino, lost in thought. He instinctively flinched, ducked to the side, apparently seeking cover from an imaginary approaching shell.

As a member of Regiment 361, the former foreign legionnaire witnessed the merciless fighting on the Gustav Line and around Monte Cassino. The war had reached an unimaginable level of cruelty, and death struck mercilessly every day.

Altmann was quickly trained as a sniper and immediately sent to the front. He recognizes the faces of his victims through the telescopic sight. His hands start to shake, his heart races. Goose bumps covered his body. Fear, misery, the loss of his closest comrades and the screams of the dying made him pull the trigger despite his initial doubts.

Josef Altmann tells his story without pathos, free of heroism and frighteningly close to reality.

This book is an unflinching factual account and should serve as a memorial against war.

L. Laddy

Amazing
Animal stories
based on true events

ISBN: 978-3759722560

116 Pages, 6,99 €

E-Book, 2,99 €

Friendship between humans and animals is almost as old as humanity itself. Some of these friendships and experiences are unique. Like that of Sergei, a forest inspector from Siberia, who received unexpected help when he was in desperate need.

Two poachers overpowered the animal rights activist and chained him to a railroad track in revenge. As a freight train approaches, Sergei is suddenly surrounded by a pack of wolves. Can the driver of the approaching freight train recognize the living shield and stop it in time?

Moroccan Salim and his mare Kala share a deep friendship. When Salim falls ill and is left for dead, Kala senses that he needs her help. Can the horse save Salim from being buried alive?

These two and five other exciting stories based on true events tell of extraordinary friendships.

A book that will captivate readers from the first page.

YOU ENTER GERMANY □ was a warning to the US-Army

It was the hardest battle the US Army had ever had to endure.

W. T. Wallenda

Fields of Death
–
The Battle of
Hürtgen Forest

244 Pages
11,99 €

ISBN: 978-3769315509

also available as an
E-Book 7,99 €

Information - original Photos - Novel
contemporary history of the Second World War

Topics presented in bullet points:

-Key dates in the Battle of the Hürtgen Forest
-275th Infantry Division
-Original photos help illustrate
-The novel section reflects the events of the time from the perspective of a German sniper and a grenadier.

The five months of fighting in the Hürtgen Forest went down in history as one of the longest and bloodiest battles ever fought on German soil. It is also known as the 'Verdun of the Eifel'.
It was the biggest defeat in the history of the US Army, but it was also hell on earth for the German defenders.
The Hürtgen Forest became a killing field for soldiers on both sides.

The battle of Stalingrad – told coldly and without any pathos

W. T. Wallenda

14,99 €
318 Pages

ISBN: 978-3759722393

also available as an
E-Book

In the midst of the inhuman and brutal battle for Stalingrad, German and Russian snipers roam the ruins like angels of death, spreading fear and terror.

Katja Kalikova lost her husband to German bombs and her youngest son, Boris, to a Soviet bullet. Since then, she and her 8-year-old son, Grisha, have been fighting for their daily survival.

Major Erwin Koenig is an officer in the Wehrmacht and was stationed in Stalingrad. When his son Rolf is also sent to Stalingrad and falls victim to Russian snipers, Koenig has only one goal left. To avenge his son's death, the former sniper instructor sets his sights on living Russian sniper legend Vasily Saizev. Koenig blazes a bloody trail through dying Stalingrad, quickly turning from hunter to hunted.

When Katja and Major Koenig's paths fatefully cross, they make a pact to defeat Saizew.

The fate of the soldiers fighting in Stalingrad, as well as that of the Russian civilians forced to remain in the city, is portrayed bleakly, coldly, and without pathos.